Melissa Lucashenko is a Goorie (Aboriginal) author of Bundjalung and European heritage. Her first novel was published in 1997 and since then her work has received acclaim in many literary awards. *Killing Darcy* won the Royal Blind Society Award and was shortlisted for an Aurealis award. Her sixth novel, *Too Much Lip*, won the 2019 Miles Franklin Literary Award and the Queensland Premier's Award for a work of State Significance. It was also shortlisted for the Prime Minister's Literary Award for Fiction, the Stella Prize, two Victorian Premier's Literary Awards, two Queensland Literary Awards and two NSW Premier's Literary Awards. Melissa is a Walkley Award winner for her non-fiction, and a founding member of human rights organisation Sisters Inside. She writes about ordinary Australians and the extraordinary lives they lead. Her latest book is *Edenglassie*.

Also by Melissa Lucashenko

Steam Pigs
Hard Yards
Too Flash
Mullumbimby
Too Much Lip
Edenglassie

MELISSA LUCASHENKO

KILLING DARCY

UQP

First published 1998 by University of Queensland Press
PO Box 6042, St Lucia, Queensland 4067 Australia

This edition published 2023

University of Queensland Press (UQP) acknowledges the Traditional Owners
and their custodianship of the lands on which UQP operates. We pay our
respects to their Ancestors and their descendants, who continue cultural and
spiritual connections to Country. We recognise their valuable contributions to
Australian and global society.

uqp.com.au
reception@uqp.com.au

Cover design by Jenna Lee
Author photograph by LaVonne Bobongie Photography
Typeset in 11.5/15 pt Bembo by Post Pre-press Group, Brisbane
Printed in Australia by McPherson's Printing Group

 University of Queensland Press is supported by the
Queensland Government through Arts Queensland.

 University of Queensland Press is
assisted by the Australian Government
through the Australia Council, its arts
funding and advisory body.

A catalogue record for this book is available from the National Library of
Australia.

ISBN 978 0 7022 6610 2 (pbk)
ISBN 978 0 7022 6750 5 (epdf)
ISBN 978 0 7022 6753 6 (epub)

University of Queensland Press uses papers that are natural, renewable and
recyclable products made from wood grown in well-managed forests and other
controlled sources. The logging and manufacturing processes conform to the
environmental regulations of the country of origin.

For Bill, who dreamt the camera

NOTE

Astute readers may detect a similarity between 'Shelley Beach' and the coastal New South Wales town of Byron Bay. Yet the language employed by Darcy, Granny Lil and others is that of Queensland First Nations people – 'Murri' and 'Migaloo', rather than the Bundjalung terms 'Goori' and 'Dagai'. There can be only one explanation for this discrepancy, which is that Shelley Beach is a figment of the author's imagination, with no geographical reality whatsoever. Similarly, no Yanbali or Agadja clans will be found on maps of Aboriginal Australia.

I am your blundering kind companion.
I am your home that keeps out bitter weather.
I am the perilous slow deposit of time's wisdom.
You are my threat, my murder. And yet remember,
I am yourself. Come, let us live together.

—Judith Wright, *Flesh*

Chapter One

The fight was over almost before it started.

'You're dead, ya prick,' Cam snarled as he sprang for Sean Lovejoy, loser of the year.

When Cam smelt the sour ammonia coming up at him off the cement floor under Admin Block, he didn't know what had happened. He was still concentrating on bashing Sean's head against the metal base of the basketball hoop. But even if he had been thinking clearly instead of being in shutdown survival mode, grunting and thumping, the dampness of his grey cotton shorts would still have been strange and unfamiliar to him. *So:* if the good news for Cam was that he won his first serious fight at Federation High in thirty seconds flat, the bad news was that he'd definitely lost his cool in the process. While no one worries too much about pimples after eighteen, or about boyfriends or girlfriends before about thirteen, there is no age at which it ceases to matter that you have pissed your pants and have hot urine running down your legs in public.

After Sean passed out, eyes rolled up in his

waste-of-space head, a few of the braver onlookers grabbed Cameron, who was bent over sucking air from a universe of pain.

'Jesus Christ, Cam,' said his friend Jordan, awed, 'I think you've killed him.' Sean's face had gone very white. A small pool of dark blood was collecting underneath the butt-brain's head. Cam looked at Sean's stillness and contemplated spitting on his toadlike face. He decided not to; there were limits. Then Sean's eyes fluttered and he gave a low painful groan.

'He's not dead,' Cam said in the toughest voice he could muster. He shrugged off Jordan's restraining hands, and looked around defiantly at the circle of spectators who were shuffling their feet now the action had finished. Lucy was still there, looking pretty in a horrified way, Sean's red fingers still etched against her cheek. Those who before and after the fight called themselves Sean's friends now came to life, and went to him with their aid, their excuses and their lies. A second bunch of sycophants made a beeline for Cam, hero of the moment with his savage victory and his broken nose, streaming with quick-drying blood. Any temptation to stay and glory in the moment was lost for Cam by the piss. Quickly he turned so that the darkened front of his pants was facing away from the crowd, Lucy in particular.

'Look, seeya when ya get back, I better go,' Cam muttered to Jordan, then bolted from the scene, jumped the wire-mesh fence in the ostentatious heel-flicking way he'd learnt from his father, and made for home. Fuck the year's last woodwork class. With any luck he might have got out, he hoped, before too many of them noticed the piss. Now he just wanted to go get cleaned up. What a joke. Jump in and play the hero and end up shamed out, wetting himself like a baby. Home beckoned to Cameron like a finish line.

Jon Menzies just said 'Hi' when his fourteen-year-old son came through the kitchen flyscreen panting and close to tears. Jon stood in front of the stove, god-like, shirtless, in his black roadie jeans that he wouldn't throw out despite the gaping holes. 'Sentimental value,' he claimed, 'I wired Joe Cocker in these.' (Cam could never tell if he was joking or not.) Jon's dark hair, worn long, was tied up in a small pigtail with one of Filomena's pink childhood hairbands. You'd have to be Dad, Cam always thought, nearly two metres tall and eighty-five kilos of rock-like muscle, to get away with wearing the stuff he did: chiffon scarves in winter, earrings in both ears, once a Japanese cotton kimono and bare feet down the main street of Federation. Most kids at school had to fight their parents tooth and nail to get grudging permission for nose-rings; on his fourteenth birthday, Jon casually took Cam to the local Black Ulans clubhouse and allowed him to pick out a leather jacket and a CD player from their stash of hot goods. The only thing he came down hard on was drugs. 'If I catch you doing anything harder than dope,' he told Cam pleasantly on the day he started high school, 'I'll put you in hospital. I'll pulverise you. You'll wish you'd never been born.' And Cam knew he meant it too.

Now Jon glanced quickly at his son, then turned away to the stove, stirred tomatoes into the pasta sauce and cursed whoever hid the fucking salt a-fucking-gain, stopping abruptly when he discovered it was him-fucking-self. 'Want some bolognaise? Late lunch?' he asked as Cam slipped past en route to the bathroom.

'Nah, I'm right thanks.'

'You're mad. Smell that.' He sniffed a long extravagant sniff. 'Meat and sloth. My only two vices – and may it be an example to you all,' he declaimed as though to an audience of hundreds, and didn't ask why Cam was home. Nor did he explain how the alleged sloth had given him a gym-junky's build in early middle age.

'Yeah, and the rest!' said Cam, sidling past. 'You should hear Mum talk about your sins! The edited version takes half an hour.'

'Ah, your beautiful mother, bless her heart, never did understand that dishonesty is the only real sin in marriage. I had thought to educate her ...'

'Yeah, she reckons living with you was a real education,' Cam replied from the hall.

Half an hour later, Jon's steelcapped boot crashed against Cam's bedroom door. An aural blur of hardcore music filtered out.

YO! MO FO! YO! MO FO! MY HO! MYMOFOHO!

Jon winced, and kept banging till his son swung the door open, using his rope and pulley invention. He was still on the bed, eyes shut, pulley-rope in hand.

'Yeah?'

'Give us a hand in the shed for a minute?' Jon shouted.

'Okay.'

Cam didn't know whether to be relieved that Jon

hadn't noticed his nose and (an added bonus) was in a school-is-an-institution-for-the-mass-production-of-mental-defectives mood. He'd washed the blood off his face and shirt at the Ampol garage on the corner; as it was the height of summer in hot, steamy Federation no one would think a wet shirt anything extraordinary. As for him not being at school, Jon had been the talk of the town when they'd first moved here a year ago. A doctor, Federation had whispered, and his kid wagging school more days than not. Jon had laughed, quoting Nietzsche and Lenin at the scandalised dairy farmers' wives who thought he was an M.D. not a PhD.

When the man from the Education Department came, Jon cheerily ignored his protests and gave him Glenfiddich and his best Scots burr. He pointed out that Cameron had an excellent report card and was already fourteen. By the time a bureaucratic wrangle was resolved, Jon noted, he would be of an age legally to do as he pleased. Then he called Cam into the lounge.

'This is Mr MacDonald. He thinks you should be at school more often,' he'd said. Cam had raised his eyebrows at Jon's newly acquired accent. *'Oh aye.* I expect he thinks you're an ignorant whippersnapper and a bad example to others. I'll leave it to you to convince him he's mistaken. On at least one count.' Jon's tone was deceptively light.

Cam had turned sweetly to the man in grey and performed. 'Mr MacDonald, I imagine that around Federation you encounter a great deal of anti-Establishment rhetoric from the feral offspring of braindead suburbia. My father and I are different. No, wait – we are no pseudo-anarchists, finding meaning through confrontation for its own sake. We value knowledge and respect the quest for Truth, complex though that can be in a postmodern age. Further, I can understand that following the strictures of Weberian rational-authoritarian bureaucracy, you have to insist on my attendance at school. You lack, no offence, the personal autonomy to do otherwise. However, I would suggest that my case falls within a different category. A difficult one for you, an annoying one also. I suggest you go away and lose my file. You already know, I expect, that if pushed we'll simply register under the home schooling program. Maybe we should anyway. I'm tired of tactfully correcting my English teacher's grammar, and doing calculus the slow way.'

Jon had splashed a little more whisky into his own glass. *'Into the valley of death rode the six hundred,'* he intoned dramatically.

Mr MacDonald had rolled his eyes, slowly panning from Cam to the overflowing bookshelves and back to Jon. He sighed and held his glass against the light, where the golden liquid swirled gently. Mr MacDonald was a sensible man in spite of his grey suit.

'This certainly is the true malt, isn't it, Dr Menzies?' he remarked in mournful Edinburgh tones.

'Aye, isn't it just?' Jon had agreed, happily topping him up with another wee dram. Since then, Mr MacDonald still visited occasionally, the level in the whisky bottle sank steadily, but school wasn't mentioned overmuch. Cam went most days. Jon rarely made a fuss when he didn't, and since the report card Cam came home with in November was mostly High Achievements and a Very High Achievement for English, everyone, with the exception of Dirty Harry, Principal of Federation High, was happy.

Cam hit the button of his Marantz CD player and went outside to the yard where Jon had just invented an urgent need to shift 44-gallon drums of fuel away from the sunny side of the shed. It took twenty minutes for the tall man and the getting-taller boy to swing the heavy, dangerous drums between them across the sand. The job made Cam's back hurt. Could the stretched white tendons of teenage legs and arms snap under such strain, he worried. When the drums at last sat fatly on the other side of the shed, they were both sweating and Jon's arms, pumped by the exercise, were more impressive than usual. Cam looked enviously at his father. Veins stuck out under his skin, snaking symbols of his strength.

Jon was tall enough to bridle their biggest horse, Governor ("cos he's a treacherous bastard, Cam, watch him') without stretching. His deep tan was the result, he said, of his rides to Shelley Bay to swim Picasso illegally. Filomena said her father was dark because he was a Romany, and that made Cam and her gypsies too. When Cam asked about this, Jon paused, then said, mysteriously, that while Aboriginals and the Irish were natural horsemen, only Mongols, Arabs and the Romany could never live without a steed, so take your pick. To Cam, Jon looked more a pirate than a gypsy, with a diamond in one ear ('a story too old and sad to tell, I'm afraid.') two gold sleepers in the other, and a habit of horizon-scanning that made Cam think of tall ships and

Moby Dick. Whatever Jon was or wasn't, Cam idolised his father.

But turning into a man was taking like forever. Since his fourteenth birthday, Cam had been expecting puberty to give him a body like Dad's any day now. He had the pimples – luckily not as catastrophically as poor Fil at fourteen – and the broken voice, even the beginnings of facial hair. Jon's hooting laughter when he'd discovered him shaving one morning wasn't enough to stop Cam scraping off the bum fluff a couple of times a week. And up he'd certainly gone, till he nudged one hundred and eighty-three centimetres. Growing out was another matter. He was sixty-six kilos, the same as last year. His arms were … okay. He worked out with weights four or five times a week on the back veranda. And there was always the work around the riding school, hauling hay bales, forking straw from stables, helping Dad break in strong young horses. And he'd been drinking the bodybuilding drink from the Federation Health Food shop for six weeks now. But Cam didn't want arms that were okay, he wanted to bulge like Mr America. He wanted a sixpack like the floppy-fringed rock star on Rage. He wanted girls to look at him the way women looked at his father when he rode down the street on Picasso, straight-backed and glorious as only a horseman can be. Still, Cam consoled himself, Dad said when *he* was fourteen he'd been much skinnier than him. That had to be a good sign. He flexed his right arm and wondered if it was, maybe, a millimetre bigger than last week …

'Gonna sweep up for me?' Jon asked, brandishing a rake from the other side of the shed.

'Okay.' Cam liked to rake the sandy floor. Neatness appealed to him. Neatness and order helped him feel the world wasn't in total chaos, with home the only sane place. He'd almost finished the shed, just starting to feel good again and forget about the pain of his face, when Jon gently wrapped his fist around the top of the rake, put his other fist on his hip and asked in an everyday voice who *exactly* had broken Cam's nose. While Cam's hand went to his face in a useless cover-up gesture, Jon waited. 'Well?'

Cam flushed, saying nothing. There was no safe answer.

'Look, son, you're home at,' consulting a diver's dial on his right forearm, 'two–fifteen on a Thursday, and unless you've finally been expelled, I'd bet there's some connection between that and the bloody great bend in your banana. Hmmm?'

Cameron was floundering. Even with the best dad in Federation, probably in Australia, how could he tell him about the fight?

'I ... there was ...' He stopped. Dad was gonna kill him. At the very least.

'Spit it out, lad!' Jon cried in exasperation.

'There was a fight,' Cam admitted.

'Ah ... now we're getting somewhere,' Jon said. His voice held ominous undertones.

'Yeah.' Cameron was shamefaced as well as nervous.

'And what happened was ...?' Jon prompted, unsmiling, as he manoeuvred a heavy, waist-high diesel drum to pin Cameron between two others in a blatant gesture of dominance. The boy didn't struggle, just gripped the rusted rim of the offending barrel with his fingertips and stared at the oil-streaked sand under his feet.

'I don't want to talk about it,' he said in a sulky voice, while inside him another Cameron screamed: *I do! I do!*

Jon bared his teeth humourlessly and rested one scuffed boot on the drum. 'But I'd like to. For starters, did you win, or lose?' Jon wore an expression Cameron didn't like at all.

'Won.'

'Bully!' Jon leaned his grim battered face closer and went on the attack. 'Thug! Criminal!' he spat. His son recoiled.

'But what if I'd lost ...' Cameron wailed in protest. 'He was bigger. Heaps bigger.' Sean played league for Federation High, and was rumoured to be trying out for the Seagulls.

Jon smiled in sour triumph. 'That would make you a fool, Cameron. An imbecile. An idiot, though not strictly in the Ancient Greek meaning: one who takes no interest in the public life.'

Cameron stared at his father, then crossed his arms and tucked his hands defensively under his armpits. Jon was telling him there was no reason for fighting that would satisfy him. And yet ... Cam had a trump card to play, glimmering under the surface. He swallowed and almost whispered: 'I had to.'

'Had to?' Jon mocked. He broke into song. 'Sometimes ya gotta fight when you're a maaaan ...'

'He slapped this girl, this little girl, in the face. Hard.'

Jon reared back, releasing the drum. He hated

violence, but he especially hated blokes hitting girls. It was the epitome of gutlessness, he said once, watching someone on the news marched into court. 'The bastard! What happened?'

Cameron relaxed a bit and unfolded his arms. He thrust his fists into his pockets. 'His name's Sean Lovejoy,' he said, the name sour on his tongue. 'He's in Grade Eleven, and he was just, oh, being a dickhead at school, saying stuff about migrants, stuff to these girls, especially Lucy Tran from Grade Nine, and she told him to fuck off back to England with the other white trash. So he hit her.'

Jon's eyes gleamed. 'Brave girl. And did the troops follow where Lucy led?'

Cam considered. 'Lucy just sort of fell back. Didn't do anything really. She's a really tiny, skinny little Asian girl. She was crying. We were ... it was on, by then.' He shrugged. 'Look Dad, I had to. He needed it, he's a real prick. And anyway, I won.'

'Who won or lost isn't my real concern. Was it you that needed to give it to him?'

'Maybe.'

'And maybe not. Ah, Cam ... I don't want to pick you up at Casualty one night with half a face. Or jelly for a brain.' Jon became a nurse. 'This is your son, Dr Menzies, care to switch him off?' And probably Lucy can learn to fight her own fights. Haphazard violence is for people who can't think. Or,' and he pointed straight at Cam's face, 'choose not to think. You wanna be a hero? Take up kickboxing.'

Cam nodded, waiting tensely for the consequences. His Dad was very big on consequences. 'Do what you like, son,' he'd say, 'if you can handle the result. And if you can't do the time, better not do the crime, eh?'

'Well, by rights I should kick your silly little arse, I suppose, but I'm not in the mood. Go on. Mix the afternoon feeds – eight of oats, and leave Angel to me. I'll finish here. And for the love of God, stay out of trouble, will ya? I'll talk to Dirty Harry for you tomorrow, though no doubt he'll simply add it to the list of reasons you should get the boot.'

Cam was speechless. His father developed an impatient look. 'Go, go! Find another maiden in distress. Or better still, go and learn something useful. But do those feeds.' He flapped the rake at Cameron.

Walking outside, Cam began to breathe again. The last fight he'd had, he was thirteen, and that time Dad had put one gloved hand behind his back and tapped him around for ten minutes with the other. Not hard enough to break anything, but hard enough to sting. Hard enough to remember. 'When you can beat me, boy,' he'd said afterwards, 'then fight who you like. Till then, forget it.' Cam had crawled to his room and cried. Not from the bruises, from the shame. And now this. But it looks like I'm home 'n hosed, Cam thought in bewilderment. Specially if he's gonna talk to Dirty Harry, the Principal from hell. *Excellent.* He went to the feed shed with its intoxicating rich grain smells and began to measure out oats, horse nuggets, bran, chaff and pollard for the twelve horses and one donkey that lived at Aonbar's Rest. Maxwell, next door's mongrel, followed him from horse to horse, hoping to scavenge nuggets, or better still, a hoof paring.

★

12

Slowly and methodically Jon swept the disturbed sand in the fuel shed into pleasing symmetrical lines. It was a far cry from Ryokan's artistry but as a soothing mantra it was fine. Boys, he thought to himself, fourteen-year-old boys, and the stories we tell them. My nose, he thinks, was born crooked, came from that bashing in Washington D.C. for my white skin. Cheekbone battered by coppers in Sydney for peace signs and pot in the sixties. Half an ear gone in an industrial accident and lucky to keep the eye. Plus the ordinary scrapes and cuts of a soft-skinned creature that had spent forty-two years in a hard-edged universe. Jon shook his head. The little bugger, finding bigger blokes to fight and beat. That'll keep his spark alive a bit longer. And yet we're weak as piss, all of us. We just fight to prove we aren't stupidly, futile. Welcome to the swings and roundabouts, Cam, it'll be the ride of your life. Till you try to get off …

Jon looked out at the fields in sad contemplation, then put the rake away and headed for the stables. And to top everything off, he told himself without pleasure, that anal-retentive Principal was going to have a field day with him over this one.

After Cam had washed up the dinner plates that night and was about to do some developing in the dark room, his father called him into the lounge. He was standing by the computer desk holding a cheap plastic ballpoint pen.

'Time to keep your beauty, sunshine,' he said.

Cam didn't understand. Nor did he like his father's tone.

'As you well know, your mother was always delighted that you'd got her looks, not mine. When she sees your bent nose, like Steinbeck's woman she'll make the bloody welkin ring. Eleven years of that was quite enough for me, so let's fix your face.'

'With a pen?' Cam snorted.

Jon grinned unpleasantly. 'It's not dot-to-dot. Close your eyes. This might hurt a bit. But then, that shouldn't bother a pugilist of your stature, should it?'

Cam put the bottom of his basketball shirt between his teeth and shut his eyes tight. If Dad said it might hurt, then hurt it would. But Cam trusted his father. Jon put the pen up Cam's swollen nose and wiggled it. Cam flinched.

'Stand still!' Jon barked. Then with a sharp crack he hit Cam's nose sideways with the heel of his palm. Cam reeled, and the hand he put to his face came away red.

'*Aaaargh*. Whaddya DOing?' he complained from a safe distance, wiping blood onto Michael Jordan's number twenty-three. He felt even sicker than he had that afternoon. The room was heaving.

'If I'd left it you'd have a wonky nose for the rest of your days. I broke it again, straighter this time. The pen was to align it.'

'You *broke* my *nose*?' Cam asked.

'The first time's the worst. You'll thank me when you're eighteen.' Jon was unperturbed, turning the TV on to Japanese baseball. 'That's it.'

'Yeah, right, thanks Dad,' said Cam through his shirt. 'Maybe tomorrow night we can bust both my kneecaps and knock out all my teeth.' He parodied his father, 'I'll thank you when I'm sixty.'

Jon threw his head back in laughter. 'Planning on taking on the Mafia tomorrow? Which reminds me, Fil's coming tomorrow afternoon, not on Saturday. Michelle's off to Italy a couple of days earlier than she planned. Alitalia came through with the date she originally wanted.' Jon sucked his teeth as a Japanese batter hit a sizeable home run.

'Uh-huh,' Cam replied on his way to wash more blood away and take yet more Panadol. 'That's good. Why not pick on her next time?' His words were gruff but he was pleased his older sister would be here early. She lived in Melbourne with Michelle, her mother, and visited in the holidays. She was his half-sister, really, but they never said that. Just sister and brother and mates, in spite of Filomena being two years older and looking like a dark Italian city girl, addicted to caffeine, designer clothes and foreign films, and him an overgrown freckled Scot with no-colour hair and his father's fey yellowy eyes. He turned from the doorway. 'Can I come with ya and meet the train?'

Jon creased his forehead and gave a loud snort. 'Oh, I don't *think* so, pal. I've got to square your account at school, remember, and Dirty Harry's gonna be hard enough to talk round as it is.' He adopted an exaggerated Black American accent. 'Get yo honky ass to school, boy, and stop troublin' ol folks.'

Cam grimaced, then disappeared to inspect the damage to his face.

Chapter Two

Filomena woke up sweating in Jon's house on Saturday morning. Off that bloody train at last. *Clickety-clack,* she'd ended up thinking as the train swayed and rattled at speed through the back paddocks of Victoria and New South Wales, *clickety-clack, this train will break my fucking back.* The ditty stayed with her from before Sydney all through the long daylight hours to Federation. She sighed and looked around the lemon-painted walls of her tiny room. An almost triangular space, crammed (a last minute gesture – Dad: In my father's house are many mansions, and *all* my children shall have a room to call their own) between the laundry and Cam's extensive darkroom. The oily backside of the washing machine poked through opposite her bed, where practicality had won out over aesthetics.

Dad claimed that anyone could build a house if they had the patience. Looking at the weird results of his efforts to reconcile genteel poverty with the building regulations, Filomena could only agree. Cam reckoned that Dad and Craig were drunk when they drew up the plans. Jon said nonsense: sublime originality was worth a thousand brick boxes in Mortgageville. Besides, it was cheap, made of fibro, secondhand timber and beautiful stained-glass windows that Cam and Jon had salvaged from a demolition site, all cobbled together in a way that worked when the light was right. When the light was wrong, Cam sometimes felt like putting one of those dumb stickers on the front gate that said: 'At Least It's Paid For.' Jon wouldn't let him. 'Not least,' he argued, 'because it isn't. I am yet slave to the Gnomes of Brisbane. Ask me again in a couple of years.'

Filomena lay on her sagging bedsprings, examining the idea of holidays. Mostly her conclusions were good. Six weeks in the sun at Aonbar's Rest, working on her tan. Six weeks of horses-on-tap, the beach, seeing Jon and Cam. Six weeks of no school, no work and no arguing with Mum. Then, she thought, playing Devil's Advocate to her own happiness, six weeks away from Melbourne's shopping and arthouse films and Drago. None of that mattered, Fil eventually decided. Hokey though the country was, Aonbar's Rest was where she wanted to be for now. And Jon wasn't hokey, he was cool, man, cool.

The knowledge that she was at last old enough to demand to go to Jon's at Christmas only added to her pleasure. Years of battling Michelle's belated Catholic disapproval of him were finally coming to an end. When she finished school next year, Fil thought dreamily, maybe she'd move North for good. Escape as soon as she qualified for Med. And head up here to the surf and sun. Even if it was the sticks, there was a warmth and peace surrounding Jon's life that might rub off on hers. Was it possible? Could she really leave behind the aggravation of Michelle, the Melbourne smog and the cold, rainy weekends that trapped you indoors, dying of boredom? Fil sighed. That little war with her mother was a fair way off yet.

She sat up in bed, breathing the subtropical heat. Maybe she should move here in winter, so she could acclimatise better. Her skin was beaded with sweat despite an overhead fan that was making her giddy when she followed it with her eyes. *Stop it,* she told herself, shaking her head to try and clear it. *Why is it this hot, anyway?* she wondered, pulling on jeans and a singlet before she went out to the kitchen to look for Cam and Dad. The house was empty, with only Giggles under the kitchen table for company. Great. Thanks a lot, guys, she told the cat silently, my first day here and they shove off before breakfast and leave me.

But the clock on the wall read ten-twenty.

Filomena blinked in astonishment. She'd slept for thirteen and a bit hours. No wonder the house was quiet. Cam and Jon would both be miles away with the weekend trail-riders. She spied a note on the kitchen bench in her father's writing:

To sleep perchance to dream? You were still dead to the world at eight, Filly, so we had to leave. Back at lunch. Ciao, Bella. PS Check out the chestnut gelding. His name's Angel but don't be fooled.

She grabbed a banana from the fruit bowl and flew outside to the stable-yard. Crossing the moss-blackened bricks between tack shed and loose boxes, her heart beat faster. She whistled loudly, once; instantly a chestnut head popped out inquisitively over one door, small ears pricked. Filomena gaped at him. The horse was stunning. She didn't usually like chestnuts, but Angel was the colour of a eucalyptus fire, coat rippling in the sun over a stallion's muscles. She checked underneath him from outside the box. He was a gelding all right, even though he held something of a stallion's power in his stance. He looked down at her with a patrician eye. Who are you, girlie, he seemed to say, and where is that man who is my real master? He pawed fretfully at his door, making the yard echo with its banging.

Filomena immediately itched to ride him. She could, she fantasised, take the gelding on her favourite trail, along Desperation Creek to the Falls. The thing was, who did he belong to – the school, or someone who'd sent him to be trained? She ran through the possibilities in her head: too short at fifteen hands for Dad to buy as a personal hack, even if he had any spare money. Cam's? Possible, but Cam had got his mare Garbo only last year – and again, he had no money to spare. Too old to need breaking ... Logically, and given what the note said, Angel was in for some remedial work. Which meant Filomena had no right to ride him. Dad was always quite dear about that: ride our horses, not the clients'. Professionalism and insurance both demanded that he keep others off the horses he trained. She could have kicked the brick wall in frustration.

Then she noticed the stillness of the yard. It was unnaturally quiet. All the weekend warriors were out on the bush trails, or else long gone to whatever gymkhana was on. Two thoroughbred mares with their foals cropped the grass of the Small Paddock. Fil could hear their crunching teeth. Flies flickered blackly over the manure pile. But there was absolutely no human around. In this silence, the horse snorted explosively over his stable door, clearing his nostrils and regaining Filomena's complete attention. Well, he seemed to be asking, what's it to be? She ignored her hammering nerves, snapped a striped lead onto his halter and led him out of his box. He danced on the bricks, lifting his hooves high and snorting. The girl steadied him with her voice and hands, smoothing his arching neck. She'd just take him around the paddock boundary for a bit. No harm in that.

'You were gelded late, weren't you, boyo,' she said, trying to sound normal despite her excitement. 'Still a bit toey, eh? Well, that's testosterone for ya.' The horse rolled his eye at her, pretending fear. Then he half-reared, testing her mettle.

'None of that, now, none of that,' she soothed firmly, tying him to the hitching post and trying her best not to show him she was nervous of his sharp hooves edged in steel. She saddled him with difficulty, leaping out of the way when he kicked as she did the girth up tight. 'You little shit! We'll have fun in a minute, mate! Want to trot all the way up Mount Avalon? Or will I take you down to the soft sand for an hour and tire you out?' she threatened, slipping the bridle over the halter. She got one foot into a stirrup and lightning fast was mounted.

Angel tossed his head and skittered sideways, but his efforts at rebellion were now only token. He seemed to have decided he liked Fil, for as she settled deep into the saddle and rode him out of the yard into the open paddocks he responded easily to her commands. She was grinning like a loon with exhilaration. Angel turned and halted when she asked and after a couple of minutes Fil's normal caution went. She shortened her reins and squeezed with her legs. Angel leapt forward eagerly and they pounded out of sight of the house. Only when she was opening the gate onto the Mill Road did it occur to Fil that she hadn't told anyone where she was going. It didn't matter. She'd only be gone an hour at the most; she'd be back before anyone missed her. Or Angel.

At twelve-fifteen the trail-riders clattered into the stableyard, soaked in sweat and smelling of horse, horse, horse. The midday sun gleamed off bits and stirrups. Two of the overheated riders stuck their heads into the horses' drinking trough and emerged bedraggled sea monsters, chaff in their hair. The other two, girls, preserved their beauty, hoping vainly for Jon's attention.

'Okay, Cam, you know what to do.' Jon dismounted, taking off Picasso's tack.

Cameron let his Appaloosa mare into her loose box and took charge of the other four horses, unsaddling and hosing down while the riders paid Jon in the tiny office that was also the tack room. It was nearly one o'clock before Cam finished and went inside.

'Fil around?' he asked his father.

Jon was putting the final touches to Thompson Specials for two – fried egg sandwiches with grated carrot, cheese, tomato, Vegemite and sprouts. He shook his head. 'Nope. She's been a naughty girl. Angel isn't in his box, is he?'

'Ah ...' Cam hesitated to drop his sister in it. '... not that I saw.'

Jon banged the wooden tabletop with a large flat hand and exploded. 'Jesus! How many times do I have to tell you kids?'

'It's not me, Dad. I'm here. Tell Fil,' said Cameron calmly, taking his lunch.

Jon nodded. 'Yeah, you're right. I'll be telling her something all right. She could at least have stayed in the paddock. That horse threw a good rider last week, and bloody well nearly threw me yesterday.'

'She'll be right,' said Cam, doubtfully.

Jon stuck the bread knife savagely into its jar and sat down to eat. He loved his kids dearly, but there was never a dull moment ...

Filomena waded into the clear waters of Desperation Creek and rubbed at the mud on her arm. Her jeans were too filthy to even begin to worry about. She washed her face and wondered what on earth to do now. Five minutes ago Angel had trotted clearly out of sight, tail high, with Filomena's own saddle (representing nearly a year's tedious work at Box Hill Maccas) skewiff around his belly. He'd probably follow the trail back the way they'd come, but how was *she* to get the eight or so kilometres home? She sat in the water to think, then succumbed to temptation, and lay down completely. Cool water streamed around her arms and legs and her shirt billowed with air. After an interval of that glorious pleasure, she wearily stood up. Only one thing for it. She started walking. After a hundred metres, her stomach reminded her she'd had nothing except a banana for almost a day. Hungry, wet, tired and about to face her father's fury, Filomena still didn't regret her rash impulse in the yard. Riding a horse like Angel was worth it, even for half an hour that ended in an ignominious fall.

After three squelchy kilometres of trying to retrace her steps, Fil was having second thoughts, and was enormously grateful she hadn't decided to curb Angel's energy on Mt Avalon. Even a city girl like her knew it was harder work going down a mountain than along a gently undulating country trail. She trudged along the creek bank in her wet elastic-sided boots, looking for fresh hoofprints and hoping the landmarks she was recognising were the right ones. Trouble is, she mused, when you're on horseback you're much higher and things look different to the way they do from ground level. You wouldn't think it'd make so much difference, but it does. You can't see as far, for one thing. She trudged on. A blister was beginning to develop on her left heel.

After another fifteen minutes, chafing in her wet clothes and beginning to suspect she was completely lost, Fil stopped for a rest under a large lilly pilly tree. She sat, panting with her efforts, and looked out despairingly over the three or four broad, shallow valleys which stretched to the horizon. The hills in front of her were a uniform dull green as far as she could see, with some rainforest outcrops showing darker. No houses, no roads, nothing. The only glimmer of hope was a dark blur far away to her left. With any luck, that was the outskirts of Federation, and the Mill Road would be between the third and fourth valleys. She decided to head that way as soon as she got her breath back.

As Fil sat, it slowly dawned on her that there could be an easier way. She could see an old fenceline – rickety half-rotten posts leaning at all kinds of angles – running past the bottom of Mount Arthur and disappearing into some slightly thicker bush. Well, Fil told herself, hoping her geography had improved since last summer, I *think* it's going due east … if I followed it I'd have to cross the road earlier that way, assuming the road really is over there, and the fence reaches it, that is … She felt a quick surge of hope that she might yet get home in time to avoid Jon's wrath. The sixty million dollar question: was going off the beaten track worth the risk?

Fil took some tentative bearings. Geography really wasn't her strong point, and she didn't want a repeat of the time when Jon and Cam had mocked her mercilessly for getting lost on the way home from Craig's. She was standing at a point midway between Mt Avalon's distinctive peak and the dip where the closest valleys met. She couldn't see the ocean, but it was presumably glittering away beyond the furthest valley. Closer to her left, Mt Arthur threw a dark shadow across the deserted hills.

Looking out at the empty landscape, Fil suddenly shivered. It seemed bizarre that she was wandering here alone. Only two nights ago she'd been eating pizza at North Carlton with Drago. This country was nothing like Melbourne. It looked completely different, smelled different and felt somehow strange, as though *(stop imagining things!* she told herself crossly) there were malevolent spirits crouching under the grass, watching her ramblings, giggling at her wild crisscrossing of the bush. Hearing a snapping sound, she turned and glanced quickly behind her and up into the scraggy gums. Nothing. Even the gurgling of the creek had been left behind. Now there was just her and the cicadas, and the vast spreading hectares of half-wild that separated her from home and family.

Fil fought down a sudden irrational urge to bolt, anywhere, just to run from her aloneness. *Don't panic.* She jumped to her feet, left the graded track and started across the rough once-cleared bush. She began thinking about whether or not she'd be spending the night out of doors. It's not cold, she reasoned, trying to calm herself. It's not as if there's lions and tigers and bears waiting to spring, and it takes longer than a day or two to die of thirst, surely. Anyway, the creek's back there somewhere. They'll find me in time, if I don't find them first ... She was still busy with reasons to convince herself not to worry when, to her relief, she spied a small tumble-down building in the clump of rainforest ahead. Good, she thought, a proper landmark. And maybe somewhere to stay tonight if she did end up not finding the road. Feeling slightly more cheerful, she went to investigate.

As she walked closer, she realised she'd been lucky even to spot the old building. It hid at the mountain's foot behind a thick fringe of lantana and lawyer vine, and it certainly wasn't going to offer much in the way of shelter in a thunderstorm. In fact, she thought in dismay, you could scarcely call it a building. A ruin would be more like it. The shabby structure was almost swallowed by the tangled undergrowth and half concealed by the shadow of Mt Arthur. Fil's sense of unease returned as she stared at her discovery.

In the dim light she made out gaping black holes in the walls, and vines sneaking out of every crack in the brickwork. It looked centuries old, but that was impossible. The first white settlers in Federation came in the 1860s, which meant that at the *very* most this house was one hundred and thirty years old. But if it was that old, Fil thought, it'd be a local tourist attraction for sure with a Olde Shedde Bistro dwarfing it, a bus parking area and postcards for sale. More than likely, it was just some old holiday place from the fifties or sixties gone to seed in the dimness of the subtropical rainforest. Everyone knew how fast the rainforest grew, how easily it covered the remnants of civilisation. So why did she have this sudden horrible, shuddering sensation when she looked at it? Feeling slightly sick with apprehension, Fil stepped closer into the shadows. Her heart was thumping around as if it knew something she didn't.

'It's okay,' she said out loud, testing this proposition, 'it's okay, it's just an old shed or something. Nothing to be scared of.' Even if those funny slit windows did look like hooded eyes, staring at her from under the tangled vines. Even if it did feel like the earth itself was running with electricity, a weird powerful buzz making the hair on the back of her neck stand on end.

'Don't be such a dickhead!' she told herself fiercely,

'Go and have a look.' Her legs seemed reluctant to obey. 'With any luck,' Fil cleverly tempted herself, 'there might be some old junk lying around the antique shop in town will buy. Now come on, don't be such a gutless wonder.'

The building, she soon saw, pushing and kicking her way through the scratchy lantana thicket, was at that stage of decay where it would very soon cease being a structure. Maybe next year, or the year after, it would slowly begin the organic reversion to rainforest, but for now it still clung to its former identity. It wasn't, she realised once she was past the lantana, just a crappy old farmer's shed or holiday cabin. It was the remains of an old *house*. She stepped closer, curiosity fighting the buzzing fear which grew stronger. Finally, she stood nervously in front of the house, trying to ignore the shrill voice in her head that was unmistakably warning: *Danger, run while you can!*

The ruin was tiny. No larger than a big caravan. The chimney was mostly intact and there were those small, creepy window spaces set high in the walls. Fil avoided looking at them. The walls were – or had been – brick, set into heavy, rough-trimmed corner timbers. Cedar, she thought instantly, now that's worth money. You'd be flat out trying to get it to the road though, without a bulldozer. She tried to circle the building, but could only reach the other end of the front wall. On the far side the lantana was far too thick and the rainforest had grown right down off the mountain to meet the back wall. Half-house, half-jungle, she thought, the ferals'd love this …

A Strangler Fig spread its destructive roots across the ruined roof; its magnificent canopy throwing the inside of the house into even deeper shadow than the surrounding area. Fil peered into the blackness. Who could have lived here in this hideous place? There was no sign of former life. No paths. No fences, stockyard or well that she could see. The house was set on a flat piece of ground almost directly beneath the sheer rock cliff, the north face of Mount Arthur. The ground began to slope away smoothly towards the valley floor about twenty metres from where she stood. What kind of weirdo would live here? Then again, if you wanted to build a *fortress,* with a mountain at your back and a protective incline in front of you, this would be the place. Fil shuddered when she accidentally looked back at the windows' gaping blackness. She'd heard of haunted houses, but this was ... it wasn't something *in* the house, it was the house itself that was weird. Just take a quick look inside, she ordered, now you've come this far. Be brave, peek inside, then go. *Fast.* The voice in her head was getting louder and more insistent with its warnings – *you'll be sorry* – but Fil fought it away.

She squeezed through the largest wall-hole, being careful not to knock the crumbling brickwork. She didn't want to be found lying there concussed in a week's time. The inside of the house was dim with dirt, vines and the debris of years of neglect. A very faint line of sunlight trickled through the frail lace of the part-tin roof that remained. Where the tin had gone the fig's sinuous aerial roots twisted into corners. Fil couldn't quite stand upright, since the roof had fallen on an angle. *What am I doing here?* she thought, crouched in the dirt, trying to squint through the roots. *Why does it feel like someone's watching me? And what about snakes?* Snakes love old buildings. There could be a million black snakes in here, she thought, and I wouldn't be able to see them. Suddenly a toad croaked from underneath her feet, making her cry out. Something else scuttled away in the darkness and Fil fought down the urge to bolt outside.

It was difficult to make anything out in the darkness. There, almost covered in ropy spider's web, was the brick chimney she'd seen outside. This must be the kitchen Fil thought. She picked her way unsteadily across the room, brushing aside the trailing fig roots that grasped at her face and stroked the back of her neck. A rotted door with wooden slats stood on the other side of the chimney. Fil reached out to the handle and tried to heave it open. Silted and overgrown with fig roots, it was impossible to shift. She used her wet shirt to rub a patch of encrusted dirt off the tiny glass circle still set into the door and peered into the other part of the ruined house. It was even dimmer and blacker. Through that deep doorway over there, where the rainforest had almost reached, must be a large bedroom, and in front of it the broken-down skeleton of two small rooms, maybe for kids.

Skeletons? At that instant the hair on Fil's head began to prickle. Goosebumps sped up her arms and legs. Quickly she took a step back from the glass. The ridiculous feeling that someone – or *something* – was looking back at her got stronger. She looked around. The darkness was thickening; it was as though, outside, the sun had gone behind a cloud. Fil stopped a scream in her throat. Breathing hard, she had the sudden horrible realisation that this was a very old place that, as far as she knew, no

29

one knew about. No one knew where she had headed, or where she was now. If anything happened she was completely alone. And was it impossible there really were skeletons inside? Or ... other things? How old was this house?

Don't be so bloody stupid, she told herself fiercely. She wasn't hot any more. She felt quite chilled. And despite the fact (she told herself) there was nothing here, and certainly nothing to *worry* about, terror seeped inexorably into her. The bush outside reverberated with the angry creaking of cicadas. Inside the blackness of the tangled ruin, Filomena felt the beginnings of panic.

With a massive effort she forced herself to breathe more slowly. What she'd do was to walk calmly away, then come back with Dad and Cam, and show them the ruin. When there were three of them, she would feel quite normal, she wouldn't feel that something was about to step ghostlike out of the last century and put its twisty hands around her neck. That decision made, she started slowly stepping backwards to the entrance, retracing her steps in the dark. She had almost reached the hole and the safety of the clean sunny bush when she heard something large rustling outside, something about to get her. She leapt blindly away, stumbled and tripped over.

Fil screamed, and scrabbled wildly at the red dirt floor. She crawled over broken bricks, fig roots and an ancient metal box before finding herself outside the ruin, looking up from inside the lantana thicket in terror at ... Angel. He stood just beyond the vines, head lowered, ears forward, mildly interested in her activities.

'Angel!' yelled Filomena, gasping raggedly for breath,

her heart pounding, 'You … are definitely … bad news.' She crawled out and dragged the reins over his head, ready to flee. Then stopped dead in her tracks.

An ancient metal box?

Oh no, Filomena told herself. *Definitely not.* That place is creepy. There is Something Wrong in there. *Yes,* said another part of her, the part that had thought about the antique shop a few minutes earlier. *An old metal box!* If it hasn't rusted away then what's inside might still be okay. So why not just pop back, grab it and go? It'd take less than a minute. Filomena looked at Angel. He stood quietly. Horses can see ghosts, she thought. If there was a ghost, he'd never come within miles of here. And an old box … it was like something out of an adventure story. Jewels, she thought wildly, doubloons. Treasure to make us all rich, or something to sell and put towards my Horse. Fil felt a tiny bit braver with Angel standing next to her. He was a reminder of the world outside the ruin. Standing beside him in the bright sunshine, with a magpie carolling in the nearest gum, it seemed ridiculous to be frightened just because the house was old, broken-down and covered in the darkness of shadow and rainforest.

She decided to compromise, and play the YesNo game. This was her own invention, a way of letting gut instinct tell you what to do. Nothing could be simpler. You just shut your eyes, repeated the options to yourself and let something outside of you decide when to stop.

Yes. No. Yes. No. Yes. No. Yes. No.YesNoYESNOYESNOYES!

Fil opened her eyes, and before there was time to

change her mind she clambered as fast as she could through the lantana, back through the hole and grabbed the old box. Instantly it fell apart and she was left stupidly holding the thin metal handle. A few pieces of strange material, maybe rotten leather, flopped onto the floor. The only other thing inside, dimly visible, was a smaller metal container, the size of a lunchbox. Filomena grabbed this, stuffed it down her shirt, then bolted back outside. She dragged herself onto Angel and didn't hesitate to put the boot into his ribs. Startled, Angel half-reared then sprang forward into an enthusiastic gallop.

The two of them flew down the slope. When Angel eventually began to roll with the effort of going flat out, blowing flecks of white foam, they were across the flatter ground and Fil could see that they were headed safely towards the distant ribbon of Mill Road. Only when they reached the gravel edge did she feel safe enough to pull her heaving mount to a walk. She trembled in the hot sun. What *was* that place?

Before she could begin to answer herself, she groaned inside. Picasso was cantering along the road towards her, and Dad's face was a picture of displeasure. Uh-oh … out of the fire, into the frying pan.

CHAPTER THREE

'It's not as if I got hurt,' Fil said miserably to Cam, sitting on her bed.

He shrugged. It wasn't him who'd taken a horse and got banned from riding for a week. He felt sorry for Fil, but at the same time it was like: *Stiff shit. If ya can't do the time* ...

'Yeah,' he answered, 'but Angel could have. What'll ya do?'

'Dunno. Go swimming, I s'pose. Hitch into town and hang out. It's too fucking hot to do much anyway.' Filomena scowled at her punishment. 'Is Jon going up to Brisbane next week?'

'I think so,' said Cam slowly, 'but if you're thinking of riding while he's ... look, I don't wanna know, okay?'

'Nah, I won't, don't worry. Anyway, I'm too bloody sore. Look!' She displayed the large purple bruise on her upper arm where she'd hit a rock falling off Angel.

'Looks major,' agreed Cam. 'Now what's this box you wanta show me? Where'd you get it?'

Fil explained as best she could about the old house,

but it didn't come out quite right. Impossible to explain how frightened she'd been without sounding wussy.

Cam's eyes widened. 'Oh *cool*! I bet it *is* haunted ... hey, I wonder who lived there? Was it like, convict-built or anything? I wonder how come I've never seen it.' He was all enthusiasm.

When she thought about the ruined house with its overhanging fig tree, trailing lantana vines and shadowy deep holes, Filomena felt less confident than sixteen. 'It's really well hidden in the forest, like a fortress or something. And there's something yukky about it – not just the spiders and things. It's real weird. It's not *cool*, Cam. It's ... scary.'

'I'll go up on Garbo later and have a look. Show us the box first,' her brother demanded, not really listening.

Fil sighed and retrieved it from under her bed. The two of them looked at it. Made of a dull silver metal it was unornamented except for the clasp, an intricately tooled Celtic knot in brass.

'Pretty,' said Cam, touching the knot. 'Looks old.'

'I've tried to open it, but it's locked. And there's no keyhole.'

Cam already had out his Swiss army knife.

'Don't break it!' Fil exclaimed. 'It might be worth a lot. Do you think it's silver?'

Cam was concentrating on the clasp. After fiddling for a couple of minutes the lid of the box lifted. He blinked and brushed hair out of his eyes. He took a deep breath before speaking. 'Is this some big joke? Did you just make up all that crap about the haunted house?'

'No! Of course not. Why – what is it?' She looked at

what he was holding. 'Oh, a camera.'

'It's not a Box Brownie ...' Cam replied in a puzzled voice.

Fil's expression was blank. A *camera*? She'd wanted rubies and emeralds. Maybe someone's antique revolver. *Shit*.

'It's not a what?' she asked crankily.

'An old camera,' Cam elaborated. 'Like, really old. This might even be an Eastman Vistaview. I'm sure Box Brownies were bigger than this.' He looked at Filomena, excited. 'This baby could be eighty or ninety years old, Fil. They haven't put that sort of slide-out lens into cameras for a million years.'

Irritated, his sister grabbed it off him and turned it around in her hands. The odd little camera was cube-shaped, with a tight-fitting case and strap made from old leather, which, frankly, smelled bad. Compared to Cam's high-tech hobby equipment, it looked to her like a dinosaur of the photography world. A thin layer of grey dust covered it, dulling the brass fittings. Filomena handed it back with a wrinkled nose. Cam was the photographic expert. Her hobbies in Melbourne were soccer and saving for her dream horse. Oh well, she should have known better than to think anything good would be lying in that spooky old dump ... She grimaced. 'Is it worth anything? How can you tell how old it is?'

Cam was noncommittal. 'Well, I've never seen anything exactly like it ... might be worth a bit, but we should take it to Brisbane where the proper – hey, look, there's still film in it! This is unreal ... that box must have kept out just about all the moisture. Can I have it?'

'The camera? Oh, why don't we sell it? The antique shop might—'

'Nah,' said Cam, 'the box. I need a decent waterproof box.'

'Oh. Um. I suppose it couldn't really be silver, could it? Must be tin or something. I guess so,' said Fil reluctantly. 'But you owe me. And if there's a missing horse one day when Dad's not here, you didn't see it, right?'

Cam tilted his head, working out the risks. He fingered the box's clasp. Putting one over Dad was extremely tricky. But if he was in Brisbane ... and a box that was so watertight ... 'Okay.'

'Good.' Filomena smiled. She'd ride Gunner (or just possibly Angel) when Dad went to Brisbane on Wednesday.

'So long as you don't sell the camera,' her brother added. 'At least, not straight away. Let me find out about it first.' He was excited by the idea of finding a real Eastman, hidden in the bush for so long.

That was only practical, Fil thought. Knowing what it is will help us to know its real value, and not get ripped off. 'Rightyo.'

Jon pushed his empty dinner plate away. 'Well, I see I've taught you something, Filly. What do you reckon, Cam, will we keep her?'

Cam was still shovelling his lasagne in. He nodded and grunted enthusiastically.

'Mum taught me to make lasagne long before you did,' said Filomena tartly. Then she softened. 'I've been doing a lot of vegetarian stuff lately. Stuffed eggplant, blackened peppers, fettucini pesto, roast honey-glazed veges …'

Jon pretended to swoon off his chair.

'Of course, my cooking is very much a reflection of my emotional health,' she added, 'which is enhanced by high quality recreation. Like *riding.*'

'Oh good-oh,' said Jon, falsely bright, 'I'll look forward to even better tucker next week. Who wants some tea?'

'Not for me,' Fil said from the fridge.

'Yes please. Hey, *The Simpsons,*' said Cam, leaping into the lounge and flicking the remote. Bart skated across the screen. Homer dropped his nuclear rod.

'Yaaaaaay!' Fil joined him, opening her beer.

Jon stacked the dishes and began to wash up. 'Hey, Fil!' he shouted over the opening music.

'Mmm?'

'What was in the box?'

Cameron and Fil exchanged glances, then yelled back together: 'Nothing!'

Jon appeared, soggy Chux in hand. 'The kind of nothing I should know about?'

Filomena played it cool and replied offhand, watching Marge buy Maggie at the supermarket. 'Nah, just some old raggy bits of leather and a few brass fittings.'

Her father grunted and went back to the dishes. He muttered to himself as he slopped in the sink. 'Pity. We could have done with a few pieces of eight or big bank rolls. I guess people just don't drop stuff like that on country roads any more. In my day … hey, kids!' He reappeared in the lounge. Cam and Fil looked up. 'Didn't tell you about the mortgage, did I? I got a statement today. I owe the bank just another five and a half grand ... and it's ours! Aonbar's Rest will become Menzies' Rest as well. Just think, Cam, if we sold Picasso and Garbo, we could just about be landed gentry at last.' Jon's face shone with the knowledge that he would soon own his patch of paradise.

Cam paled. 'You wouldn't—'

'Oh, don't be a bloody goose, of course I won't,' Jon grinned. 'But it won't be long ...'

'That's great, Dad,' Fil said, nine-tenths of her attention on the show.

Cam was more impressed. He'd watched Jon struggle with the riding school on a daily basis and overheard more than one heated phone call to the bank, Jon demanding more time to conjure mortgage money out of thin air. 'Way to go, Dad!' he crowed. 'So do we get that trip to the States next year?'

'Son, if we have enough money to go to Noo York next year, wild horses won't keep us away.'

'Me too?' asked Fil.

'You, me, the whole bloody lot of us! I'll take Picasso if I win the Pools, too,' said Jon, grinning, 'cos that's the only way we're gonna have enough dough.'

Cam's face fell.

'Don't look sad, Cam,' teased Fil from the floor, 'when I start playing footy professionally in Holland I'll send you a ticket.'

Cam threw a pillow over her head and began to pummel it. Fil played dead.

'Worse things than poverty – not that this is poverty,' said Jon. 'Think of all the suckers in Shriekertown, riding their commuter buses to work, pumping out carbon dioxide in their one-person cars, coming home to watch tit shows and thinkin' they're alive.'

'He means Brisbane,' said Cam.

Fil sat up and threw the pillow back. 'I dunno about youse, but I'm gonna be *rich*. Richer than Kerry Packer or Rupert Murdoch. As rich as the Queen. And then I'm gonna buy the Bulls for ya, Cam,' she said. 'And Alan Shearer for me,' she added, licking her lips and opening her eyes in overacted lust.

'Oh, that's nice,' Cam said disbelievingly.

'What about me?' called Jon, 'What do I get?'

'A walk-on part in *Upstairs, Downstairs*,' Filomena laughed. He threw the tea-towel at her, then sat down on the floor. The three of them watched the rest of *The Simpsons*, dreaming their separate dreams.

It was Tuesday morning, early. Filomena was already bored. Only boring people get bored, Michelle always said, but that was crap. Why hadn't she stayed in Melbourne? She could have gone to town, met Drago and had lunch, gone to the movies, looked at clothes. When she whinged to Jon, he silently handed her a book by a guy who'd been locked up in Baghdad for years in solitary confinement. *Thanks for nothing,* she thought sourly as she took it, if it wasn't for your dumb rule I could go riding. Cam helpfully offered to find her some jobs around the farm. 'I don't think so,' she snapped, slamming her door. *Jesus.*

Aaarrghhh! Fil stared at the harrowed looking man on the book cover. She didn't feel like reading. She'd come here to ride horses. Now that wasn't available she was bored out of her tiny skull. How did Cam stand it here, stuck in the middle of nowhere? She lay on her bed and wondered what would be worse, to help the guys muck out the stables, knowing she couldn't ride any of the horses, or stay in the house and try to forget about them. The thing to do, really, was find something completely different to do. At home she would have gone to the gym, maybe for a jog if she felt energetic, but here it was way too hot for that. If I was Cam, she thought, I could go around taking photos of stuff. Where did he put the camera? She rolled over and looked under the bed. *Gotcha.* She examined the little machine.

'You stink,' she told it, testing the leather to see if it would peel away from the body of the camera. It didn't. Then she held her breath, put it to her eye, and swivelled around like a film director. As the door to the lounge came into view, she pressed the large black button at the back. The camera gave a satisfying *clunk*. Fil was pleased with herself.

'Hey! Do you really work? After all that time in the old house?' she wondered aloud. Surely it was impossible. 'Only one way to find out, I guess.'

She spent the next hour walking around Aonbar's Rest, carefully deciding what to photograph, clicking and clunking at whatever took her fancy. After the sixth photo, the camera stopped clunking and only clicked. When Cam came in from the morning's mucking out, she waved the camera at him. 'Hey, it works, I think.'

Cam made a face. Girls were so dumb sometimes.

'That's impossible. It's been in that box for a zillion years,' he said, as if to an idiot.

Filomena's face fell. She'd been enjoying herself composing 'artistic' shots of wheelbarrows in the yard, and the interior of the house. 'But it's been clicking away when I take pictures,' she whined.

Her brother sighed. 'That doesn't mean anything. Come and look.' His tone was authoritative. He grabbed the camera and took it into the darkroom, with Fil following. He folded something and unclicked something else. Then he dipped a wide, short roll of film into a fluid that smelt almost as bad as the leather case.

'What a stink!' Fil said, holding her nose.

'You get used to it,' replied Cam, 'Check this out, there's only six exposures on these old ...' Suddenly he stopped, then said in a different voice. 'Well, bugger me! You might have something here after all. Look at that, there's gonna be a *picture*. It'll be crap, though.'

He showed Fil where a fuzzy image of an animal was blurred onto the film in the tray. She was intrigued. Either she or the camera had made tall thoroughbred Picasso look like a pony, perhaps even a cow. Cam took the film out and pegged it onto a mini-clothes line that stretched across the room. He shook his head in disbelief as he looked at it. Unreal. 'I wonder ... well, it's got to dry for a long while yet. Come on.'

'Where are we going?' asked Filomena when they got outside.

'Library. I wanta look it up and see if I can identify the model. Then I'll know if that film can still be made up by a specialist photo place.' Cam shook his head. 'It's amazing, Fil.'

'It must be worth more because – if – it works,' said Fil, thinking hard.

Cam frowned at her. 'But don't sell it, Fil. It's ... history. That'd be like finding a Roman helmet, and melting it down for scrap.' He wore a pleading expression.

'I'll see. Let's find out how much it's worth first.' Fil had no doubts that she would sell it. No point arguing with Cam, though. He was a fanatic. She kicked him out of her room while she put on togs and a sarong. If it was worth less than fifty dollars, she decided, she'd pay off that red party dress at Cue. If it was worth more, she'd keep it for her horse piggy bank. And if – by some miracle – it was worth more than five hundred, she'd give the money to Dad, to help pay off Aonbar's Rest. Dressed, she looked at herself in the mirror. Long dark hair fell around her face. She had a soccer player's calves, muscles jutting. Training had kept her fairly fit, even now in the off-season. *You'll do,* she told her reflection, *you're not thin but you'll do.* Just stop eating so much chocolate, and drinking so many beers. She put her sunnies on and struck a pose for the mirror.

'Oh ... Linda Evangelista!' mocked Cam from the door.

'Fuck off!' she roared, leaping at him, but he was too fast.

'We're going to town, Dad, okay?' Fil told Jon from outside the lunging ring.

'Halt!' The young grey horse he was lunging slowed, then stopped completely.

'Good girl, good girl ...' Jon turned around.

'How are you getting there?' he asked. 'I want the Yammy this afternoon to go to Craig's.' Craig lived on the other side of Mount Arthur, and the trip to his amazing tree house was twenty minutes shorter through the bush. Otherwise you had to drag ass all the way around through Shelley Bay with its traffic and tourists.

'I'm ... hitching?' said Cam, tentatively, his plan to double Fil on the motorbike shot.

'Both of you?'

'Yep. We're gonna have a surf, then lunch at the Hare Krishna's. That okay?'

'Yards and looses boxes all done?' Jon continued. 'Yep.'

'I thought you were gonna help me with this one?' he asked his son.

Cam's face fell.

'Don't hitch if you split up. Ring me,' Jon ordered sternly. 'Okay? And be back by four, or we'll never get all these horses done. Go on then. Oh, here, Cam, your pay. Don't spend it all at once.'

Cam grinned as he pocketed eighty dollars. 'Thanks, Dad.'

'Scram, I'm busy. Someone's gotta work around this joint. Move on, sweetheart, move on ...' Jon refocussed on the young grey, which walked forward obediently for him.

★

Filomena and Cam stood outside Goddards Photographic on Cook Street, arguing.

'I don't want to show him the camera,' said Fil. 'Just ask about the film. I'll be in next door.' She had spotted a shirt she liked in the St Vinnies window.

'But why?' complained Cam. 'What harm can it do? And he might be able to tell us how old it is ...'

'I just ... I dunno. I just don't want to show it to him. He's a fuckin pig, all right. He looks at me like I'm a pro.' Fil was immovable. When she took a dislike to someone, she kept it. She'd been into Goddards Photographic with Cam on her last visit.

Cam heaved with irritation. 'So I'll just go in and ask for some eighty-year-old film, will I? Great.' He pushed past her into the icy air-conditioning. Nikons and Minoltas were arranged in expensive displays throughout the shop. *I wish, he* thought, looking at the latest models. Then he had an idea of how to solve the film problem. 'Hi, Glen,' he hailed the shop's owner.

'G'day son. What can I do ya for?' Glen Goddard sat splayed on a small stool at the back of the shop, beer-gut hanging loosely in his shirt. 'New lenses in yesterday. Nice.'

'Mmm. Bit much for me,' Cam replied frankly. 'But, listen, can I get some uncut material, about ... oh, three by ten? Say five sheets?'

The shopowner lifted his eyebrows. 'Funny size.'

'Just experimenting, mucking around at home,' said Cam quickly, then with a flash of genius: 'I'm trying to build my own wooden camera, based on the Box Brownie. That material should work, shouldn't it?'

Goddard smiled, showing gold teeth. Even in the air-conditioning beads of sweat rolled down his fat neck. 'Always the innovator, eh? I was the same, till the Japs beat us at our own game. Yeah, it's pretty primitive but it might do the trick. Here you go ...'

Cam paid him, then asked as if it was an afterthought: 'Hey, you know about old cameras, don't you, Glen?'

'Yeah, I've got a small collection. Why?' Glen licked his lower lip in an interested fashion. 'Got one, have you? How old?'

'Not ... exactly. And we don't know how old it is,' said Cam. 'A friend of mine has it.' He described the camera.

Goddard leaned forward with narrowed eyes. 'A little round viewing hole, you reckon?' He dragged an enthusiast's magazine out from under his desk. 'Anything like this?'

Cam examined the picture. 'Yeah. Like that, only ... I think the fittings are a bit different – on the corners, here, see? They're brass. And it's a bit smaller. About ten centimetres square. I wondered if it might be a Vistaview.'

Goddard's watery blue eyes widened. He became even more ingratiating. Cam expected him to start rubbing his hands together any moment. 'Well, well ... you could be right. Except that they were made in the States, and not many got over here.'

'Yeah, it's a bit of a mystery,' said Cam.

Irritatingly, Goddard assumed ownership of the problem. 'Your best bet is to bring it in, give us a look. Or should I come out to where it is? Might even be worth a few bucks to your mate,' he said importantly, as though

Cam wouldn't have already thought of that. I know it makes sense to show an expert, thought Cam, taking a step backwards, but how come you're so very interested all of a sudden?

'Oh, my friend's in Shriek – I mean, in Brisbane,' said Cam quickly, not knowing why he was lying. 'She'll take it to someone up there, I think. I just thought you might know, that's all.'

Goddard regarded him with a less friendly eye. 'Well, I can't really help unless I see it. How's that sister of yours, anyway?' he asked.

'Good,' blurted Cam. 'Real good. Well, seeya later.' He bolted out of the shop, with a feeling of disquiet that he could only put down to Goddard's excessive interest.

'Didn't I tell you?' demanded Fil in St Vinnies. 'He's a bloody snake, and he'd rip us off in his sleep.' She hung the shirt back on the rack – at twelve dollars it was too dear.

'Yeah, okay, you win. But now we're stuck. Better try the library.'

The Federation Library was a high wooden building that dominated the south end of Camelot Street. As they went inside, Cam looked casually around at the staff. No luck, Ann wasn't here. Filomena flicked through reference books on the large laminex-topped tables. Cam went over to a computer and was soon plugged into the Internet, on the specialist photography pages.

'Hey, did you know that modem photography was invented by a French guy? Louis Jacques Mandé Daguerre in eighteen *zirty-nine*,' said Filomena in her throatiest French accent.

'Oh ... durr,' Cameron responded in a moron tone. 'Where did you think they got the name daguerreotype from?'

'Just asking,' she said sniffily. 'Found anything?'

'Not yet ... hang on! Hey, check this out! I've got it!' Cam cried, then ducked his head in embarrassment as the male librarian frowned at him. 'Look,' he whispered, reading to Fil off the screen. 'The Eastman Pictureview preceded the Vistaview. It was an experimental model with a small production run of only two thousand, of which only a few hundred are known to have survived. Problems with the operation of the differentiated lens were subsequently solved by the addition of blah, blah – This is it, Fil! Look!'

Fil looked over his shoulder as the illustration appeared on the screen. Yep, that was her camera, down to the loopy stitching on the shoulder strap and the clever brass fitting that held the body closed. 'Only two thousand made,' she murmured. 'It's rare.'

'It must be valuable,' said Cam, 'and it's ...' He made a rapid calculation. 'Jesus, it must be ninety-five years old. Production was between 1902 and 1903. Not long before the First World War. Someone must have brought it out from the States. Eastman didn't internationalise until well after that.' He looked at his sister. Her eyes shone.

'No wonder Goddard wanted to get his greedy paws onto it,' she said.

'Lucky you had a hunch,' Cam agreed. 'Well, we

know what it is now, anyway. D'ya wanna go and get a drink? I'm melting.'

'Let's go to the beach before the Hare's,' she suggested when they'd bought drinks from the snack bar outside the Library, 'then we can have a think about what to do.'

They spent the middle of the day swimming and bodysurfing. By the time they'd hitched back home, Filomena had decided that she would definitely sell the camera to the highest bidder. Even if that was Cameron. He wasn't talking to her.

Chapter Four

At six-thirty, just as the summer day was about to make itself felt, Jon began loading his gear into the Transit van. Wednesday was his day to work in Brisbane, breaking in horses for what he called the 'unspeakables'. Already hot and sticky, Fil handed him his plain, uncarved Western saddle.

'Dad,' she said diffidently, not sure she should mention it, 'did you know there's an old ruined house at the foot of the mountain?'

Jon lifted his eyebrows and slid the saddle onto one of the fold-down racks he'd installed in the van. 'I should think there'd be a million old ruins. It's a big mountain, after all. Shepherd's huts, cattle shelters, humpies where the first whites squatted with the Murris. But the short answer is no. Where?'

Filomena paused, not knowing if she really wanted Dad to know everything. 'It's ... well, you know Desperation Creek – where that huge lilly pilly tree is, just past the second crossing? It's in the bush near there, about four or five kilometres in.'

'What the hell were you doing in there? Or do I want to know?'

'Took a short cut out riding,' she muttered. He still didn't know that she'd temporarily lost Angel, just that she'd fallen.

'I reckon,' he said seriously, 'I wouldn't go anywhere in the bush around there that was too far off the track.'

Fil looked up quickly. Maybe Dad had a logical reason why the house felt so gross. 'Why?'

'Use your brain, Bella. The mountain's riddled with plantations. Stumble over someone's green superannuation crop and you're likely to get a bullet first and questions second. You're not just a skinny kid any more, you know.'

'Oh, I didn't see anything like that.'

'Just as well. They always have a fence up, but still … And *please,* don't go looking!'

'Yeah, yeah … I was wondering who the house could have belonged to. It's – I mean it was – a real house, not a shack.'

'What's it made of? Timber?'

Fil shook her head. 'It's mostly brick, with a tin roof.'

Jon was surprised. 'Brick? Well, unless you've stumbled on Great-grandfather Costello's long lost dream home, I really don't know. This area's got a long and tangled history. Chuck us that blanket, please.'

'What do you mean, dream home?' Fil was staring.

'When I was growing up in Shriekerville, my father used to talk to me about his grandfather, Hew Costello; how he'd gone off into the wilds around Mount Arthur to carve an empire in the bush. I think he always regretted that he couldn't do the same. Of course,' Jon the anarchist added, 'he could have. He just thought he couldn't.'

'Really?' said Filomena.

'Really. In fact, that's partly why I moved here, to find where the old Costello place was ... who knows, we might even still have some sort of a bodgie claim to it. Somehow, I haven't got around to looking yet, but I know it was in this area. It must have been within a day's drive by bullock wagon of Shelley Bay, 'cos he used to farm cattle and pan gold in Desperation Creek. At the end of each month he'd take a bullock, if he had one, and whatever ore he'd found, and trade them for subsistence rations down at Shelley Bay. It was a big centre in those days, when the whaling station was still running full-time.'

'What happened to him?'

'Ah, now, he was a bit of a mystery man. Don't know for sure. He came to a bad end, I'd say, seeing as how the family stories stop with his goldmining. He was wealthy for a short time, but probably either starvation or the Murris got him. Farming's a hard line of work. Just another in a long line of imperial failures.' Jon didn't seem too concerned about his ancestor's demise.

'How long ago was this?' asked Filomena. It was a fantastic story, and typical of Jon not to tell it until he was asked. Could she really have stumbled on to her great-great-grandfather's house?

Jon slid the van door shut and glanced at his watch. 'Oh ... let's see. Dad was thirty-two when he had me, and if his father was, say, thirty ... *his* grandfather would have been born in eighteen seventy-three or four ...' He gave her a despairing look. 'I can't do it in my head, Cam's the mathematician. I think it would have been just before the turn of the century. You work it out on paper. A generation was about twenty years or so in those days. I've gotta get going now. Take me and show me one day. You never know.'

He got into the driver's seat, started the shiny maroon van with 'Jon Menzies – Master Horseman' painted inside a large upturned horseshoe on both sides, and turned it around. Before driving out, he stuck his tanned face out of the window. 'And Fil—'

'Yeah?' She smiled innocently.

'Since I know you wouldn't be thinking of going riding while I'm safely in Brisbane, you'll have plenty of time to help Cam paint the foaling shed, won't you? I told him to get out a brush for you. Made his day. You should be finished by four or so.'

'Mmm,' said Filomena, expressionless. 'I bet.' How did Jon always know?

'Cheer up. I might let you come to the beach with me tomorrow on Gunner.'

She brightened. Gunner was their little bay quarter-horse stallion, and everyone's favourite. Gunner wouldn't hurt a fly.

'Okay! See you tonight.' He waved and left in a cloud of dust.

Filomena trudged back to the stables, where Cam was grinning nastily at her fate. She snatched the paintbrush he was holding out. 'Not one word, you,' she threatened as she stalked off to start painting the other side of the shed.

★

Shortly after lunch, the phone rang from the tack shed, making both of them jump. Jon had it turned up loud enough to hear from the schooling yard. Since he was the one painting inside, Cam answered. 'Aonbar's Rest, can I help you?' He made a few comments, then came out to where Filomena was painting, pressing the receiver to his chest. She gave him an enquiring look.

'Bill Barton. Wants to know if he can send someone over for that grey filly. Did Dad say anything to you?'

'Oh, yeah! I forgot. He said she's ready to go, but bring her back in a fortnight for shoes.'

Cam nodded and passed the message on. 'He's sending a bloke about fourish. Name's Darcy. We'd better get her in before then.'

Fil grimaced. 'Yuk, what a name.'

'Jane Austen. To die for,' said Cam. 'Look, I've had enough of this shit. Let's have a break.'

'I'm staying. I'm nearly finished. Give it another half an hour.'

Cameron sighed melodramatically and started work again. 'Paint the fence. Scrub the floor. Polish 'da' car,' he complained loudly.

'I was gonna jump Governor over the log this arv,' Fil moaned in sympathy. 'Jon's a slave-driver.'

'Ha! Says she, who visits for four weeks a year. I get it all the time. Eighty bucks a week for eighty hours work, practically.'

'At least you get paid,' Fil told him. 'You got to buy Garbo, and you're two years younger than me.' She put a limp hand to her forehead as she passed him to go outside to her half-painted wall. 'Give me a yell at half past. If I'm alive by then.'

'That'll do it,' said Cam after another hour, when the foaling shed was gleaming white inside and out, with blue trim. 'Let's party, dudes.'

Showered and depainted, they opened beers and collapsed in a heap in the lounge. Cam gave the phone the evil eye. 'You Will Not Ring,' he ordered. Instead, a loud banging sounded at the door. He rolled his eyes. Less used than Cam to the hard work, Filomena didn't even move. If she did, she thought, her arms and legs would definitely fall off. Would you love me if I was a stump, she imagined asking her kind-of-boyfriend Drago.

'Ah, fuck, we forgot that fucking grey,' Cam said wearily, getting up, beer in hand, to answer the door.

He opened it to find an impressive young Aboriginal standing outside. He wasn't dressed like the Aboriginal kids in Shelley Bay. They wore surf shorts, dreads and Bob Marley T-shirts. This kid had on fawn moleskin trousers, elastic-sided boots and a faded blue button-down shirt. His haircut would have pleased the army, it was so short. The only thing about him that hinted at trendiness was an earring. He could be any age, thought Cam, from sixteen to almost twenty. He had a friendly smile, and he stood straight, shoulders squared, like Jon. Probably Bill Barton made him wear those clothes on account of the snobby racehorse owners coming to inspect their investments on the weekends. They'd like an Aboriginal working for them, Cam thought, so long as he was dressed right. Make them feel really ... high class, or something.

'Hi. How ya doing?'

'Hi. I'm Darcy. Come for a horse of Barton's,' the boy said.

'Yeah. Ah, look ... we'll have to get her from the paddock. You wanna wait here, or come?' Darcy looked pointedly at the beer Cam was holding. Cam followed his gaze, and noticed that Darcy's forehead was wet with sweat where his hat had been. 'Oh, sorry. You want a drink? Look, come in. We've just finished work. Are you in a hurry?'

The dark youth hesitated. 'I've got to get back before five, eh.'

'Coke or VB?' Cam asked.

'Oh, better be a Coke, eh. Thanks.' Darcy stepped inside and saw Filomena watching TV through her splayed legs.

'G'day, I'm Darcy.' She's pretty, he thought. Like a city girl's pretty. Clean. Fresh.

'I'm Fil. That's Cam.' Darcy sat down uneasily and sipped from his can. Cute, observed Filomena, very very cute. Dark curls, black eyes, skin like golden syrup. Tall, too. And nicely dressed. Yum, yum. 'Have you been with Bill long?' she asked, sitting up and brushing her fringe back. Please say yes. And that you haven't got a girlfriend. And that you lo-o-ove soccer-playing wog girls. Drago, whispered her conscience, but Fil had suddenly developed hearing problems.

'Since last Monday,' said Darcy.

'What'd you do before that?' asked Cam, being friendly.

Darcy bit his lip. 'Ah, nothing much. Hooned around in Adelaide. Bit of cattle station work. I'm from the bush.'

'I thought this was the bush,' said Filomena. 'Christ, it feels like it after Melbourne.' She attempted to sound like a world-weary sophisticate, adrift without her cafes and art galleries.

Darcy grinned. 'Federation? The bush.' He laughed as though Fil had cracked a great joke. Then, suddenly serious, he spoke very quietly. Reverently. 'Where I come from, there's nothun. Nothun for yufla.'

Something in Darcy's voice made Cameron hold his breath. Filomena could sense it too. Mile after mile of dirt stretching away in front of her. Didgeridoo music played in her head.

'Youse see that film *The Red Centre?*' said Darcy. 'That's my country. Red dirt country, eh. Beautiful. Here's okay though. Too many fucken whitefellas, but.' He was grinning again, being deliberately over-the-top to see how they'd react. They both smiled, unoffended. Darcy upended his can, then crumpled it. Enough talkin' to these kids. He had work to do. 'Let's get this horse, eh?' Filomena got up to join them outside. Cam looked at her, surprised. Five minutes earlier, she had said that she was never going to move again. The three of them walked towards the paddock where the newly broken thoroughbred filly grazed, unaware of her hoped-for future as a racecourse star.

'Youse live here, or what?' Darcy addressed himself to Cam.

'Yeah, well, my dad, I mean, our dad owns the place and I work here.' Cam tried to emphasize that he didn't always sit around swilling beer. Something in Darcy's dark face and sparkling eyes made Cam want to impress him. 'I help with the yardwork and the breaking. Plus school, of course. Fil just visits in the holidays. She's my sister.'

Most people did a double take when Cameron said that, but Darcy didn't blink. 'Nice place. Good yards,' he said approvingly, looking at the thickness of the timber Jon had used. Wired and bolted, not nailed. 'Did ya help break this one?' he asked Cam. 'She's beautiful, ch.'

'Uh ... yeah,' Cam lied. Well, he would have, if they hadn't gone to town so much since Fil arrived. He *had* helped the first couple of days, before Fil got here. The dark boy hung off a heavy rail while Cam went up to the filly with a handful of oats. She was a gentle soul, and didn't budge when he held her mane.

Standing by herself, Filomena tried to think what to say to Darcy that wouldn't sound stupid – So, what's it like being Aboriginal? Um, my boyfriend's a wog and I am too, and we get racist comments at school from the skips sometimes. What do you think of Barton? – She couldn't think of a single thing.

'Coosh, bonnie girl, coosh.' When the horse was haltered, Cam handed her to Darcy. 'She's all yours, mate. One broken filly. She needs shoeing in a coupla weeks.'

'Thanks.' Darcy looked the filly over very carefully, running hands down her fine thoroughbred legs. He tightened his grip on the halter rope and leaned his body weight onto her back. She flicked an ear but stood firm. Cam wondered what he was doing. To his surprise, Darcy then gave what looked like the lightest of hops and was astride the horse's bare back. 'Well, nice to meetcha. Bye.'

He rode out of the open paddock gate while Filomena's jaw dropped. Cam stood stock still, waiting for the horse to freak. If there was one thing you didn't do with newly broken horses, it was ride them outside the paddock bareback and unbridled. As if in confirmation of this, the filly began to plunge and buck. As though he was on a quiet old carthorse, Darcy hauled her head up and used the end of the halter rope to whack her ribs. She snorted in surprise. He readjusted his Akubra with one hand while the horse whirled in a circle.

'Gerrout of it, you cheeky bitch!' he reprimanded her, hooking a heel into her chest to steer her. She walked forward, behaving herself this time. Darcy turned and waved, then set off. Yerra fucken showboat, Darcy Mango, he told himself. Silly bastard. You'll getcha self killed one day. He laughed to himself and rode the filly home with only half his attention on her, the rest of him filled with the lustful thoughts of sixteen-year-old boys always have when they see an attractive stranger.

Cam raised his eyebrows at Fil. 'And I thought I was pretty good.'

His sister smiled, starstruck. Good-looking, exotic and a rider too. Wow. Did she have plans for him. 'He's *cute*. What a hunk. I have to make sure we get to Barton's soon. Did he leave anything behind?'

'Oh, puh-lease!' Cam said, dismissing her girlish

sentiments. 'There's a dozen horses here to feed and groom.'

'Be nice,' Fil said sweetly, 'or I won't tell you what Dad told me this morning about the old haunted place …' She trailed off, knowing Cam hated suspense.

'What? What!'

On the way to the stables she told him about Hew Costello, and his wilderness home at the turn of the century.

'What's for dinner?' Cameron asked as he and Fil took their boots off outside the kitchen.

'You tell me!' she retorted. 'Since when did I become chief cook around this joint?'

'Okay, okay … you got any money? We could get a pizza. They deliver out here now. But they charge an extra five bucks.'

Fil handed her money to him. The pizza would be redneck shit, of course, but it'd save her cooking. 'The twentieth century comes to Aonbar's Rest, yip yay,' she said.

'Do you reckon it could really be Hew Costello's place?' Cam asked as they waited in growing darkness on the front steps for the food.

Filomena shrugged. 'I don't see why not. It's got to be somewhere around here. And it looked real old. The only thing wrong is the roof. Tin would have rusted out much longer ago — if it was built — when did you say?'

'If it was twenty to twenty-five years between generations, he'd have been born about 1880 and lived there about 1900 or 1910. But I'm just guessing. But what if someone else lived there since and replaced the roof? That's possible.'

Filomena considered this suggestion. Of course, why didn't she think of that. Hew Costello could have built the house in 1900, lived in it (died – yuk – in it), then someone else might have lived there before abandoning it to the rainforest.

'Why would he live so far from the road, though?' she wondered aloud.

'Roads shift,' Cam pointed out. 'The creek bed might have flooded and they might have moved the track. Anything could have happened in eighty years. You know how things change around here.'

Aonbar's largest paddock had been cut in two only last year when the creek broke its banks, and since then they'd had to detour around a swampy patch every time they brought horses up.

'It's spooky. What if it is our own great-great-grandfather's house?' She shivered melodramatically. 'It's really creepy in there, Cam. I was shit-scared, hey?' As she spoke, the cane toads started ribbitting in the wet ground near the water trough. Moths and other insects were already flying kamikaze style around the light bulb above them.

'Forests are always a bit creepy when you're by yourself, even if you're used to the bush,' Cam said, in a tone of maddening superiority. 'The thing is, to find out for sure if it was his. What if it's our land? What if he owned it and there's a title to the property, and Jon, you and me are the only living heirs? We'd be rich!'

His mention of riches reminded Filomena of the camera. 'Hey! What about the photos? Will they be ready yet?'

Cam leapt up and came trotting back a minute later, holding the prints. 'Maybe the solution is too strong for the old film,' he said in a disappointed voice. 'Can't see very much. Just blurs. Look, there's the one of the horse ...' He handed a photo to Fil, who examined it under the glare of the light bulb. It sure didn't look like Picasso. 'And this is inside the house, I think. It's pretty dark.'

None of them looked like she'd expected. Even accounting for the poor developing, there was something – different about them. None of the shapes looked right.

'And this ...' Cam turned it around, trying to decipher it. 'Who is it? Did you take one of Dad?'

'No.' Filomena suddenly felt chill. She hadn't taken any photos of people at—

'You sure? It looks like him.'

'Positive, dickhead,' she said, getting angry because she was frightened.

'Look!' He thrust the photo towards her and she took it reluctantly. She had that yukky feeling again, the one she'd had inside the ruin. Like someone was watching her from the shadows. Like something bad was going to happen. She avoided looking out to where the night was getting very black. Instead, she turned around on the step to face the house with its comforting TV noise and brilliant lights. A night bird made its call close to where they sat.

The photo she held was slightly clearer than the others. In it was a man, a man she'd never seen, although Fil could understand why Cam thought it might be Jon. He was about the same height, standing in a doorway. and his hair was also longish and dark. Above the doorway she struggled to make out the very faint lettering: *Robinson's Emporium*. And a date. After a long moment, her hand began to shake. Cam saw that something was wrong. Fil had gone pale under her tan.

'What is it?' he asked urgently. taking the photo back and looking at it. 'Who is it?'

'I don't know. Read it.' Filomena said in a terrible whisper. *'Robinson's Emporium*. Wasn't that the old name of the arcade where you and Dad got the wood for the house?' Cam and Jon had taken the van last summer, when they were still living in the Thunderbox, as they called their old caravan, and bought secondhand timber for the house. On the phone that night, he'd told Fil it would build a beautiful house, and was still in good condition since it had been used only for the inside of Federation Arcade, which was being ripped down to build a hotel. The Arcade, he realised she was saying, used to be the old Robinson's Emporium building.

'What d'ya mean?' he asked, puzzled.

'Cam,' Filomena blurted in horror, 'listen to me, listen! Look at the picture – that's not Dad. That's not anyone we know.'

Cam's scalp tingled; he was beginning to get infected with Filomena's fear. 'That's someone standing *in Robinson's Emporium*. Read the date on the sign – *1896* – it's a photo of how things were a hundred years ago.'

Cam snorted. 'Don't be ridiculous.' But his voice wavered. 'It's just an old photo that was already in there …'

'When I picked it up to start taking photos, I checked. The counter read zero.'

'Zero,' Cameron repeated. '1896. Am I going mad?' He ran his fingers through his short spiky hair.

The man that looked out at them from the photo wore old-fashioned working clothes and a hat that could only have been worn in the nineteenth century.

Cam fought his sudden panic. 'There has to be an explanation …'

'It's awful!' Filomena said fiercely. 'There's something about that house.'

Then Cam saw something that made his mouth go dry. 'Look at his eyes.'

The black-and-white print showed the man's strange pale eyes. Cam had never seen those weird eyes on anyone except himself and Dad. 'I bet,' he said slowly in a choking way, 'I bet you anything you like, that's Hew Costello.'

Filomena nodded weakly. 'Cam, I'm frightened.'

Before Cam could confess that so was he, they heard a car approaching.

'The pizza,' said Fil in relief. But it was Jon returning from Brisbane. Cam put the photos away, and he and Fil agreed to talk about it after dinner. It was all much too weird to tell Jon right away. Maybe if we go away and come back, Fil secretly hoped, the photos will be of Picasso and the house and the wheelbarrows, and everything'll be okay.

★

'*Uhh.*' Jon groaned as he sat in his lounge chair. He stretched a stiff leg in front of him.

'You right? Get hurt, Dad?' Cam asked in concern, bringing him a cup of tea. They'd made short work of the pizza when it finally arrived.

'Oh, a bit.'

'Just a flesh wound?' Cam said. It was their private joke. No matter how badly Jon got hurt, he'd stagger to his feet and say it to prove to himself he wasn't getting old. Cam had started saying it too. It made him feel more like a man.

'Bit more, maybe.'

Cameron stopped laughing. 'What'ja do? Fall?'

'Bloody green arsehole of a strapper at Hendra let a rein go when I was putting a crupper on. The horse was frightened and kicked. That didn't get me, 'cos I rolled out of the way, but then the fucking thing stood on my leg. Big gelding, too. It's enough to make me go back to Uni some days.'

Cam made a face. His father hated working inside. He'd only stayed at university so long – most of Cam's childhood – because they needed the money, and when he'd got almost enough to pay for Aonbar's Rest, he quit. By then the rot had set in between him and Mum, but that was a different story.

'What I really need,' Jon told Cam, 'is for you to be a couple of years older and my full-time assistant. Then I wouldn't have to rely on knaves and fools.'

Cam glowed. 'Say the word, Dad.'

Jon shook his head. Cam was still too young. He knew his son was going to be an outstanding horseman, but no one else did. And he couldn't see the flinty trainers in Brisbane letting a babyface like Cam near their expensive charges, even with him there. A rare few of the yearling horses he broke were almost worth their weight in gold.

Jon peeled his trouser leg up away from the ankle. Filomena sucked her teeth when she saw the cut, a purplish-black crescent on her father's calf, surrounded by puffy red flesh. 'Da-a-ad! Shouldn't you see someone about it?'

'I might go and see Craig in the morning.'

Filomena pursed her lips. Craig, her father's hippie friend, lived in his treehouse in a haze of ganja smoke and esoterica. He advertised himself as a herbalist, naturopath and acupuncturist. Filomena had as little faith in him as Jon had in conventional medicine.

'It's just muscle and skin damage,' Jon reassured them. 'Lucky he didn't get my shin or the bone might …' He made a two-handed snapping gesture.

'Oh,' said Filomena sarcastically. 'I'm sure Craig has a magic potion to knit broken bones overnight.'

Jon looked steadily at her. 'Western doctors nearly killed me once. For all Craig's … peculiarities, he's never done that.'

'Give it time,' she replied. 'What'll you do when I'm qualified, insist I prescribe you dope and daisies?'

'If and when you become a doctor of medicine, my dear,' Jon said, 'I'll haunt your corridors day and night.'

'Yeah, scabbing money. Here's the tea-tree oil, Dad.' Cam handed Jon the bottle and he smoothed the oil tenderly onto his bruises.

'So, how's the shed look?' Jon enquired. 'Get it done?'

Cam nodded. 'Yeah, it looks good. Fit for another Phar Lap.'

'You wish,' Fil said. As well as breaking Bill Barton's thoroughbreds, Jon and Cam continued to sink their little spare money into breeding the three thoroughbred mares Aonbar's Rest owned. Fil considered it collective lunacy on their parts; there was no surer way for small fry to lose money than to be associated with racehorses. They'd sold one colt for a few hundred last year, recouping the season's outlays and intensifying their mad scheme to breed the area's first Melbourne Cup winner. Cam was always scouring the racing magazines to find which horses were standing at stud close enough and cheap enough for them to consider.

'Good,' Jon said in satisfaction. 'And what about that filly?'

'Yeah, this guy picked her up,' Cam said. 'Fil's new boyfriend.'

'Oh, shut up!' she snapped, blushing.

'A black kid,' teased Cam mercilessly, 'tall, dark and handsome, hey Fil? She was drooling,' he informed his father.

'Leave her alone,' Jon said. 'Or I'll tell her about Lucy.' Cam shut up. Lucy had rung him twice since the fight, and he was eagerly waiting for another call. Fil looked at him with narrow eyes. Who was Lucy?

'Given the state of this leg,' Jon told them, 'you two had better exercise Picasso and Gunner tomorrow. We'll lunge the others if I can't ride.' His tone was deadpan, as if he wasn't offering them the two best horses (bar Angel) on the place to ride.

'Wow! Excellent! Thanks, Dad!' Filomena was overjoyed. 'Who gets Picasso?'

Jon sniffed. 'Cam. He's ridden him a couple of times lately. And your little escapade on Saturday isn't entirely forgotten.' He drained his teacup. 'I better have an early one, I think.' He got up with difficulty and limped off down the hall.

Cam stuck his tongue out at Filomena, who had only ridden the elegant Picasso once, in the ring on her fifteenth birthday. 'Hey, let's go up the bush tomorrow.'

'Why not the beach?'

'You know, up the mountain,' he said meaningfully.

Fil understood him, and froze. 'Uh ... maybe,' she said reluctantly. She still remembered the cold fear the old house had given her.

'We can take the camera,' Cam whispered.

She looked at him. He just didn't have a clue.

CHAPTER FIVE

Filomena took Cam's photo standing in front of the tangled bushes that hid the ruin.

'That's the six.' he told her. 'There's a good view from here. You don't notice how high you're getting till you've arrived.'

'No, it's five,' Fil said humbly. She felt a bit silly. From a distance, and with Cam and the two horses there, as well as Maxwell crashing through the bushes after scrub turkeys, the house didn't look nearly as frightening. Lonely, yes, and decrepit, but not skin-crawlingly yukky like the other day. Cam hadn't said anything about her being chicken, but she knew he was thinking it. She shivered anyway. It was cooler up here.

'You in your room. One,' Cam said, sticking his thumb out.

'The stables, two.'

'The creek crossing, three.'

'Back of Dad's head in the kitchen, four.'

'And this one, five. You're right.' Cam agreed. 'Will we take one of the inside?'

Fil was silent.

'Fil?' he insisted.

'Oh … shit, all right. But you go first. Let's tie the horse up here.' Filomena wrapped Gunner's reins around a young gum tree while Cam took care of Picasso. Then they stepped cautiously into the lantana thicket. Still scratched from the other day, Fil dragged her shirt up over her face as she crawled after Cam. A tingle of apprehension ran up her spine as they reached the open ground.

'Wow,' Cam breathed when they emerged on the other side. 'You went in *there*? Alone?'

Filomena suddenly felt braver. She noticed how much quieter it was on this side of the lantana. As though the mossy house was marooned by its undergrowth. Those windows still had the look of eyes, even with Cam here. A cool wind brushed over her and she wrapped her arms around herself. 'Yeah,' she tried to sound offhand.

'It is a bit … spooky, isn't it?' As Cam spoke, he was walking towards the same hole in the wall that Fil had squeezed through.

Fil stared angrily at his back. Couldn't he sense it? The feeling that they weren't the only ones here? Picasso neighed sharply from somewhere out of sight, startling her. Suddenly, instinctively, she just knew it was dangerous to be here.

'Um … Cam?'

He turned, his freckled face looking more like Jon's than she'd ever noticed before. She really was the odd one out.

'Yeah?'

She could see it was no use. To him, this was just an old, ruined building.

'Nothing.' She swallowed her fear and went after him. When they were standing inside the first room (the 'safe' room, Fil called it to herself), Cam sounded disappointed. 'It's way too dark to snap,' he said. 'Nothing'd show up.'

Fil held the camera up. Her hand trembled. 'It's dark,' she said. 'But if it really is … doing what we think … then it won't matter.'

Just talking about the camera made her want to bolt outside and ride for her life. Cam, on the other hand, cheered up. Fil didn't know whether he completely lacked imagination, or whether his world was so full of fantasy from living with Dad that the camera confirmed his basic world-view.

'Good thinking, Fil. Where do you want it?'

Hesitantly, Fil peered into the dimness. 'Anywhere. No, wait. Do one of that room there.' She didn't know what made her point to the small room, furthest from the horrible dark doorway beyond the kitchen.

'Hokey-dokey.' He took the picture through the glass in the door.

'Let's go.' Fil felt claustrophobia racing in on her. They stepped outside to the clearing. The cicadas thrummed; otherwise, she and Cam seemed to be the only living creatures there.

'I wonder …' said Cam thoughtfully. 'If it was Hew Costello's place, wouldn't something be left? Clothes, books or something? So we could tell?'

Fil, in a hurry to be gone, pooh-poohed the idea. 'It

was so long ago. Clothes or books would have rotted. Pots or pans could belong to anyone. If the camera ... the photos might tell us, but who'd ever believe *that?* Come on, let's go.'

'Yeah. But what if there was a — a gravestone or something,' Cam suggested.

Filomena swung on him. 'Just stop it!' Her brown eyes flashed angrily.

'Okay, okay ... just an idea. Let's go, then.'

They crawled back to the horses and rode across the cleared hills to Mill Road, the camera safely stowed in Cam's saddlebag.

At Bill Barton's stables Darcy sat lightly on a bay gelding waiting for the word to gallop. The trainer standing beside the railings took out a stopwatch then signalled him to start. Darcy cantered, bum high, towards the finish post then started scrubbing with his hands and feet. The horse snorted heavily through reddened nostrils as they rounded the track, throwing mud and turf behind them. Darcy loved to ride; best of all he loved to gallop. This was living, he thought, as he brought the horse to a halt beside the Boss.

'One eighteen,' Barton said. 'Not so good. How was he feeling?'

'Okay.' Darcy was shy of the Boss, and with good reason. Bill Barton was a decent man, but even the most decent man would have flinched at Darcy's secret history of thievery, vandalism and assault.

The trainer frowned and looked the horse over. No

injuries. No stone bruises. No cold. 'What did you say you weighed, son?'

'Sixty-two.'

'Sixty-two.' Barton was impassive. 'Okay, take him inside. Then come and see me.'

Darcy took himself unhappily to Barton's office. He knew he was about to be sprung.

'Jump up there for me.' Barton pointed to a large set of racing scales. Darcy sighed and stepped on. 'Sixty-seven,' said Barton in a tight voice. 'No wonder the horse couldn't perform. Look, son, you're not the first heavy kid with a crush on horses to tell porkies about your weight. And you're not too bad a rider. But a racing stable's no place for you. You'll have to pack your bags. Sorry.'

Darcy slumped from the room. With no job, his parole was gonna look pretty shaky at the next interview.

Jon hobbled towards the lunging ring, Angel's lead in one hand, a walking stick in the other. Not the safest way to travel, he thought, but I'll be right. The leg that had horrified Fil on Wednesday night was now, on Friday, beginning to worry him. The bruising wasn't coming out, and he didn't know what to think of the red streaks around the cut. Well, that wasn't really true. He did know. Infection, and danger. Angel pranced, excited in the belief that he was about to be ridden. 'What do you reckon, old boy?' he asked the horse. 'Should I risk it?' Angel tossed his head up and down. Jon laughed. 'You're on. I'll go to the quack this afternoon.' But there were nine more horses to lunge, he thought, and Cam could only do three, four at the most. I should have made them lead a couple out riding. Then someone coughed.

'G'day, Boss.' Darcy's words made Jon jump. He'd thought he was alone. The black boy stood just beyond the fenceline of Aonbar's Rest, half-hidden by a big eucalypt.

'Christ. Didn't see you there, come in. What's up? More precisely, who are you?' Though he already had a suspicion before the boy spoke. Good-looking black youths didn't grow on trees around Aonbar's Rest.

'Darcy Mango. I was working for Bill Barton, till this morning.'

'Oh, yes?' Jon said cautiously, remembering Cam's remarks about Fil's interest in this lad. He could see why — he was as yet an unformed work, with an unsuitable haircut and shy manner, but Darcy would one day be a beautiful man. And he dressed like ... well, like a male model. Blunnies, Akubra, chequered shirt. Fil was wasting her time, alas. Jon scratched his head, amused.

'Umm, turns out I'm too heavy for track work, eh. I was wondering if you had anything going, breaking and that. I've got a reference.'

Jon unsnapped Angel's lead and left him loose in the yard. He examined the piece of paper Darcy was holding, in which Bill Barton spoke highly of his abilities. 'A piece of paper's not worth very much now, is it?'

'Guess not,' said Darcy softly. 'But I used to break horses and do stock work outside Alice Springs. Bill Barton said to give you a try.' There wasn't the slightest hint of begging in his voice.

'You Pitjantjatjara. Aranda or Agadja?' Jon asked.

Darcy's eyes widened. 'Yanbali, by blood. But I was raised Agadja since I was five.'

'Local boy, eh? What are you, eighteen?'

'Seventeen. Just turned.'

'Buckjumper?'

'Lil' bit.'

'Country races?'

'Yeah, a few.'

'Cattle work or sheep? Please don't say camels.' Darcy's lip curled in disdain.

'Cattle.'

'Got a criminal record?' That stumped him. The kid didn't know what to say. 'I'll take that as a "yes". Well, you're not the only one.' Jon closed one eye, looked out of the other critically at the boy. 'It might be your lucky day, Darcy Mango. I've hurt my leg and I could use an extra pair of hands. These aren't all quiet old riding-school horses, though. Let's see you lunge this fella before we sign you up.'

Inwardly Darcy smiled to himself. He stepped towards Angel's head holding the lunging rein unobtrusively behind his back. The horse tensed and shifted his weight almost imperceptibly to his hindquarters, ready to jump. Darcy changed his angle of approach very slightly and stopped about two metres away. He looked in a bored fashion at his feet and ignored Angel. Intrigued, the horse swung his head to face the boy. Darcy still didn't look at the horse. Angel's ears came forward and he took a hesitant step fowards. Darcy shuffled backwards, very slowly. The horse's confidence grew. By the time Darcy reached the middle of the ring, Angel was sniffing him all over and wondering what the hell was happening. Only then did Darcy slide a dark arm around the chestnut's sleek neck, bridle him, and begin to send him around the ring. He trotted the horse, cantered him, halted him, turned him in the other direction. Then he shot an inquisitive look at Jon.

'Got yourself a job, son,' Jon said, pleased with Darcy's obvious skill, and – just as important – gentleness. Someone on those outback stations hadn't subscribed to the belt 'n bash school of horsemanship. 'Part-time, I'm afraid, we're not terribly financial around here. You can come in three times a week. How's that?'

'Good.'

'What did Barton pay you?'

'Two hundred a week.'

Jon winced. He could use some help, but it was a luxury on Aonbar's Rest's small cash-flow. And yet, to let the boy go ... a vague guilt nagged him with visions of Darcy at the dole office, or mouldering in the parks of Federation. And, he suddenly thought, Fil could use being shaken out of her I'm-a-Big-City-Smoothie act too. This boy might be just the shot. 'Less than you need, more than I can afford ... I'll give you one fifteen a week. Okay?'

Darcy nodded. Beggars can't be choosers, he thought. And he liked this muscly dude with the sharp eyes and long hair. He was pretty hot for an old guy. Something powerful hovered about him; an underlying strength rested beneath his good looks and easy manner.

'Oh, and Darcy.'

Darcy lifted his chin.

Jon was still smiling. 'If you fuck up – if anything goes missing, or anyone gets hurt – watch out. Okay?'

'Yep.'

'So long as you're clear about that. Welcome to Aonbar's Rest. Lead him back for me, will you?' Jon limped beside Darcy, explaining the operations of the school.

When Filomena rode into the stable yard she knew she was dreaming. Darcy had rolled his shirt sleeves up and was busily forking straw out of Angel's loose box onto the manure heap. Jon was grooming Angel, and the two were discussing the music of Tupac Shakur. She did an instant appearance self-analysis. Hair – okay. Clothes – her red tab Levis and elastic-sided riding boots were fine, the cream Portman's shirt a bit daggy. Zits – the only serious ones she had were out of sight in her hairline and on her shoulders. She was, thank Christ, over the terrible volcanic pustules that had made her life a misery at Cam's age.

Then Cameron came up behind her on Picasso; lost in thought, Fil didn't notice Gunner putting his ears back. His squeal of anger was matched by Picasso's grunt of pain when a pair of neatly shod quarter-horse hooves thudded into the larger horse's chest.

'Can't you two control your bloody horses?' snapped Jon. Pain was making him irritable. 'That's a thousand-dollar animal, Cam, not a lump of catfood.'

'It's Fil ...' wailed Cameron, embarrassed and angry. Filomena's heart sank. They looked – and sounded – like a pair of quarrelsome kids. She didn't sound like someone Darcy might awkwardly ask to the movies in Federation sometime, say this weekend.

'Sorry, Dad.' Then she glanced, oh so casually, towards Darcy. 'Hi, Darcy. Whaddya doing here?'

Jon answered for him. 'Darcy's going to do a bit of work around the place for me. While my leg's sore, anyway.'

I've died, Fil thought, died and gone to heaven.

'Way to go, man!' Cam congratulated Darcy. There was no jealousy in Jon's son. On the contrary, he was delighted he'd have a bloke his own age around.

Jon heard the pleasure in Cam's voice and smiled. His children were innocents, both of them. Oh, he knew well enough that Cam smoked a little dope with Jordan from time to time, and Fil thought she knew the city rave scene but they were still babies really. Should he have a word to Cam, or let Darcy handle it himself? Jon decided to butt out for the time being. 'Where've you been?' he asked Cam. 'You've been gone for two hours. That Glen Goddard from the camera shop rang asking for you.'

Cam shot a look at Fil. 'We went up Mount Arthur. Looking at that old house Fil told you about.' He unsaddled Picasso and slipped the camera from the saddlebag into his backpack.

'Our ancestral mansion?' Jon pricked up his ears. 'See anything new?'

'Just this old dump. Man, it's history.'

'Cam, can you and Darcy lunge the other horses after lunch?' Jon began a detailed description of the afternoon's schedule. Cam computed it all and smiled at Darcy, who wore a worried expression.

Surrounded by too many whites for very long, he began to get a big edgy; right now it was three to one. Cool it, bud, he told himself, don't go freakin' about it.

'What are you gonna do, Fil?' Jon asked as he felt Picasso's chest for lumps and bruising.

What Fil planned on doing was to be wherever Darcy was for the rest of the day. After she changed into clean shorts and a sexy halter top, that is. But she could hardly say that, could she? 'I've got something to do for Cam in the house.' Cam looked at her. 'Developing,' she explained.

'Don't want to come to Federation with me?' Jon offered. 'I'm going to see the quack. It'd be good if you'd drive me as far as Norfolk's Bridge.'

Fil considered the temptations of town versus those of slim, attractive Darcy with his Akubra tilted back over his short black curls. Was it true what they said about black guys? Was it even okay to wonder about that? Despite Jon's efforts, Filomena's colour consciousness was limited to a vague, sentimental disquiet about Aboriginal poverty and an appreciation of black rappers' bodies and style. After all, people were all the same under the skin, weren't they? 'How long'll you be?' she asked Jon.

'Not long, I've made an appointment for two.'

Right. She could go surfing, and be back in time to hang around afterwards. 'Okay.'

As Jon and Filomena prepared to go to town, an exercise that provided Fil with a good excuse to change into her Sportsgirl miniskirt, Cameron quickly dashed to the darkroom and immersed the prints from that morning. He'd take them out in an hour or so, have them ready to show Fil when they got back. Then he slipped out the laundry door to the stables. For the rest of the busy afternoon, he and Darcy groomed, lunged, hosed and fed the eleven horses in their charge. By five o'clock, Cam was exhausted. Darcy, with a history of alternating crushing labour on cattle camps and lighter work in prison, was feeling as fresh as a daisy.

'Your old man's taking a while,' Darcy commented as darkness began to fall. Cam agreed. He knew Fil would be spewing. She had a major crush forming around Darcy. He couldn't get any sense at all out of her yesterday, just endless questions about what boys thought about girls who wore make-up, girls who didn't, what he felt on the issue of earrings, what he would look for in a girl ... What had set her off about Darcy, he wondered? He was pretty cool, but to Cameron's eye he didn't look any more attractive than half a dozen kids in Fil's age-group they'd seen in Federation the other day. Then she'd started reading some of Jon's books on Aboriginal topics.

'Hope the van hasn't broken down. It hasn't for a while now.'

Darcy sat atop the railings of the stableyard, his hands braced on the white-painted wood. Below him the sawdust was a broad golden desert, clean and sharp-smelling. Everything about this place reminded him that he was far from home – the greenness, the seemingly constant rain, the noise, the strange rainforest trees and birds. Looking out at the emerald hills of Aonbar's Rest, he couldn't make himself feel this might have been his home. It was his country through his dead grandmother. Didn't feel like it, but. Sometimes it felt like Mars. He turned to Cameron.

'Well. I'm goin' now. That's okay, isn't it?'

'Shit, don't ask me … I reckon it is, yeah. Dunno where they've gone off to. Where do ya live?'

'Place at Norfolk's Bridge.' Darcy thought Cameron was a nice enough kid, but he wasn't going to let on to the Boss's son that he had spent his last twenty dollars on two night's caravan accommodation at the downmarket Norfolk Bridge Van Park, home of local junkies and alcos.

'I can give you a ride on the Yammy if you like,' Cam offered in a tired voice. Darcy wisely refused, and went off to hitch on Mill Road. Cam dragged himself inside for a bath, and it wasn't until he was fully immersed, soaking his soreness in Radox, that he remembered. 'The photos!' He ran naked and dripping to the darkroom to rescue them. Standing wet and alone in an otherwise empty house in the depth of the country at night was not the ideal situation for discovering that something pretty fucking weird was definitely going on with the old camera.

The photos – they'd turned out clearly this time, their extended soak apparently having done them good rather than harm – confirmed what Cam had tried desperately to disbelieve, and what Filomena had tried to ignore. The first, of Filomena's tiny room, showed a wall of a quite different house. The stables and the creek crossing were replaced by bush. Where Jon should have been leaning backwards on his chair in the kitchen

80

at Aonbar's Rest. was a pastoral scene with horses and cattle. This was unsettling, to say the least. But it wasn't until Cameron reached the two photos taken last, in front of and inside the ruin, that he began to feel truly frightened.

The exterior shot displayed the ruin in its glory days. The walls complete. Grass instead of the jungle and lantana. Wooden shingles on the roof, not decaying tin. Glass in the little slit windows. And standing in almost the same place that Cameron had, the man from the Emporium photo, pale eyes staring out at the future. There was no evidence of a family, of wife or children. Just the man, and at his feet two mongrel dogs. Long-shanked, high-browed, heavy-muscled, pale-eyed. It was him all right, just as it was also Jon, and Cameron. Hew Costello.

There was once a bush-dwelling fellow
Who went by the name of Costello,
He lived in a house,
That was grouse, later louse,
And his eyes were a startling yellow.

Cameron often composed limericks in times of stress.

That photo was bad enough. Cam gulped and was forced to rethink his position. Something extremely bizarre was happening. Either to the camera, or else to the boundaries of space-time. (The alternative explanation, of course, was that he and Fil were simultaneously going mad.) Cam examined the last photo. It was even more bizarre and worrying. As Fil had expected, the gloomy darkness of today did not intrude, but what was probably the interior dimness of 1898 (or whenever) did. The result was a slightly blurred image of a person – he thought it was probably a child or young man – lying down and someone else with their back to the camera holding ... a stick? Or a gun. Yeah, a gun. And on the ground lay a hat, or maybe a hat-shaped rock. Was this inside the house, or was the house in those days differently built, and this picture an outside one? It was impossible to tell. But what was on the feet of the person lying down? And why would anyone lie with their arm at that odd angle, facedown? As he answered his own questions, Cam's wet naked skin began to crawl with goosegumps.

The child was wearing spurs on bare splayed heels. No one, outside cowboy movies, ever goes to sleep wearing spurs. A dead person would lie like that, arm-twisted, wearing spurs. A dead person who had just been shot. A dead person, who had just been shot by the other person in the photo, carrying a gun. A dead person ... a dead *child,* who had just been shot by a man who was probably Cameron's great-great-grandfather.

Murder!

Cameron dropped the photos and ran out sobbing for light, for the twentieth century, and for his father. Slamming the darkroom door, he saw with fear that the van still wasn't home. After he'd pulled on some clothes he pounded to the lounge and turned the TV on loud. The news program was discussing some protest or another; its familiar, bland tone brought him to his senses. He sat watching the TV and avoided looking out into the darkness beyond the windows while his heart-rate returned to normal. Where were Dad and Fil? *What* was going on?

Cameron grasped the arms of his chair tightly. Maybe it was time to ask Dad for help ... no matter what Fil said. He was getting frightened, and he and Fil were only kids. He'd tell Dad everything when they got home, he decided. About the house, the camera, Goddard's interest in it. Fil's determination to sell it, the photos, the dead body. And Dad would, as always, know the best thing to do.

Cameron sat, and watched, and waited ...

At seven o'clock he wanted to know why they hadn't rung.

At eight o'clock he desperately wished Darcy hadn't gone home.

At nine o'clock, he thought of calling the police.

At ten minutes past nine, a car came up the drive. With relief surging through him, Cam went to the front door, to find Filomena getting out of a cab alone. The van was nowhere in sight.

'Where's Dad?' Cam asked, pricked with other tendrils of fear.

'In hospital.' Fil's face was tired. 'He's had his leg operated on. It's infected and they think the infection might have got into the bone.'

This isn't happening, thought Cam, it's impossible. Dad's immortal. Invincible. It's Dad who comes to the rescue, not us, not doctors. 'But it's not ... serious?' he asked.

'I guess he'll be all right, if he stays there. But you know what he's like. The doctors wouldn't tell me anything 'cos I'm a kid. They wanted to know who my *guardian* was. But I wouldn't worry yet.' Be cool, Fil, she told herself, be the big sister. Don't reproduce the concern on the doctor's face. Don't tell him Dad screamed when they manipulated his leg.

'What'd you say?'

'I told them I was eighteen, that my mother was dead and that when there was any news, to ring here. Dad said if there was any problem we should ring your mum, and not to worry, he'll be home in a couple of days.'

'Where's the van?'

'At the hospital.' Fil smiled an exhausted smile. 'So what's for dinner?'

Cam was bewildered. He had already been tired at five o'clock; now, at ten, his poor brain wouldn't work at all. He'd had a nasty shock from the whole weird camera business which he still hadn't figured out, had probably discovered a murderer in the family tree, and now Dad was lying in hospital. Cam was fourteen years old. He was tired and frightened. He gave up. 'I haven't made anything, sorry. There's tomatoes there if you want a sandwich. I'm going to bed.'

Lying in bed, the vivid death-images of his skull-rock poster gave Cam the willies. He got up, turned it to the wall and fell asleep listening to the radio. Dad was gonna be all right. The alternative was unthinkable.

Chapter Six

Darcy woke up homeless. To be more precise, he had four hours until ten o'clock, then he and his few possessions had to be out of the Norfolk Bridge Van Park *(Clean self-contained Cabins from $39 Casual or Perm Vans From $10 Apply Within No Pets Thank you)*. The owner was a large fifty-year-old woman well used to dealing with the low-lifes and sob-stories who couldn't afford anything better than her place. She'd heard every excuse in the book in her time and had long ago lost patience. She'd heard it all: the imminent good fortune of the drunks, the misplaced wallets of the druggies. When Darcy first fronted in reception, handsome, clear-eyed and immaculate in his moleskins and Akubra, her heart soared, until it became obvious that he, too, was scratching for a dollar.

Mrs Long had kept a soft spot for young lads ever since her Nick had left for a girl in Ireland. Recognising the small intimations of poverty from fifty paces, she'd let Darcy stay for four days on terms she kindly described as credit. He'd accepted gratefully, hoping Jon would front-up with some money sooner rather than later, but he couldn't rely on her charity any more. It was time to be off. He rolled with teenage energy off his bunk and picked at the shrivelled remnants of last night's fish 'n chips.

At least I got a job, he thought. He could survive. He'd have money to ring the Parole Board in Adelaide, money for a taxi to see the parole officer in Lismore. Money for laundry so he looked respectable when he fronted court. Probably even enough (once Jon paid him) to come back and buy a few more caravan nights off Mrs Long, so he could claim a fixed address – another point in the Shall We Lock You Up Again stakes. It was just a matter of roughing it, finding an empty house or something until pay day. An old car would do, if it didn't rain too much. Pity his swag had got flogged on the train. He'd loved that swag, eh.

This business of his pay was a bit bloody tricky. If Darcy had been a white boy, or perhaps older and more confident, he would have simply asked Cameron about his money. But seventeen-year-old Darcy had been raised in the bush. English was technically his first language, but Agadja and Kriol were what he'd spoken exclusively until a couple of years ago; and all his life Darcy had been taught that children (which is what he'd resemble until he'd been more fully through the Law) did not speak much to adults. Let alone virtual strangers. Let alone *whites*. Life in traditional Aboriginal families is an intricate web of iron-clad rules, at least where the grog hasn't hit too hard and busted everything the fuck up. At home, Darcy's mother's brothers would have been responsible for noticing that he had no shelter, very little food, no one lookin' out for him. But here, Darcy was outside the web, stranded. He was in charge of himself, and he had to work it out.

One year in the white man's city and a second hanging around in prison had educated Darcy about the world beyond the Agadja homeland; and it had done nothing to make him think that asking white people for things would get him far in life. After a week on the streets of Adelaide, Darcy had found – to his great surprise – that there was not one but many types of whitefella. There were those who hated him for his blackness no matter what. They were to be strictly avoided. There were those who wanted to buy him, and who were manageable if they stuck to business. There were some who wanted to 'help' – provided they decided what 'help' he needed. And then there was the best sort, that didn't care and didn't bother him unless he asked them to, and then were usually good for a couple of dollars or a smoke.

Darcy had survived in this new world by making up his own rules as he went along. His main rule in Federation was that Jon was his man. Darcy had risked looking stupid by asking Jon for work, and the gamble had paid off. Jon was cool. He knew he'd been locked up, and didn't appear to care. So, if any whitefella was safe, that whitefella was Jon. Cam, on the other hand (while just a kid) was an unknown quantity. Potential shame lurked in their every conversation. (*Where* were you living last year? How come you talk like you do? Can you show me how to play the didgeridoo?) Darcy wasn't about to risk either his job or their slender relationship by introducing money to the equation. For Darcy, employed but still broke, it was not only much easier to be homeless than to talk to Cameron about the wages that would buy him a roof, it was the obvious path to take.

For the thousandth time, Darcy wondered if it would just be easier to go home. There were fewer white ways to worry about at home, no pain-in-the-arse whites falling over themselves to be nice, or to show how much they knew about you because they'd been on a bus trip to Uluru ten years ago. But despite the culture shock of white Australia, Darcy was inexplicably drawn to this saltwater country. Something kept him away from the desert, and every time he felt like running to the nearest main road and starting to tramp west, another part of him said: *Wait.* Invisible hands had beckoned him here, to Yanbali country. He would sit on the headland at Shelley Bay, watching the surf, throwing his spirit down there until the thundering of the waves made him dizzy. He still couldn't accept that it was safe to go into all that turmoil; he loved the waves, but he feared them too. The traffic, the tall buildings, the whitefellas who swarmed like termites everywhere he looked, shops full of shining toys for the rich, streets full of other things for the poor … it was all strange and frightening. And yet even though the saltwater country was as foreign to him as Africa would have been to Cam or Fil, there was still a connecting thread somewhere, teasing, waiting for Darcy to discover it. He sighed. It was hard being Agadja, not because of the racism, or because you were poor (though these things were of course tedious). It was hard because you had to do things and you didn't understand why.

Once he was dressed it took Darcy only two minutes to roll his blanket and few things together. Shouldering his bundle he went to say goodbye to Mrs Long. 'I'll give you that money next week, missus,' Darcy promised. She smiled and pressed sandwiches on him. Her cheap plastic beads swung as she gave him an unexpected peck. 'That's good, do your best, Darcy.'

She was sorry to see him go, and not only because there went four nights caravan money hitching down Mill Road. Forty minutes later, when he arrived at work, Darcy noticed that the van wasn't in its usual spot.

At eight o'clock, the sun bored into Cameron's pale head as he stood grooming Governor. The horse leaned ecstatically into the brush, head nodding.

'G'day. How's your Dad's leg?' Darcy asked in genuine concern.

'They operated on it last night, he's gotta stay in hospital while his leg heals up a bit more. Filomena told him not to try and escape. Normally he'd just take off by now.' Cam rolled his eyes. For a Sensitive New Age Guy his Dad was a bit reckless with his body sometimes.

'Yeah, I can relate to that, I hate fucken hospitals. How long till he gets out?' Darcy sweated on Cam's answer.

'Tomorrow, maybe. Or Sunday. Fil says he's got this fucking great bandage on his leg and nurses all over him like a rash, lucky bastard.' Cam grinned. 'Listen, I've done Picasso already, and let Garbo and Babyface out, so how about you do Gunner and Angel? Then we can start lunging, maybe? They're all fed.' Darcy wouldn't argue.

'Yeah, no worries.' Darcy's heart sank at the news about Jon. He could always sneak back into the stableyard at night, he thought, and crash in the straw as a last option. But what if they discovered him there? He might get the sack. Oh, worry about it later, he chastised himself, ya getting so white about things lately! Fuck, you can sleep anywhere, can't ya? He shook his head. Uncle Frank was right – it didn't take long to get spoilt.

Cameron led Governor back into his box and stood watching Darcy pick out Gunner's little black hooves. 'He's nice, Gunner,' Cam said, trying to make friends. Darcy hadn't opened up much yet. He must be the shy type. 'Dad bought him two years ago. He was being neglected by this rodeo guy, he just stuck him in a paddock and let him rot. There was hardly any grass or anything, and he was real skinny. Just a skinny colt. You wouldn't think so now, hey? Dad was going to have him gelded and give him to me. But then we found out his pedigree, and he fattened up like this. So we decided to breed from him. He serviced eighteen mares last year. Two hundred bucks a pop.'

Darcy straightened up and smoothed Gunner's gleaming coat. He was a blood bay, deep red-brown with glossy black mane and tail. A broad blaze, ugly on some horses, gave character to the short, deep face. Gunner was stocky, with a muscular neck and bum.

'That's eighteen more'n me,' Darcy lied with a grin.

'Yeah, wish someone'd pay me to fuck em,' Cam said wistfully. He was still a virgin, just. He'd been getting close with Mae, but the idea of pregnancy frightened her off, and then she moved away to Sydney.

'Oh they probly would, eh, good lookin lad like yerself,' said Darcy matter-of-factly.

Cam smiled, then returned to the subject of Gunner. 'You can do anything with him. He was servicing this mare last year, and she wasn't ready, she was kicking out at him like mad, and Dad had to drag him away. He just went with Dad like a little lamb.' Cam grinned coarsely. 'Poor bugger, he was raring to go too, he had a stiffy like that. But he's gentle. Not like that sod.' He jerked a thumb at Angel, whose beautiful sculptured head looked out from the box opposite.

'He's okay, isn't he?' asked Darcy, surprised. 'Seemed all right the other day.'

Cam shook his head. 'You think he is, then he turns on ya. I reckon he's got something wrong in his head. For days he'll be fine, just perfect, then boom! A big fucking buck out of nowhere, or else he'll try to kick you or something. You want to watch him.'

Darcy nodded his thanks, then started brushing out Gunner's tail.

'You haven't got a car, eh?' Cam asked, not feeling any need to hurry the morning's work.

Darcy shook his head. 'Nah, got nonna.' He rubbed forefinger and thumb together in the air. 'I had one once for a little while, but a real deadly one,' he reminisced.

Cam brightened. He wasn't a revhead, personally, but if Darcy was he could talk cars. He'd gone through a hoon phase a while back, and got the shits when Dad wouldn't put extractors and flares on the van. 'Oh, yeah ... what sort?'

'Commodore. Oh, it was a fucken beauty, eh. Red. V8—'

'Oh yeah, they're excellent,' Cam agreed matily.

Darcy shot him a sly glance. '—but then they caught

me.' He and Cam burst out laughing together. *He's cool,* thought Darcy in relief. *He's funny,* thought Cam. It didn't occur to the younger boy that Darcy hadn't been joking. It didn't cross Darcy's mind that Cam might think he was. How the fuck else would *he* get a V8 Commodore?

An hour later, Darcy and Cam were leading their horses across the lumpy turf of the Small Paddock away from the lunging ring. Sawdust fell from Governor's hooves, leaving a faint yellow trail on the grass.

'... Dad's superannuation, and once we bought the wood it took us about three months to get the place so we could live in it. We had a caravan we slept in meantime. We've been painting and patching bits up ever since.' Cameron finished the tale of Aonbar's Rest, from Dad's drunken declaration that he was going to leave the university, and avoid witnessing its rapid decline to Degrees-R-Fucking-Us, to the equally drunken day they moved in and christened the joint with Craig's home brew.

'What's superannuation?' Darcy asked.

Cam looked at him, trying not to look surprised. Fancy not knowing that. 'It's money they give you, or really it's your own money, that you save up while you're working. Then you get it when you retire. It's mostly if you work for a big company or something. See, Dad used to work at the university till two years ago.'

'Oh.' Darcy couldn't see why a university would need a horse-breaker. Never mind. Cam's story had given him an idea. 'What happened to the caravan?'

'It's parked on the other side of the fuel shed over there. It's pretty rotten now, just an old wooden one, not metal. The roof's all caving in. Why?'

'I was thinking of buying meself a caravan to live in,' Darcy half-lied.

Cameron hooted with laughter. 'Well, that one isn't worth much … it's full of spiders and toads and dry rot. You could ask Dad, I s'pose.'

'Yeah … I might. I used to live in caravans a lot.' He didn't mention that the donger had had locks on the outside of the door, and sat inside a high wire fence with guards on the other side.

Filomena wrinkled her nose at the hospital smells and tried not to look at the poor kid with all the tubes coming out of her nose. Jon waved enthusiastically at her from the end of the ward.

'Come to rescue me at last … Grab my bag there, will you, let's go! There's life in the old dame yet, archy.' He was on his crutches in an instant.

'Dad,' Fil warned. 'Did they say you could go home?' She scoped the room for nurses.

'Yep. Definitely.' Jon asserted, hurrying down the aisle.

'Have you at least got some antibiotics?'

'Thousands, my love.' Jon was disappearing into the foyer.

Filomena followed him reluctantly, sure he was lying. What was it with him and doctors? She helped him into the passenger seat of the van then slid herself behind the steering wheel. She took a big breath, and drove out into the traffic of Federation, praying she wouldn't hit anything.

'Let's sneak up on them,' Jon suggested when Filomena turned the van off in front of the house. She grinned and followed him on sneakered feet along the path to the horses. This ought to be good.

'MALINGERING on duty, ten days detention, Corporal MenZEEES!!!'Jon shouted as he silently crutched his way around the corner of the stables. Cam and Darcy were sitting with their backs against the tack shed, having morning tea. Angel snorted, Picasso threw his head and whickered. Darcy jumped up and stood trembling on the other side of the yard. A wet trail showed where his mug of tea had gone. Jon's military manner was a bit too familiar for his comfort. Cam's tea went in his lap and he flung his boots in all directions, dancing the hot-groin jig.

'Dad!' he said, 'you arsehole! Did they let you out?'

'Come on, Darc,' Jon said. 'I won't bite ya. Siddown. Better still, let's all go inside.'

Darcy hesitated, still a bit shaken. Then they all went into the kitchen, where Jon entertained them with horror stories of hospital while Filomena got the coffee grinder down from the shelf with a flourish. Ten minutes later she put a steaming silver jug of coffee on the table, and four pottery mugs.

'Darcy's got something to ask you, Dad,' said Cameron. 'Quick, while he's off guard,' he advised his workmate *sotto voce*.

'Cam said you had an old caravan around the place,' Darcy muttered, wishing Jon would mention his pay.

'Yeah, the old thunderbox. In Xanadu did Kubla Khan a stately pleasure dome decree, and, said the Menzies caravan, that stately dome was not like me,' Jon recited joyfully. 'Are you in the market for some old timber, Darc? Wanting to build a bonfire? Or have you got a pet termite collection to provide for?' His yellow eyes flashed with delight at being home, at being out of hospital, at being alive.

'Oh, I was just looking around for something to live in, eh,' Darcy said in a low voice of shame. Jon would have jumped to his feet, but instead had to settle for thumping the table dramatically with his palms.

'Hear that, Cam! The lad just needs somewhere to live. And do we happen to have a large, expansive property with mountain views, conveniently situated to town and less than twenty horse minutes to the beach? Is Aonbar's Rest not the home of the brave and the land of the free? Filomena, is our new project cleaning up the caravan for Darcy to stay in, or is it not?' Both his children grinned at Jon; this mode of rhetoric was nothing new to them. Darcy merely stared. It *sounded* good, but what exactly did Jon mean? Was he giving him the van? Confusion was obvious on his face.

Filomena explained. 'Jon's saying that we should clean the van up and you can live here.'

Darcy's face lit up.

'It's now a condition of the job,' Jon declaimed, 'that you live-in. What do you say? Want to join the madhouse?'

'Oh, yeah, I guess!' Darcy liked Jon, and Cam, and Fil was okay too. But living with whitefellas? What next?

★

'Phone, Cam!' Jon called as he was preparing chicken Marengo that night.

'Who is it?' Cam shot up from the table where he sat greasing saddlery, desperately hoping it would be Lucy.

Jon shrugged, slicing the mushrooms with extreme care and attention into exact quarter-inch thicknesses. 'Some bloke.'

Alarm bells rang faintly for Cam underneath his disappointment.

'Glen Goddard here, how are ya, son?' Cameron flinched visibly. 'Okay ...'

'I've been doing a bit of research. Looks like that old camera you spoke to me about is an Eastman Vistaview. Makes it a genuine antique, son. Not worth all that much, mind you, but definitely an antique.'

'Really?' Cam replied, wondering what the difference in value was between a Vistaview and a Pictureview, and whether Goddard had made a genuine mistake. Somehow he doubted it.

'So I was wondering if I should pop out with this article on it I've dug up for you—'

Cam thought on his feet and put a puzzled tone into his voice. 'Hullo? Hullo? You there, Goddard?' He depressed the button on the phone several times and dragged it along the bench top to make a scraping sound. Cautiously, he spoke again. 'Hullo, you there?' Silence. Relieved, he hung up and went back to his tack. When Jon went to dump some onion skins outside in the garden, he sneaked back and surreptitiously took the phone off the hook. Jon would kill him if he knew he was cutting their lifeline, but Goddard was bad news. He knocked on Fil's door.

His sister lay reading on her bed in Levi's and a striped fashion shirt. She was in a particularly good mood. Darcy had just gone, he said, to pay back some money he owed someone, then he was coming back. For good. It had taken her forty-five minutes to decide between the striped shirt and her tight black singlet.

'What's up, dude?' she greeted Cam, sitting up and brushing her hair for the umpteenth time that night. Not bad, she decided, a nice glossy dark brown and past her shoulders now. Cam sat on the floor, stretching his legs apart to accommodate the washing machine. It was in a quiet part of its cycle, luckily. When it wasn't, the room shook.

'Just got a phone call. From Goddard.' He gave the name the most sinister interpretation he could.

'Geez. What'd he want?' Fil asked, twisting her hair this way and that. She began plucking her eyebrows with the tweezers from Cam's Swiss Army knife.

'He wanted to come out here and show me some article about the camera,' Cam said. 'I fobbed him off. But Fil, we need to talk about it.'

'What, Goddard? Might be our ticket to the States. Hey – what about those photos? Did you finish them?' She forgot her face and swung around to Cam. After the drama of Jon's operation, then Darcy's decision to move in, the photos had slipped her mind.

Cam, on the other hand, hadn't stopped worrying about the 'body' in the last photo. Should he tell Jon? Or Fil? He'd even considered asking Darcy's advice. 'Yeah. They're not good. Take a look.' He pushed them into her.

Slowly Fil examined them. She made a funny face and her flesh began to creep. 'I was right, wasn't I? These aren't of now … they're old.'

Cam waited for her to comment on the body.

'So that's what the ruin looked like. This one's a bit weird, isn't it?' she asked. 'Wonder what it is?' She pointed with a shaky finger to the person lying inside the house. But her wavering voice gave away what she half-suspected already.

'Um …' Cam bit down hard on his lower lip, 'I think it's a dead body.'

'*Dead*? It's just someone lying on the ground.'

Cameron pointed out the spurs and the child's bent arm. When Filomena looked more closely she could see he had to be right. No live person would be lying that way. And that could easily be a gun the other figure held. She started to feel sick and turned a worried face to her brother. Then she had a brilliant idea. 'Cam … why don't I just sell it? Get rid of it? It's too weird … I should just let Goddard buy it, then give the money away – then maybe nothing bad will happen. I mean, nothing else. Look at Dad's leg. That doctor said it was a thousand-to-one chance that an injury like that would get infected. What if it's a family curse or something?' She spoke urgently. 'I *have* to sell it.'

'Nothing bad would happen? Fil, something bad *has* happened. Someone was murdered! We can't just pretend it didn't happen.' Cam was outraged.

'Why not?' she argued, fear rising in her at the word *murdered*. 'It was a million years ago. Who cares? I don't want to know about it, Cam.' She leant away from him and hugged her pillow to her chest. 'It's too scary.'

Cam jumped to his feet. 'You gutless cow! I'm not going to let you sell it. It's not even yours, anyway. And give me my knife!' He snatched the photos and the knife and slammed the door behind him. Blood pounded in his ears as he stalked to his own room. She can't, he thought wildly, she just can't! It's … wrong. We have to find out what's going on, we can't just ignore it. Worst of all, he thought, we're related to him – we're the descendants of a murderer. Me. Dad. Fil – we're all tainted.

A family secret most horrible
Provoked a discovery terrible
The boy did not know
When the blood first did flow
And his sister was ever incorrigible.

Yuk, he thought, it doesn't even scan.

In her bedroom Filomena stared miserably at her reflection. Just when things were starting to improve. Just when gorgeous, desirable, hunky Darcy was moving in, and Dad had come home from the hospital, this shit had to happen. In spite of what she'd said, Filomena knew deep down that selling the camera wasn't really going to fix the problem. Let's face it, she told herself, if some sort of terrible, ghostly presence was stalking them (magic? – that sounded too like a kid's storybook … how about *demons*?) then the camera was just a useful object for the overall purpose. Getting rid of it wouldn't stop the stalking. She heaved herself up and went to speak to Cam. They had to work together on this one.

★

A few days later Fil sat impatiently at the kitchen table waiting for ten o'clock, smoko time. Bay FM played upbeat Mexicano and she tapped the table with light palms. She'd made fresh coffee, even baked scones, some effort in this heat. So where the hell are ya, boys? At ten-twenty the three banged their way through the flyscreen and collapsed onto chairs.

'Mmmm, looks good,' said Jon. 'Michelle ring yet?'

'Nah. Else I'd be outside, wouldn't I? I'm boiling in here.'

Darcy and Cam started eating with both hands, mopping up the fresh whipped cream with their scones and washing them down with great buckets of strong coffee. Jon had only one scone with jam. 'At my age, Bella, you get fat just looking at cream.'

Cam immediately leaned over to grab Jon's gut and was promptly put on the floor for his trouble. Laughing, Jon held the cream bowl over his face, threatening to dump it on him. Cam opened his mouth wide, shut his eyes and waited.

Filomena grabbed it back and put it on the table. 'That cost money, and I need it for my almond cream layer cake. What've you lot been doing?' She'd had to stay near the house waiting for a call from her mother telling her the date she was coming back to Australia next month. Or, maybe, Filomena thought optimistically, telling her Italy was so wonderful she had decided to stay there for a year or two. Fil could join her at her convenience. Off in a dream of living between Rome and Aonbar's Rest, she paid little attention to Jon's reply.

'... so if you want to go into the Bridge you can take

Babyface and Governor,' he was saying. Fil wondered what he was talking about. Why would they ride along the main road into the Bridge when the bush was so much prettier and cooler? And Darcy was looking uneasy, for some reason.

'Ah … might go after work, eh?' Darcy suggested. 'When it's cooler?'

Jon instantly agreed, chastising himself for not realising Darcy would want to go alone. Or at least not with whitefellas. 'Yeah … take the Yammy if you want.'

Darcy nodded gratefully. If he had to turn up out of the blue, not knowing anyone, then arriving on a fairly inconspicuous and battered trailbike would be better than on the back of a prancing horse. They'd think he was a real big-noter if he did that.

'Hey, Darcy, do you know anything about ghosts?' Cam said out of the blue.

Darcy gave him a swift glance. 'Oh … little bit.'

'Ever seen one? Are youse 'sposed to be able to see them better than us or something?' Cam blurted.

'I seen 'em …' Darcy said softly to his coffee cup.

Filomena listened intently from the sink, but Darcy just fidgeted in his seat and wouldn't say anymore.

Jon broke in. 'Look, there's work to be done before storytime. Tell us about the ghosts afterwards, Darcy. If we get Gunner in the float and over to Lismore, we can start fixing up the Thunderbox this arvo, eh?'

Cam looked at his father resentfully. Darcy might have a great story to tell, one that would shed some light on the camera business. Jon stared him down, hands clasped behind his head, his biceps popping under a T-shirt that read *Hard Rock Cafe Port Moresby*. Cam met Jon's yellow-grey eyes for a few seconds, then lowered his own. He was no match for his father, not yet. Obediently he got up to go.

Later that afternoon, when Gunner had been delivered to the mares in Lismore, Jon drew his son to one side. He had some difficulty explaining why, for Darcy, some conversations were no-go areas. 'What are ghosts and goblins to us, are the spirits of the dead to him,' he told Cam. 'If he's had the life I think he's had, then for him that stuff is real, not fairytales. And maybe he's not allowed to talk about it. So tread carefully. There's lots of stuff he can't talk about to us.'

'But Dad—' Cam began, wanting to say I *know* it's real. Boy, do I know it's real!

Jon cut him off with a gesture, then went up to Darcy, who was playing tiggy with Maxwell. For the first time Cam felt a tiny tinge of jealousy for Jon's attention to someone else.

The kangaroo dog crouched, waiting, with his fluffy mongrel tail waving in delight. Darcy leapt athletically for Maxwell's hind leg but the dog was too quick. He bounded forward, leaving Darcy to do a belly flop on the mown grass behind the house. A button had torn away and where his shirt flapped open the brown skin of his belly was showing, glowing with sweat. The boy was lightly built without any spare fat at all, muscles sharply defined by years of work. Just this side of skinny, Filomena thought, watching him avidly. An unfinished homemade tattoo on his neck, a roughly outlined snake, would have marred his appearance more if he was pale.

As it was the markings didn't stand out very much on his cocoa-coloured skin; it was only when he came to the house and stuck his head under the tap near the steps that Fil could see clearly what the design was. He wore a coloured necklace and a silver earring; these and the tattoo were his only offerings to vanity. Filomena felt she was about to burst with not being allowed to touch him – he was the most desirable thing she'd ever seen.

The object of her lust grudgingly conceded victory to Maxwell. 'Ah, ya too good for me, ya—' Darcy stopped himself just in time from saying 'white bastard'. The dog panted from where he lay in the shade of the house.

'Getting a bit of a tan there, Darc,' Jon said.

Cameron instantly flushed crimson while Filomena watched silently, wondering if it was okay to joke about Darcy's dark skin. But Jon was perfectly serious. Darcy was darkening up now that he didn't have to wear flash clothes for Bill Barton's clients.

Darcy glanced down at his forearms. 'Yeah, I was gettin' real white, before, too, eh.'

'Well, maybe not white,' said Jon, 'but you can see a difference. Your hatmark isn't so bad.'

Cam looked at Jon and Darcy standing together in front of the shed. Jon, who normally attracted attention with his olive skin and long dark hair, looked very much the white man beside the Aboriginal boy. God only knows how pale I look, Cam thought, I'll never get a tan if I live to be a hundred. He had long ago given up on trying to fry himself a better colour in the hot sun.

Jon suddenly grabbed Darcy's slim arms from behind, marched him a few yards, then turned him to face the caravan disintegrating slowly behind the fuel shed. 'Renovator's delight? Ideal first home?'

Enjoying the contact, Darcy began to grin. He could really go for Jon. Sometimes he felt himself on the verge of saying something stupid, something he'd really regret as soon as it was outta his dumb black gob. 'Too right.'

'I'll get the flame-thrower, will I?' Fil offered from the back steps.

Darcy and Jon both turned on her, offended, loudly proclaiming the virtues of the van.

And it was true: by five o'clock, it was almost fit for a dog to live in, as Cam said. Sub-let it to Maxwell, was his suggestion. The roof was propped and patched, the floor swept and mopped, the toads evicted. Darcy had stated his intention to paint it – a stark white outside, pale green within. Fil instantly developed a secret passion for painting, one she'd let Darcy in on very soon.

As they observed the results of their afternoon's labour Jon invited Darcy to stay that night. 'For now, son, crash in the lounge. Can't have you living in squalor – what would the neighbours say?'

Fil snorted. The nearest neighbours were three kilometres away.

'Hey, Fil.' Darcy hung one-armed off the kitchen doorframe and lifted his weight high.

She turned from the TV and smiled. 'Jon can do that. He does weights too. Those ones out the back.'

Darcy grinned, eager for information on his charismatic employer.

'And I do aerobics when I'm not training for soccer.' Fil flexed her arms comically. 'But Cam's the real weightlifter.'

Darcy dropped onto the kitchen floor. 'Yeah, I seen him with his shirt off, must be workin'. He's real big for fourteen, eh? Hey, any tucker going?' Since he'd come to an agreement with Jon about board, he'd been eating like it was going out of fashion. No more starving and trying to be jockeyweight, specially not with Fil's cooking.

If Cam had said that, Fil would have made an acid comment and sent him to the fridge. But for Darcy nothing was too much trouble. 'Feel like an omelette?'

Darcy shone with expectation. 'Yeah!'

He and Fil chatted easily for the time it took her to cook and him to eat. Fil soaked happily in the look, the feel, the spirit of Darcy. She could summon up his dark eyes and curls no matter where she was in the house. At night in bed, she reproduced the sound of his voice and the conversations they'd shared that day. Every morning she dressed with exceptional care; any comment on her appearance from Darcy made her glow for hours. Filomena was in love.

'You play much sport?' she asked him, hoping to steer their conversation onto her own prowess at soccer – captain of the boys' soccer team in grade eight, State Rep last year and a good chance of the same when the season rolled around again in March.

Darcy's mouth was full of egg, so he mimed basketball – that was easy. The next one took a while to guess – hockey. When Fil stopped laughing she had learned that he played five different team sports, plus boxing.

'No wonder you can do one-arm press ups,' she flattered him shamelessly. 'All the girls in Federation'll be chasing you.' Butter wouldn't melt in my mouth, she thought.

'They'd have a long run,' Darcy replied.

Fil's hopes soared. Could he mean he was already interested in someone else … like her?

They heard the van come into the yard.

'Jon and Cam back from the shop, eh,' Darcy observed.

Fil quickly whisked Darcy's plate into the sink. If Cam saw her cooking specially for Darc she'd never hear the end of it. Then she joined Darcy flicking channels in front of the Friday night TV offerings.

'Just some spaghetti crap,' he said, dismissing a Wim Wenders film on SBS that Fil had been looking forward to.

'Want to go to the pictures in town?' she asked before she had time to think.

'Oh, yeah … what's on?' Darcy replied, as if it was no big deal. Filomena's heart flew into her mouth. She had just asked him out, and he'd *accepted*. A date, a real date. She found her mouth wouldn't work and fled to the toilet to hide her lack of composure. Fuck, shit. What could she wear? How could she make sure that all her holiday friends saw her with Darcy? And what was on at the Federation Twin that a male would like? She hoped she wouldn't have to sit through two hours of bombs and guns. Although even that would be interesting if Darcy liked it.

'What are you all dressed up for?' Cam inquired as he passed her on his way to the shower ten minutes later.

'We're gunna see a movie,' Fil said, praying for Cam's cooperation.

Darcy shut the fridge door, holding a samosa in one hand and a can of coke in the other. 'Wanna come?' he asked the younger lad, to Fil's dismay. Cameron noticed Fil's eyes shooting black nuclear sparks at him. He was obviously expected to decline. Would he tease her, or be nice?

'Oh, are youse going on the bike?' he asked, deciding to do the brotherly thing. 'No room, hey? And there's heaps of cops around on Friday nights, so we better not drive the van. I think Jon might be taking it over to Bill Barton's, anyway. Nah, you two go.' *There*, he smirked to Fil, you owe me. She gave him a low thumbs-up in front of her stomach where Darcy couldn't see.

At eleven-thirty, steering the Yammy bumpily back home across the old quarry, Fil's euphoria had dimmed considerably. The movie, one about drag queens in London, had been funny. Darcy appeared to enjoy himself. But there had been no romance forthcoming. Afterwards, when they sat in the park in the shadow of the War Memorial clutching beers, and Fil had been expecting Darcy to *do something*, instead he started talking about horses and his love of the bush. Which was all very well, she told herself as she lay dissatisfied in bed, but horses could only take up so much of a girl's attention.

I'm ugly, she decided in the end, flat with depression. He was just being friendly because she was ugly, and fat, and he doesn't know anyone else. If I wasn't, she convinced herself, he would have held onto me when we rode home, instead of the handrail. Miserable, she buried her face in her pillow.

On the lounge, Darcy went to sleep smiling. He'd had a deadly week, he had a job *with horses*, and now had somewhere to live. The movie was filth, and Fil and Cam were becoming proper friends, too. There even was some blackfellas hanging about in town; he'd gather the courage one of these days to go and introduce himself, find out if any of his relations still lived around here. It's all downhill from here, he thought happily.

CHAPTER SEVEN

One of the thoroughbred brood mares had been walking around uncomfortably for the last couple of days, nose down. 'She'll drop tonight,' Cam had said confidently, not letting on to anyone that he'd seen her bleeding and cleaned her up on the sly. Darcy wasn't about to admit it, but he was impressed when Cam was right. The big bay had foaled in the Small Paddock just after dawn, a spindly black colt with a tiny white star on his forehead. Now, with Cam and Fil both asleep, Darcy was sitting on a bale of straw as Jon sacked the mare down. There were deep poverty lines down either side of the old girl's rump and hollows under her eyes. Full bag of susu for bubba, though. The foal's coat was still curled from being wet inside. He had dark eyes big as saucers. Strong pasterns, four black hooves. Snuffling soft muzzle white from drinking, and legs less tottery by the second. Looking at the beauty of him made Darcy feel a bit like crying, even though he wasn't sad.

Jon crooned to the mare as he rubbed her with the drying sack stuffed with straw. Small shards of yellow were falling about his hair and upper body, sticking to his skin, turning him into a scarecrow. Suddenly he stepped aside from the mare, scratching furiously under the T-shirt he'd kept on for modesty.

'I gotta feel air on my skin, Darcy,' he said as he stripped his shirt off. 'Most blokes feel ties were invented to strangle them. That's how I feel about clothes. But I guess you never wore a tie, uh?' Keep it light, man, Jon instructed himself.

But when Jon reached down to bring his shirt up over his ridged belly muscles, over his spreading pecs, showing the black hair of his chest and beneath his arms, Darcy shuddered inside and had to look away. At the same time couldn't. Head saying one thing, down below another. He made himself say something, anything. 'Not likely. Not even in Court. Fuck 'em.'

Jon grinned. 'Lucky man ... Reckon this is a good foal uh? Good hooves. *Black Meaning Good* – that's a song. Can you hold him out of the way for a minute?'

Think about the horse. Think about anything else but Jon's back muscles tiding in and out with the effort of drying the big bony mare who is nervous and snorting, wanting her foal. Darcy reached a slow hand for the little bloke's muzzle. The colt shied away into the furthest corner of the yard and fell over his feet. Jon laughed gently at the clumsiness of the small creature. The mare nickered in distress.'Yeah. A beauty.' Juice rising in him now. So close. But so, so far away. He could reach out a dark finger and trace a line down Jon's chest. In a strangled voice Darcy excused himself. 'I don't reckon he's gunna let me touch him, eh. Back dreckly.'

The young man went to the toilet on the far side of the stables, where it took three fast pumps of his hand to do the deed. He achieved a little physical relief but when he went back to where Jon stood the orgasm part of it was still roaring inside him. Still in his head, making him crazy. Still locked up in Jon's big dark frame, in his face, his hair, in the man of him.

Jon drew the sack away from the mare as he finished rubbing her down. He made no comment on Darcy's sudden expedition. If you have a single virtue, he told himself, it's that you have finally learnt when it's best to keep your mouth firmly shut. He addressed the mare instead:

'That's better. Can't have you catching cold, old girl. Let's get her some gruel and leave 'em alone. Got any ideas for a name?'

Darcy shook his head dumbly, shamed of his feelings and of what his body told him. He didn't know what to say to Jon, sometimes, didn't know what to do about any of it. Some things you just couldn't fist away with brownish-yellow knuckles that read L-O-V-E and H-A-T-E in prison ink; some things needed them whitefella's words, but their words were what ya never had.

'Dad,' Cameron began, as the news finished.

Filomena sat beside him on the old leather lounge which sagged drastically at one end. Darcy was asleep. arms flung out. on the beanbag. Fil was enjoying the opportunity to study him unobserved.

'Ssh. I want to see if it's going to rain. Ah, yes, you beauty. What?' Jon turned his attention to Cameron. He had spawned two good-looking offspring, he realised for the millionth time that summer, seeing them together. Sturdy, independent Cam had inherited his own height and build, and his pretty mother's face, the best of both worlds. Filomena had taken after Michelle almost entirely with those dark eyes and skinny limbs; seeing her out of the corner of his eye, sometimes Jon forgot his failed first marriage to his Italian–Australian wife. Losing it at forty-two, he told himself, that's what you get for smoking dope for a decade, you fool. Every time it happened he felt the old stab of loss.

'You know you were telling me about Hew Costello,' Filomena said, following Cam's lead, 'well, how come he settled here in the first place?'

'Well, who knows?' replied Jon thoughtfully. 'Woman trouble? The white man's burden? Running away from debts? Frontiers always attract a motley crowd. Troublemakers, troubleseekers, nonconformists. Although he must have stayed married long enough to have Michaela. Maybe he was the black sheep of the family. Michaela only mentioned him when she was drunk. The main thing I remember is she said he was the most frightening looking man she'd ever clapped eyes on, tall and broad, with the dingo Menzies eyes.'

'Don't you know anything more about him than that?' Fil said, aggravated not by the reference to Menzies eyes, but by Jon's casual disinterest in his own grandfather.

Jon paused. 'Michaela used to say' – and here he broke into an old woman's voice – 'he lived with savage blacks surrounding him on the edge of a cliff in the middle of nowhere. But that must have been bullshit, because there aren't any farms on top of any cliffs around here. The closest thing to a cliff is Mount Arthur. You'd be flat out standing on top of that, let alone farming it.'

'What about his wife?' Cam interrupted. 'She'd be our great-great-grandmother, wouldn't she?'

'That's right. I think I remember someone saying once he got married in Washington? Or was it San Francisco? See, Hew was born in Australia, but went ... yeah, that's right' – Jon was warming up – 'I remember now, he went to California, to the tail end of the gold rush there, and made his fortune selling dry goods to the poor bloody starving miners. Smart man. Then he came here, 'cos he always wanted to be a squatter, really. Came back to Brisbane with his Yankee fortune and his Yankee wife, moved down this way, and then he sort of ... fades out of the picture.'

Or *into it*, thought Cam with a tiny shudder.

'So, he panned for gold again here?' Fil asked. Darcy stirred, and turned over on the beanbag. She had to drag her eyes off the place where his brown leg curved into rounded creamy-olive buttock.

'Hang on,' said Jon, 'I think his wife might have been called' – he screwed his face up, trying to remember – 'Bridget ... Bronwyn. It started with B, something Irish I think. Or it might have been the surname that was Irish, her maiden name. Oh, I dunno, kids. It's so long since Michaela died. I was barely older than you, Cam. Why this sudden interest?'

'We're thinking of doing a family tree,' said Cameron.

113

It wasn't a lie. The camera had pricked his interest in his background.

'Must be something about your age,' said Jon. 'Darcy's looking for his relations, too, in town.'

But he's from the bush, thought Cam, how could his relations be from here? Was he lying about where he came from?

'So there was no scandal that you know about Hew Costello?' asked Fil. 'He wasn't hanged or jailed or anything?' She smiled, as if it was a joke. Even in 1898, surely you couldn't murder someone with impunity.

'As far as I know, he was like the rest of us, pure as the driven slush. I wonder where he's buried?'

'Fil and me could have a look in the Shelley Bay cemetery,' Cam said. 'Check out the library and that.'

Jon nodded slowly. 'No reason why not, I suppose. Let me know if you discover any millionaire second cousins on the Gold Coast, won't you?'

Cam reassured Jon on that point as he and Fil retreated to his bedroom for a war council.

Next morning Filomena and Cam donned their wet-weather gear and hitched into Federation. Rain streamed down the windscreen of the Nissan that picked them up, turning the landscape into strange blurs of trees, cows, fences. When they escaped their Christian Fundamentalist driver ('Have a great day with the Lord.' 'Oh, we will.') and were standing outside the library, Cam shook raindrops off like a wet dog. Carefully he smoothed his white T-shirt over his chest so that it stuck to his skin. His pecs were actually beginning to stand out, he rejoiced, after all those bench-presses. He didn't want to waste the opportunity of showing them off.

'How's my hair?' he asked urgently. 'Is it all wet?'

'It's too short to matter, fool.' Filomena replied. He grimaced and tried to finger-comb his hair in the dark glass of the library door.

'You look cool, don't worry.' She flicked his fringe up a little then folded her rain-jacket and put it into a plastic bag. They went inside.

'You know, there's a real resurgence of interest in local histories,' said gorgeous blue-eyed Ann Lyons from beneath a hairstyle that reminded Cam of pineapples. He liked pineapples. A lot. 'You're the third mob this week wanting to know about that period.'

Cam hung pathetically on her every word. What is it, Filomena thought to herself, that makes every bloody girl in Federation – even a *librarian* – look like a centrefold? She had no hope of attracting Darcy's attention in a town like this. Then she realised what Ann had said. 'Anyone we know?' she asked.

Ann paused. 'The first lot were just tourists from Brisbane, I'd say, people wanting to know more about the Bay … you know, round specs types.' Ann made nerdy eyeglass hands around her baby blues. To his sister's disgust, Cam chuckled as though it was the best joke he'd heard all week. 'And then Glen Goddard was in for half an hour yesterday, looking up some old magazines. You'd know him, wouldn't you Cameron?'

Cam admitted to knowing him, at the same time trying to look serious and dangerous like Mel Gibson in

Braveheart. Filomena filed the information away as Ann showed them to the historical records.

'How old do camera magazines get?' Fil asked as they crouched over the copies of the births, deaths and marriages registers.

'What?' He was still entranced by Ann, now talking to her crumbly male colleague on the other side of the help desk.

Impatiently Fil repeated her question.

'Oh, forty or fifty years, but they haven't got any that old here. They haven't got much at all except what we looked at the other day.' It dawned on Cam, as it had upon Fil some minutes earlier, that Goddard might not simply have been looking up magazines for information about the Viewfinder. It predated any camera publications by about forty years or more; the short article he'd found on the Internet had taken over an hour of searching.

'What's he up to?' Fil said unhappily.

'Let's find out.' Cameron replied. 'He might have put his books on the returns table.' They started digging through the stack. Books on gardening were out, or, if that's what he had been looking at, harmless. Books on cake decoration. 'I don't think so,' said Fil sarcastically. A monograph on translating documents from Arabic. Books on the English Lakes District. 'Hmmm,' said Cam.

A book on property law pertaining to abandoned or discovered property. 'That's the one!' decided Fil, picking it up. A pamphlet fluttered out. *Christmas Camera Sale. Goddards Photographic – Up to Forty Per Cent Off!*

Filomena fingered the pamphlet as she thought hard.

116

Property law. Property law ... 'He really wants it,' she said. 'He wants it any way he can get hold of it, I reckon.'

Her brother grimaced. 'He can keep fucking wanting it, then. It's ours.'

Or mine, actually, Fil thought, since I was the one who (a) found the house, (b) was brave enough to go in alone, and (c) brought the camera out. She didn't argue the point. It wasn't worth having a fight about.

'Hey, look, that Nikon's only four hundred and fifty bucks!' Cameron noticed.

Filomena snatched the pamphlet back. 'Will you concentrate? It must be worth *heaps*,' she said, 'for him to worry about it.'

Cameron disagreed. 'Sometimes collectors get fanatical. It might only be worth a couple of hundred, but he'd still go off his head about it. Depends how close to complete his collection is. If he needs a lot more, then it wouldn't be so important. But if he only needs this one, well ... he might murder for it.'

'Isn't one murder enough for you?' said Fil in a sharp voice. She hated talking about that stuff. Sometimes she pretended to herself that none of it was happening. She could pretend for hours, but in the end she always remembered. The camera was ... what? Something creepy was attached to it, some lingering ghost from long ago. Maybe, somewhere inside it was a murderer's victim looking for revenge. Gross. She didn't even like touching it anymore, but Cam had insisted that one or the other of them always look after it and now it sat inside her rucksack.

'There's no point worrying about Goddard right

now,' said Cam. 'Let's see if we can find out anything about Costello first.'

They spent the morning flicking through newspapers on microfiche, old Court records, and birth certificates. Cam was fascinated by the picture of Federation they discovered lying in the books and film – a world with anti-Chinese legislation, Aboriginal marauders attacking the white townsfolk, whaling dominating the town's industry, plus gold in the hills and dairy cattle on the flats. A bushranger holding a passenger wagon to ransom in 1866. The opening of a new hotel. Building of the Council Chambers in 1898. And—

'Hey, check this out. This is them building the arcade. There he is!' Cam said excitedly. A crowd stood outside the half-built arcade, many of them holding tools. Hew Costello's profile was just visible in the left of the picture, towering over his neighbours. He wore the same distinctive pointed hat as in Filomena's first photo.

'Hey, isn't that the shape of the hat in the – the body photo?' she said grimly.

'Yeah, you're right. So, it's definitely him, then.' Cam and Fil had both fostered a small hope that the gunman in the photo was someone other than their great-grandfather. They looked at each other miserably. Descendants of a murderer. Dismayed and yet encouraged by their discovery, they stayed in the library till three o'clock.

'I've gotta go, Fil, Dad'll kill me if I'm not back for stables at four,' Cam said finally.

She dragged herself up, rubbing a numb arse. 'Right-o. At least the rain's eased up.'

As they went to leave, Ann waved from her desk. 'Any good?' she asked.

'Hardly anything,' Cam answered, mesmerised by the gentle roll of her breasts.

Ann pushed a piece of paper towards him. 'Try this lot, if you like.' Family History Association of New South Wales, Cam read. A Sydney telephone number. Not much good when you can't afford to ring STD, he thought glumly. He forced a smile anyway. Was she really that much too old, he wondered hopelessly, as Ann waited for his response.

'Thanks, I'll give them a call,' he said. He was terrified that if he tried to say more, his voice might break for the first time in a year.

Since Filomena wasn't tongue-tied by hormones, she took over the questioning. 'Are these the only records in Federation?'

'They're the official ones,' Ann replied. 'You'd have to go to Brisbane for some of the very old ones, before federation.'

'Hey?' Filomena asked, confused.

'Not Federation the town, federation.'

'The federation of the Commonwealth of Australian States in 1901, durbrain,' Cam told her. 'For which our metropolis was renamed, previously being known as Miller's Corner.' He couldn't believe his good luck at being able to show off in front of Ann.

'Oh.' Filomena was constantly surprised at Cam's grasp of what she considered trivia. It came from living with Jon, of course.

'That's right. And it was only after that that the

119

official records were kept in New South Wales. But don't give up yet,' Ann said. 'History sits everywhere, not just in books. If it was me I'd try asking some of the older people in town. Once you get them talking about their younger days, and they drag out the photos, well ...'

Filomena was buoyed by this good advice. 'I'll give it a go. Come on, Cam.' She dragged him reluctantly away.

Ann smiled. Cameron was going to be a heartbreaker like his father one day, she mused.

After half an hour's wet wait for a hitch at the edge of town, Bill Barton's trainer Mark stopped for them. The three talked horses for the twenty minutes it took to get home. Bill had big plans for the grey filly they'd just broken, Mark revealed; the lads were already fighting about who got to ride her in her first country meet at Ballina. He waved goodbye at the gate of Aonbar's Rest. He liked the Menzies kids.

'Oh leave that, Darcy, better give Cam something to do if and when he gets home,' Jon said. 'Can you saddle mongrel-guts for me? I'll see if I can ride him before they get back.'

Darcy was forking wet straw from under Garbo's feet. Now he bridled Angel, put the chestnut's saddle on and led him to the yard.

'Don't you go telling Fil about this,' Jon warned, 'or I'll have your guts for garters.'

Darcy didn't comment. He couldn't see why an almost healed leg should stop Jon riding, nor, for that matter, why Filomena should mind. Where he came from cuts and bruising were a matter of course. The things that city folk worried about wouldn't rate a mention from most of his mob, not with hospital five hours away by four-wheel drive. Darcy threw the reins over Angel's head and held them near the horse's mouth, steadying him for Jon.

'I think a lot of this horse, you know,' Jon was saying as he mounted stiffly. 'Bloody cantankerous bastard and all that he is, if he'd settle down he'd be a beautiful riding horse. The owner's had it with him, though. She's got the wind up. Can't blame her.' Jon gathered the reins and gingerly put some weight onto the stirrup holding his bad leg. He winced and sucked air through his teeth. 'Ah … nup. Not gonna do it today. Give us a hand down, please.' Reluctantly Jon got off and stood watching Angel.

'Want me to ride him?' Darcy offered.

'I suppose someone should, the owner's paying me a fortune to educate the bastard. Can't just leave him in the stable … but watch him.' It was Jon's turn to hold Angel's head.

When Darcy was atop him, Angel put his ears back flat along his neck and gritted his teeth onto the bit. Darcy nodded to Jon, who let go of the horse's head. 'Get ya head up!' Darcy cursed him with a drover's fluency as Angel began backing towards the timbers. When his bum touched wood, the horse began to buck, but Darcy, well used to riding half-broken station horses and rodeo nags, clung to him tenaciously. Angel's eye showed an angry white. 'He don't like me, eh?' Darcy yelled as the horse heaved and plunged.

'He's trying you out all right!'

Tiring of the amusement, Darcy hauled his reins in very short and surprised the horse with a quick hard kick in the ribs. He forced him around in tight circles, then switched reins and whirled him in the other direction. Angel fought the bit but was outsmarted by Darcy's sudden changes of direction and savage feet. 'Open her up, Jon!' he cried. Jon swung the gate wide. Angel saw the gap and bolted for it, but Darcy was ready for him. As the horse's head was passing the thick gatepost, he snatched the right rein and booted him again. Angel's shoulder thudded into the massive wooden upright and the horse grunted in pain. Jon frowned.

'That'll fucken teach ya, ya prick!' Darcy exulted as he rode through to the paddock. He crouched over Angel's neck and worked his legs furiously, forcing the horse to go left, go right, halt, back up. After ten minutes the reins were dripping sweat and white foam dotted Darcy's black T-shirt. He brought the horse to a halt. Angel stood, lungs heaving, coat slick, yet despite his exhaustion the horse still had a malevolent look in his eye. He flared a red nostril as Jon walked up to them.

'What do you think, Darc? Is he going to make it?'

'How old is he?' the boy asked doubtfully.

'Seven or eight.'

'Nah. Too old, eh? Be different if he was just a young one, but he knows what he wants by now- his own way. Oh, you could ride him all right, but you can't relax, can't enjoy yaself. You'd have to be on top of him alla time, see, showing him you're boss. They shoulda left him a stallion. Least he'd be a breeding horse then.'

'Can't teach an old horse new tricks, you reckon? I

just hope you're wrong, son.' Jon took a sorrowful look at the lovely animal. The frightened owner had offered to sell Angel to him cheap, but who had three hundred spare dollars? Not him. 'Otherwise it'll be off to the rodeo circuit for you, me lad,' Jon told Angel. 'Or the doggers. Okay, let's put him away and get cracking with that young horse from yesterday.'

'The paint or the bay?'

'The paint. Get the lunging gear on her, will you?' As they walked the young quarter horse filly to the ring, Jon asked Darcy about his search for his family. He'd had a bit of luck, Darcy explained; he'd met an old lady named Granny Lil, who thought she remembered who his mother was. She'd come from a bit north of here, Darcy said. Her and his aunty were both dead – and Granny Lil said the rest of them lived in Lismore now.

Jon thought a moment. 'Granny Lil ... big woman? Looks a bit like Oprah?' Darcy agreed. 'I think I met her in the radio station once,' Jon said. 'She took a bit of a liking to me for some reason and invited me to a barbie, but I never got there.' He looked at Darcy with a meaningful eye. 'That's a powerful woman for you, a real matriarch. Wouldn't want to cross her, I tell you.'

'A what?'

'Boss woman.' Jon revised his language.

Darcy nodded enthusiastically. 'That's for sure.'

'Where'd you meet her?'

'At the Bridge. I went down to Knockrow Street. You see all them blackfellas hanging round the shops ... just asked 'em who knew the most about the local scene. Granny Lil lives next door to the garage. She was real nice, once she knew what I was on about. She said she'd take me to Lismore one time, introduce me round.'

'New girlfriend, eh?' Jon teased.

Darcy made a sour face and stuck his tongue out. 'No way, Josè.'

'Yeah, she's no oil painting. Wrong team, too – is that right?' Jon asked carefully.

Darcy looked up at Jon, with his crooked nose and his dark hair falling over a polo shirt packed with muscle. 'You knew that?'

'Oh, I figured. The "love that dare not speak its name" – Oscar Wilde. And they locked him up, too,' Jon said. 'Of course, Fil'll be broken-hearted.' He smiled gently. 'I'll leave it to you to tell her and Cam, when you feel like it.'

'Thanks.' Darcy's face was impassive but inside he felt huge a burden lift off him. Jon knew – and he *still* had a job. Sometimes things worked out for the weirdest reasons.

'I don't know how much you owe Glen Goddard,' Jon said to Cam when he and Filomena trudged into the muddy stableyard at a quarter to five, 'but you better ring him, 'cos he's been on my case again. And,' he added more sternly, 'if you can't shift your arse to get to work on time, you'll be flat out paying any debts, 'cos I'll be docking your pay.'

Embarrassed at seeing Cam told off, Filomena slung her rucksack over the other shoulder.

Cam reddened. 'Sorry, Dad,' he said. 'We got stuck for a lift.'

His father grunted, unimpressed, and handed him a fork. 'Muck out Garbo and put Donk's gear away. Darcy's already done most of the boxes, so I've left the feeds for you. How was town, Fil?'

'Oh … good.'

Jon came over and washed his hands. 'Go surfing?'

'Just a short one,' Filomena lied for no particular reason. 'We spent most of the day in the library.'

Uh-huh, thought Jon, aware that her togs had been flapping on the line all day. He said nothing though, trusting his kids weren't stepping too far beyond the lines in sand he'd drawn. When Cam had finished mucking out the donkey, Jon took the fork back and told Darcy to knock off, he'd had a big day.

'Fancy cooking us something for dinner?' he asked Fil. She cheerily agreed and went inside to raid the freezer.

A hum sounded from the dirt drive and someone drove around the corner past the wattle trees. 'Speak of the devil,' Jon said in surprise, picking up Fil's rucksack where she'd left it beside the trough, 'isn't that Goddard's van now?' The rucksack gaped open in his hand, revealing the camera and Fil's raincoat. Jon frowned. 'That's a funny old camera. Is it yours, Cam?' He took it out and was holding it as Goddard heaved his bulk from his van.

'G'day Jon, Cam.' Goddard ignored Darcy, who instantly developed a blank look on his face to cover his hatred. 'So this is it, eh, the famous machine?' Goddard was beaming in triumph. 'Mind if I have a look?' He took the camera from Jon, admiring it. He'll start salivating in a minute, Cam thought sourly.

Jon glanced at his son. 'Is it yours Cam? What's the story?'

'No, it belongs to – someone I know. No big deal. It's not *his*.' He whispered the last three words.

'Come on now, Cameron. No big deal? This is a valuable piece of memorabilia, it belongs in a museum, not lying around some' – Goddard sniffed – 'horse shed.' He lifted the Viewfinder to his face, and brought Darcy into focus. Darcy looked at him strangely.

'Smile up now, there's a fella!' Goddard called out in his most patronising voice.

Jon's eyes narrowed and Cam bunched his fists beside his legs. This was too much, Goddard waltzing in, then actually using the camera in front of him. He was in the act of snatching the camera out of Goddard's greasy fat fingers when Darcy went oddly limp, let out a strangled shriek, and fell to the ground.

Quickly Jon knelt beside the dark boy, feeling his pulse. 'Well, he's breathing,' he said. 'Cam, get us a blanket, hurry up!'

Goddard hadn't moved, and as Cam ran to the house he snatched the camera from the man's pudgy hands. Goddard watched him go, incomprehension turning to fury as he realised he no longer had possession of the treasure.

'Who is he?' he asked Jon, nodding towards the Aboriginal youth.

'He works for me, his name's Darcy,' Jon replied shortly. He was rapidly becoming fed up with this know-it-all who had arrived uninvited. 'Look, can you catch up with Cam some other time? It's not convenient right now.' Jon stood up to his full height and gave Goddard the evil eye. It was the kiss of death for Goddard's ill-fated expedition. 'Cam!' Jon bellowed, 'Hurry up!' He turned his back on Goddard, dismissing him as irrelevant. Darcy's chest moved up and down normally, and his pulse was regular, though very fast. Jon sat back on his heels. Curiouser and curiouser.

When Cam emerged from the house, Filomena at his side, Goddard was turning his van around to go. 'I'll see you soon,' he told Cam. It sounded like a threat.

Cam ignored him. Filomena was turning pale. 'What happened? What did he do to him?' She glared at the back of the disappearing van, venom in her heart.

'Nothing,' Jon answered. 'Settle down. He was just taking Darcy's picture. Then Darcy simply fainted, I think. Might have been working the lad too hard or something. Ring Craig, will you, Fil?'

Filomena and Cam looked at each other in horror. They knew why Darcy had fainted.

Darcy stirred as Jon felt for broken bones or other traumas. Finding none, he wrapped him carefully in the blanket and got Cam to help carry him inside.

Chapter Eight

When I die I don't want to go to heaven
I would not do heaven's work well.
When I die I pray the devil takes me to stand
In the fiery furnaces of hell.

'Ah, I wish I'd written that,' Jon complained gently to himself, eyes shut, his hat low on his forehead. Darcy lay quietly wrapped in the blanket on the lounge, also listening to *The Ghost of Tom Joad*. He kept remembering Springsteen singing low about doing straight time. *I'm doing white time*, he substituted, living here away from home, 'sick of doing white time'. Maybe that was why …

'Music to slit your wrists by!' Fil declared, grimacing.

'I kind of like it,' Darcy told her.

Jon turned around. 'Ah, he's alive. How are you?'

The boy blinked. How much did they know? 'Fine. I think. Bit tired, but.'

Jon seemed satisfied with this answer. 'You'd better have the day off tomorrow.'

Darcy agreed, sitting up. This sort of stuff always

wiped him out, even when he had family around and was prepared. When it happened unexpectedly; the shock took something out of him. In the low light of the lounge Jon didn't notice that Darcy's pupils were dilated to three times their normal size, nor that he was trembling slightly.

Filomena and Cam fidgeted on the lounge. They had to talk to Darcy – at once. Filomena beckoned to him out of Jon's line of sight. He got up shakily and joined them in the kitchen.

'You sure you're okay, Darc?' Jon called.

'Yeah.' But Darcy swayed slightly as he spoke. Cam pushed a cup of sweet tea at him. The drink surged through him; he could feel the sugar seep powerfully into his cells. Cam wanted to speak, but how to put it? Fil made an impatient gesture at him: *Hurry up*. Cam looked up from the floor and began: 'Outside, before, when you fainted—'

Ah, thought Darcy in relief, that's what they think.

'Um, did you ... see anything?' Cam whispered, his face urgent with worry.

'What sort of thing?' asked Darcy, cautious.

'Did anything change?' Fil butted in, impatiently.

Darcy got up and looked in the fridge to avoid answering. What did he do now? They obviously knew something. Should he lie? He took out a slice of ham, its edges slightly reddened and dry from being exposed to the cold air. He folded it into his mouth and chewed for a minute. Fil and Cam were still looking at him. 'Don't know what ya mean,' he compromised. 'What sort of change?' He tried to look neutral.

'Come outside,' Cam said. When the three of them were perched on the front stairs, he started talking again. 'About two weeks ago, Fil went into this old ruined house up in the hills—'

'Cam!' Fil said in horror.

Cam shushed her, shaking his head positively. He was tired of no one else knowing about it. 'He's got to know. That old camera,' he told Darcy, 'it's about a hundred years old. I didn't think it could possibly work, but Fil mucked around with it and the photos turned out.'

Darcy shrugged and made an upturned mouth – so what? He felt extremely uncomfortable.

'Except ... the photos don't show what she took, they're not of here and now. They're of this place a hundred years ago.'

That made Darcy pause. Fil watched him.

'It takes photos of things a hundred years ago?' he checked.

'Yeah, I know it sounds stupid ... but it's true. There's people in them, people we don't know.' Cam waited, hoping Darcy wouldn't sneer.

Darcy sucked at a piece of grass he'd picked from beside the steps and looked out at the bush. One hundred years ago, some of his ancestors still lived out there, hunting, fishing, dancing, sleeping, singing, living, fighting. 'Is that it?' he said. 'Is that all you found?'

Cam nodded, but Filomena said: 'No, it's not, Cam. What about the body?'

Darcy's eyes widened. 'A body?'

'In one photo Fil took in the old ruin, there's ... we think it's, I mean it might be ... a dead body.'

Darcy rolled his eyes. *What* were these white kids getting into? And what was he supposed to do? He sighed heavily and decided not to lie, but to tell as little of the truth as he could manage. 'Doesn't Jon know about this?' Obviously not, since they were perched out on the stairs, whispering.

'No, not yet.'

Darcy nodded his approval. That was *something*. 'Okay. Look, when that fat prick pointed the camera at me, you're right. Everything I could see changed. He disappeared, and so did the fences, and I think the house, but I'm not sure about that. Then I passed out.'

Fil and Cam were silent, coming to grips with Darcy's astonishing revelation. He went on: 'So, from what you said, I reckon when that camera's used on me, I'm gonna flip back too. Doesn't it happen when you use it?'

Fil thought Darcy was taking the whole thing remarkably calmly, and wondered why. 'No,' she answered, 'nothing happens except the photos aren't what we take. I mean, they go back in time. But we don't.'

Cam agreed. 'Remember that one you took of Jon in the kitchen without him knowing? Nothing happened with him, either, or with you in your room. It's just Darcy.'

The two white kids were bewildered. Darcy smiled. 'Well, that's only natural, eh?'

Fil and Cam were frowning.

Darcy gave an impatient gesture, flicking his fingers back towards his ears as he dipped his head. 'I belong here. You fellas are just bloody migloo ring-ins. I can't work out how you got involved at all ...'

Filomena didn't like that, but since Darcy had said it she tried to keep her temper. 'Whaddya mean, we don't belong here? It's our house, our place!'

Darcy laughed openly and said nothing.

'Do you reckon you've got more of a right to be here than us because you've got black skin?' she said.

'It's nothing to do with me skin – well, not the skin youse mean, anyway,' Darcy said matter-of-factly. 'But basically, yeah.'

'Rubbish!' Fil said angrily, stumped for any better response.

Darcy regarded her for a minute. He was losing patience. Living with whitefellas, whaddya expect? Ah, fuck her. 'Who that gum-tree?' he asked her harshly, pointing twice. 'Who that mountain?'

Fil screwed her face up. What was he talking about? 'Where's your grandmother live? How you sing 'im this country?' Darcy swung round to Cam. 'Where's the Men's Dreamin'? But you wouldn't know, eh, cos you just a fucken *kid* ...' He spat the word. Silly white kids playing at Business.

'Look, I don't understand what you're saying, Darc,' Cam replied with a restrained dignity that might have come from Jon, 'but I don't necessarily agree with Fil. What we really need to decide is what we're going to do.' It was the best he could do to ease the tension. It worked. It gave him a tiny shock to realise he was acting as a peacemaker, not a warrior. It felt *good*. 'Whaddya reckon? Do you know what's going on?' he added, consciously ceding authority to Darcy to balance Fil's comments.

Darcy looked at the ground. Well, yeah, he did, and

no, he didn't. Worst thing was, he had no clue why whitefellas had gotten back, even if it was indirectly. Or what he was supposed to do about it. He was really only a kid himself, after all, and a yellafella at that. 'The only thing I can think is to ask someone else, someone older,' he told them.

'I wanted to tell Jon!' cried Cameron in relief.

Darcy looked at him in astonishment. 'Not a *whitefella*, an elder. An Aboriginal elder!' These kids were real thick sometimes. Shit, as if—

'But,' Fil began, trying not to let her crankiness show. He waited. She had trouble getting it out. 'But aren't they all … gone? Around here?'

'Granny Lil,' Darcy said. 'I'll ask her.'

Cam seemed satisfied with this. Filomena felt massively confused. How could there be Aboriginal Elders in Federation? The only Aboriginals she'd ever seen were the surfies at Shelley Bay. And they weren't real full-blood Aboriginals, she thought ignorantly, not proper ones like Darcy … so who was Granny Lil? Things were slipping out of her grasp. I'm not giving the camera up, anyway, she told herself stubbornly, no matter what. It's mine, and I'm gonna sell it and buy my horse, and give the rest of the money to Dad.

Next morning, Fil stopped the transit van outside the small housing commission dwelling next to the BP station. Granny Lil's place. What now? Cam craned his neck from the window to see. A couple of dogs lay flattened in the shade of a large camphor laurel tree.

133

The yard was overgrown with longish grass and a plastic tricycle lay on its side beside the wooden stairs. A battered mini-van stood on the concrete strips of the drive. The yard looked as though way too many people had been living in the house for way too long, he thought. As he watched, a shouting chocolate-coloured child pursued by another paler one ran out from the backyard, then they both disappeared down the side of the house. Puddles of water lay between them and the stairs. An adult voice called out to them to shut up. They shrieked merrily on their way.

'Is this it?' Filomena asked, hoping it wasn't. How on earth could the solution to their problems rest in this dump?

'Yeah.' Darcy came to life, happier even just parked outside Granny Lil's. Being at Aonbar's Rest was strangely okay, for a white house, but this was his people. They were city folk, of course, and saltwater mob to boot. But no matter. Blackfellas know blackfellas. He felt more relaxed than he had for days. He began to sing as he got out. It was the loudest sound Cam had ever heard him make. 'Country roads, take me home, to the place I belo-o-ong!'

A dark head popped out of a window upstairs. 'Ay!! Darcy! Come upstairs, boy. Mu-u-m! Darcy's here.'

They picked their way through the puddles and stood at the open door of the ramshackle house. The floor was covered in cracked lino bearing a fresh trail of muddy kids' footprints. One window pane had been taped up with dear plastic to replace the glass. A foam double mattress without sheets lay on the floor, and a small brown dog slept on the lounge chair in front of the TV.

After a minute Cam put a name to the overpowering smell of the meat on the stove – corned beef. Silverside. Jon loved it with white sauce. An overflowing ashtray sat on the middle of the kitchen bench. You couldn't have called the house filthy, but it wasn't what you'd call clean, either. It was certainly different to all Cam's friends' houses. Granny Lil's was packed with the evidence of people and crowded with junk. Filomena shrank from the grimy scribbled-on walls, and tried not to breathe.

'This is Fil, and here's Cam.' Darcy introduced them to an old lady sitting at her kitchen table smoking into another ashtray made from a cutdown IXL jam tin. She looked at them carefully, folding up a form guide to the Gold Coast races. There was no sign of the person who'd stuck her head out of the window.

'Come in, come in. Here, sit-down, have a seat. Put kettle on, Darcy, willya? Teabag there.'

Darcy bustled in the kitchen, while Fil and Cam sat twiddling their thumbs. Granny Lil heaved her bulk out of the chair and went to the window. 'You kids! Go over to Uncle Joe's, gorn now! We got grown-up business to talk about here, so get lost!' The sound of shouting disappeared up the street. Cameron wondered if he should mention Jon, seeing as how she'd met him. He decided it was best to keep quiet. It might take quite a while before they could explain everything.

'So …' Darcy said over his teacup some time later. 'We thought we should ask someone older, you know, someone with experience. I wouldn't have said anything to them but …'

Granny Lil gave a very slight nod and pushed out her bottom lip, thinking. She groped for her lighter in her dress pocket. Then she swung the force of her gaze onto Filomena. 'You, girl, you found this camera, eh?'

Fil nodded, terrified.

Granny Lil looked out of a wide dark face with amazing bloodshot eyes. White hair spiralled around her head; she looked like the devil's sister.

'Why?' Lil demanded, lighting another smoke.

'I beg your pardon?'

'Why did ya pick it up?'

Filomena floundered for the right response, but someone large and heavy was standing on her tongue. 'Just ... I dunno ... 'cos it was there, I s'pose. I was frightened, in the old house, and just ... took it.' She trailed off, feeling for the very first time that perhaps she didn't have any right to the camera after all.

Granny Lil looked at Darcy, who shrugged. She frowned and said something Fil didn't understand. Something about igloos.

'Yeah, I'm pretty sure,' Darcy answered her question, whatever it was.

'What made you go in the house? How did you find it?'

Here Filomena found herself on safer ground. 'I was out riding, horse-riding, and I fell off. I took a shortcut, and then I saw the house. I just wanted to look around, I suppose.' Fil didn't mention wanting to find stuff to sell. Somehow she didn't want to mention that.

'Just wanted to look around,' Lil echoed savagely, tapping ash. 'Never mind where you are. Never mind about where you might be steppin'.'

Filomena shrivelled. She couldn't think of anything to say. Lil closed one reddened eye and leaned away, still looking at her like an insect. Then she took pity on the kid and her face relaxed. 'Ah, you can't help being hignorant, I suppose.' She grew stern once again. 'Things around here, you don't know about. Town's the place for migloos. You know' – her voice changed yet again, to a milder one, remembering – 'when the migloos first come here, there was an old man, a wise old man. They were bringing in their cattle, and their convicts and cutting the cedar. Taking over. Fightin' over land. And these blackfellas they made an—' she searched for the word '—an envoy. Went and seen 'em, and said, you white man, you take the plains for cow. And us blackfellas, we'll have the hills. My grandfather told me, they went up in the hills then and left the plains alone. Took their Business up there, too, to the cliff. See, they wanted to share. No good. White man took everything. They woulda been better off fightin' from the word go.'

Filomena swallowed. Granny Lil had both eyes shut now, and was nodding mournfully to herself. 'Everything,' she repeated. 'Everything.'

Fil shot a glance at Darcy: What now?!

Wait, he gestured. Be patient.

Granny Lil opened her eyes and took a mouthful of tea. Cameron seemed to catch her attention for the first time. 'You look like someone I met ... a migloo fella. John?'

'He's my Dad,' Cameron said automatically, before he realised he should have said our dad. Granny beamed at him. That'd be right, thought Fil sourly, women always love Cam with his pretty-boy face.

'You tell him come see me. He never come to see me after I met him, that time. You tell him to come. All right? Darcy, you bring him to see me.'

'Yeah, okay, Aunty I'll tell him.'

Granny jerked her chin just half an inch and Darcy stood up. 'Gimme smoke price, Darcy.' He felt in his clothes for money and luckily found a ten dollar note, which he gave to her. She nodded happily. 'Gorn, now.'

'Thanks. Granny Lil.'

He ushered Filomena and Cam outside.

'Is that all?' Fil asked, 'An interrogation?' She felt put upon. Bloody rude old Aboriginal woman. Anyone'd think it was her camera that had been found.

'That's a start,' Darcy replied coolly. 'She invited us back, didn't she?'

'Did she?' Cam said.

Darcy rolled his eyes. 'Didn't you hear her ask me to bring Jon around? That's an invite to come and see her again. When she's had time to think about stuff ...'

'Oh.' Cam and Fil walked back to the van quietly, thinking about what they'd seen. It was like the shows on TV about the third world, thought Fil in disgust. Mud, dogs, rubbish. Yuk.

All of a sudden Cam understood better why Darcy was more than willing to live in the broken-down Thunderbox.

'Darcy,' Fil asked when they were driving home, a bit embarrassed at raising the subject, 'do all Aboriginals live in places like that?'

'Nah,' Darcy said, 'some of 'em still live in terrible places, eh? Oh, there's some real dumps where I come from. But lots live in nice houses these days. Specially in the city.' He looked out the window, pleased with the morning's work. Granny Lil liked him, that was for sure.

CHAPTER NINE

Cam stopped his wheelbarrow in the yard and mopped the sweat off his face using his sleeve as a hanky. Then he lifted the heavy load of straw and manure again, wheeling it to the compost heap. He forked the contents out, mixing fresh straw with old rotted earthy matter full of worms. When that was done he decided to do what Fil had asked. Darcy was grooming Picasso, running a currycomb over his fine bay coat.

'Darc—' Cam began.

'Mmmm?' Darcy switched sides. Now only the top of his head was visible, the rest of him masked by tall Picasso's neck and back.

'You know how we were talking about Gunner, and you said he'd had eighteen more roots than you?'

'Yea-ah.' Oh-oh, what now?

'Well … have you ever gone out with a white girl? Would you, I mean?' This was so *embarrassing*. Cam tried desperately to sound light and non-specific. Surely Darcy would know he was talking about Fil.

Darcy didn't stop working as he laughed uproariously.

'Never in a million years, Cam.'

'Oh, okay. Just wondered.'

'He said never in a million years,' Cam reported to Filomena in her room. 'Guess you're out of luck.'

Filomena scowled. 'That's so ... racist. That's stupid. What if I said I'd never go out with a black guy or a Chinese guy?'

Cameron shrugged. 'If he won't, he won't, I s'pose.'

Fil snorted. How bloody ridiculous. All this Aboriginal stuff was giving her the shits. Indignation fizzed in her all day like ginger beer.

Fil sat on the veranda reading *My Place*. Her pride was still stinging from the attack Jon had launched last night when she criticised Granny Lil's house to him. He hadn't gone as far as he did when he argued with the politicians on TV, calling them the moronic by-products of a racist orthodoxy, but she had been left feeling ignorant and small nevertheless. 'Read, and learn and listen before you judge,' he had ordered. 'What do you know about these people's lives? Dirty houses pale into insignificance when you take a ten-second look at Australian history.' This was the same Jon, mind you, who acted like it was a major crime to leave a horse un-mucked out, or dishes unwashed after dinner. Fil had resolved to read all his books on Aboriginal stuff, then decide for herself whether having a dirty house was okay if you were black. Confused, she lowered her head, and read on.

'Good life for some,' Cam teased her as he came out from the lounge and began lifting his afternoon dumbbells. His biceps swelled and rounded with each repetition. On the down stroke, the tops of his shoulders showed deep valleys between the small linear muscles of the deltoid. He grunted as the weights grew heavier in his hands. A rainburst of sweat formed on his forehead. He watched himself with something approaching satisfaction in the long mirror propped dangerously on a pile of books, on a wooden chair.

'I'm paid to think,' Fil quoted their father in his previous incarnation as a university lecturer. 'Where's Darcy?'

'Took off again. I think he might have gone round to Granny Lil's, but I'm not sure. Dad's still inside.'

'Is he all right? Darcy, I mean.'

'Yeah, why?'

'He's just ... a bit quiet. Or something.' Darcy had barely spoken to her since yesterday after they got back from Lil's. He'd disappeared into the caravan, and apart from his quickly scoffed dinner, hadn't shown his face around the house at all.

Cam was still heaving away. 'Nah ... he's fine ... at least he was ... this morning. Maybe he misses other Aboriginals. Must be different for him, living with us, eh?'

'Or do you think he got frightened about the camera?' Fil wondered out loud.

Cam lowered his dumbbells, and considered this. 'He didn't *seem* scared. Not about the camera part of it. I think it was the fact that we found it was the big deal.' They made I-don't-know faces at each other. It was a mystery.

At dinner, Darcy had switched again. If not exactly cheery, at least talkative. He and Jon went great guns on religion. To hear Jon you'd have thought the Catholic Church was the source of original sin. Darcy was shocked, and defended the nuns who'd taught him. Strict but fair, he claimed. Oh, some of them were racist, but mostly ...

'That's what they said about Hitler,' Jon snorted. 'Beware the fanatic, Darcy. Beware, beware.'

'Especially fanatical moderates,' Cam added with a serious face. 'They're the worst.'

Jon pointed a knife at him. 'You watch your step, young Ming. Or I'll deliver you up to Dirty Harry on a silver platter.'

While Filomena was washing Jon's fish pie off the plates, Darcy drew Cam to one side. 'I got some more info. This arv.' He made as if to take Cam outside. But to Darcy's disquiet, Cam waited for Filomena to finish, then insisted that they go to his room. It was more private, he said. When they got there he switched on the CD to cover their voices. 'Well, what have you found out?' he asked.

Darcy looked at Filomena, wishing she hadn't come. This wasn't for white women. Not that he knew for sure. But then Granny Lil knew. So what was he to think? 'I went down Knockrow Street this arv and hung out with the Murris,' he told them. 'Granny Lil sent for me. She told me about Hew Costello – we think it was him, anyway, and where he built his place.'

'But we know where he built it.' Fil interrupted.

Darcy ignored her. 'When the Murris took off to the hills, them old ones, they took their Business up there with them.' He spoke to Cameron, quickly. 'Used to be it was on the coast as well as in the hills, but they had to shift everything up there, or else lose it. Anyway, only about twenty years later, Hew Costello built his house smack in the middle of a sacred area. A men's area, luckily for him, and not the major one, but ...'

'I don't understand what you mean,' said Cameron. 'What business?' He had absurd images of Aboriginals dressed in top hats, serving behind counters.

'Ceremonies, dances. Corroboree.' Darcy explained impatiently. 'Men's Business. Women's Business. Religion.'

'Oh, okay. So how come they lost it?'

'They didn't, not all of it. But if men got killed from the migloos, or died of disease, you know, if an old woman died from the new diseases, then her knowledge was gone, pretty much. They had to chop and change ... some of the women's Business went to men, Granny Lil reckons, some of the men's went to old women. Anyway, the closer the whites got, the further they had to move away from the massacres ... to protect their Business from the whites,' Darcy continued matter-of-factly. 'That's why they went up the high country.'

Cam was able to forget about Darcy being black. Right now, though, he felt as white as he ever had. He felt like a category. 'Massacres?' he asked. 'That stuff happened around here?'

'Of course,' Darcy replied impatiently. 'What did ya think happened? Think a spaceship come down and kidnapped all the blackfellas round here?'

Cameron, shamed, was silent. He'd never thought

too much about that side of the past. To him, history was goldfields, and 'explorers'. Sometimes he gave some passing thought to Aboriginal languages or Central Australian tribes. And of course he knew that the continent was taken by force, but, well, it was never stated that way, was it? Not to your face. Not about your own home. And not by an Aboriginal. It made him remember how he felt about a poem Jon had insisted he read before they went to see *Schindler's List* in Brisbane. He'd always remembered one bit of it, about someone letting a cat in. Cam pictured a rainy city street in the North of England for some reason, wet cobblestones and a cat mewing at the door. There was something about a dream of a building, too, with a thousand floors. Cam couldn't remember the words. But it meant: different treatment. How they thought the Jews were different, and even though they weren't, they killed them anyway. Like they weren't really human.

'So Hew Costello interfered with their religion?' Filomena asked.

Darcy tilted his head. 'It wasn't quite as simple as that. Business ... it's not *just* religion.' He stopped. It was near impossible to tell these white kids, with no religion, no Law, no understanding, what it meant to have sacred responsibilities. 'He had some sort of agreement with them. Granny doesn't understand why, or can't remember the details, she just knows that this white guy sort of lived – not with them, but like, among them – and they let him alone. But there was a big problem over the site of his house. Originally. She thinks maybe after a while the problem went away for some reason. No one knows the full story. She told me she'd ask around, find out as much as she can before deciding what to do.'

'So what's that got to do with the camera?' Filomena said.

Cam answered her. 'Well, if this ... this Business got interrupted by him, maybe the camera got ... maybe it went into the camera?' He looked at Darcy for help.

Darcy answered slowly. 'I don't know ... I mean, something like that musta happened, for the photos to come out the way they do. I dunno about me and Goddard, but – that was pretty weird. And if someone's been killed.' That was what really freaked Darcy. The idea of an old death still lurking around the edges of their own time. In his book, that meant real trouble. Where he came from, deaths meant payback. 'Let's just wait until Granny Lil does some asking around, eh? Leave it alone till then. It's not my ... not our, place. We just need to leave it be.' Darcy wore an expression both pleading and insistent.

Fil felt the camera was turning into a sinister waking nightmare. And to think that she'd gone looking for it! 'What would happen,' she asked, 'if I just sold the camera? It's probably worth a lot, it's so old.'

Darcy was horrified. 'You can't sell it!' How could he explain to Fil that the camera came to her because she was the right person? And that the payback belonged to her, she couldn't shift it? Selling the camera would be a big mistake. He got up to stand in front of Cam's stained-glass window and stared out tensely at the black night. Stranglers out there? Feather-feet? He didn't know what lurked in Yanbali country after dark. It sorta seemed his life was one big don't-know at the moment.

'Why not?' Fil asked.

Darcy grimaced. 'It's real hard to explain. But if someone's finished up … there's – consequences. Dunno what yet. But you're mixed up in it, see. Ya can't sell it. That'd just make it worse. Can't run from it.'

'Consequences. Dad'd love that,' Cam said glumly to Fil.

'But I didn't do anything,' complained Fil. 'Why do I cop this shit?'

Darcy had nothing to say to this. These white kids hadn't a clue that the land they stood on was soaked in Yanbali blood. They'd learn. Probably the hard way, from the look of it, but that wasn't his worry.

Chapter Ten

Cam was mooching around the house next morning in a tight circuit from the fridge to the bookcase to a kitchen chair. Hands in pockets, face downcast. He kicked furniture. Opened and shut the fridge door. Never went more than ten steps from the phone.

'Moocher!' Jon accused his son. 'What's wrong with him today? Bored is it?' Inside, Jon was grinning savagely. The boy's suffering all right. That girl hasn't rung for at least – what, twenty-four hours?

'Nuh.' Cam knew better than to fall into that trap. There were always a million jobs to be done, outside – where he couldn't get to the phone first. Why weren't they *rich*? Then he could have his own mobile phone and some *privacy*.

'Why don't you ride over and see Jordan? Or go swimming?'

'Jordan's at his Mum's till the middle of January.' Brightening, Cam suggested, 'I could go see him if you'd buy me a bus ticket.'

'Where's his mum live?'

'Townsville.'

Jon rolled his eyes. Two hundred at least, not to mention the work that wouldn't get done. 'Sorry.'

Cam scowled and went to his bedroom, leaving the door open in case Lucy rang after all. He flung himself onto the bed and looked at his posters. She'd said, 'I'll give you a call in the morning.' Didn't she? Or had it been, 'I *might* give you a call in the morning.' *Will* ring? Or *might* ring? Could he call her? But what would he say? Why hadn't she rung? The thought of Lucy and her honey-skinned gorgeousness made him almost weep with frustration. Her luminous black hair lay against her blue school uniform in a way that cried out for Cam to seize great handfuls of it and draw her gently closer to him. He lay in miserable agony on the bed, wanting to wank, but too afraid to shut the door in case she called, and Jon thought he didn't want to be disturbed. Ah, fuck it, he finally decided, he'd ring her. And if she wasn't there, or was there and said she wasn't ... too bad. Better than lying around hopelessly, dying from lack of female attention.

With beautiful, uncanny, perfect timing, as he walked into the kitchen Jon rose from the paper and said: 'Keep an ear out for the phone, will you? I'm going to have another look at Donk's back. It didn't look too good last night.'

'Yeah, no worries.' Yes, yes, *yes!*

Cam waited beside the phone until his father's broad back had disappeared tactfully around the corner, then dialled quickly. He needed to hurry while Jon was out, and whisper in case Fil was in her room eavesdropping.

At the same time he had to sound manly and authoritative for Lucy. Life was truly impossible.

'Is Lucy there, please?' he gabbled as soon as someone picked the phone up at the other end.

'This is Lucy ... who's that?'

'Cameron.'

'Hi! I was just going to ring you!'

Oh great. I blew it, lost the advantage by calling her, Cam chastised himself even as he glowed. She'd been going to call! A minute of talk, then she asked: 'Did you ring for anything special?'

Help, thought Cam. *Did I?*

'Ah ... yeah! I was wanting to know if you, if you're doing anything on Saturday. Saturday night, that is.'

'Oh.' Lucy sounded crestfallen. 'My parents are going out to dinner and I'm supposed to go to my cousins. Did you want to go to the movies or something?'

'Yeah, that's right,' Cam clutched at the suggestion like a drowning man. 'Yeah, the movies.' Thank you, thank you, thank you, for asking first. He could have wept with relief.

'I could ask them, I guess,' Lucy sounded a bit dubious. Her dad didn't like boys hanging around, especially Aussie boys, but if she insisted ... 'Look, I'll see if they'll let me, and ring you back, okay? Dad's a bit funny about letting me go out.'

'Sure. Talk to you soon.' Cam replaced the phone, feeling faint. He sat down weakly with a Coke and calculated how much money he didn't have.

'Who was that?' Fil was standing in the doorway, smirking.

Cam smiled dreamily. Lucy was gonna call him. She had been going to call him, and, as if that wasn't enough, she was going to call him *again*. She wanted to go to the movies! With him! 'Who was what?' he asked, all innocence, unaware he was blushing.

'I heard you talking about going to the movies.'

'Uh, no one you know.'

Fil smiled a slow, malicious, big-sister smile. Only one thing could make her little brother blush like that. 'It was Lucy wasn't it?'

'Nuh.' As casual as he could. Fuckin sisters.

'Yes it was – you're blushing.'

'No it wasn't! It was Jordan. Piss off!' Cam cried, knowing what sort of treatment was coming.

Just then Darcy walked in through the screen door, throwing his Akubra on the kitchen table. 'That's nice, a fella walks in and gets—'

'Not you,' Cam explained. 'Her.' He pointed angrily at Fil.

'He's shitty because I guessed his *girlfriend* rang him,' Fil teased without mercy, 'Feeling lonely 'cos Cam-the-Man's not there. Wanting a little kissy-wissy.'

Darcy smiled broadly. 'Didn't tell me ya had a girlfriend, man. She cute? Whasser name?'

'Oh,' Fil answered for him, 'She's *be-yoo-tiful*. She's got lovely brown eyes, four of em, and six hundred and eleven zits and her name's Lucy Rootalot—'

'SHUT UP!' Cam howled at his sister, chasing her around the room.

'I can see,' Darcy said thoughtfully, 'why you'd try and keep her a secret, eh?'

'YOU can fuckin shut up TOO!' Cam spat.

Darcy rolled with laughter. Fil pursed her lips and made loud kissing noises at him from the other side of the table. This was just too much. Meaning to throw only the drink, Cam hurled his Coke glass at her. She ducked and the edge of the glass hit Darcy fair in the face. Fil gasped. Blood poured off Darcy's lip onto the kitchen lino. He put a hand up to his face and looked at it, stunned and angry.

It took a single second for five problems to collide in his mind. Problem One – blood demanded action to square it back. That was Law. Problem Two – not in white way, it didn't. Problem Three – Cam was a child. He couldn't fight a child. That was Law, too. Problem Four – If he didn't fight, Cam and Fil and Jon would think he was chicken. Problem Five – Blood was pissing out everywhere.

Darcy solved these unsolvable riddles the only way he knew, by going spare. 'You fucken bastard! You stupid little dumb bastard!' he accused Cam through a sliced mouth. He picked an unripe avocado off the table and hurled it with deadly accuracy. Cam staggered backwards against the wall in shock, his nose broken for the third time in two weeks. Darcy walked up to him and casually hit him twice in the lower face. Barn. Barn. Now Cam's face was red too. Finish.

'Stop it! Stop it!' Filomena was screaming and crying at the same time, unaware in her shock that Darcy was in fact simply standing there, and, satisfied that the correct action had been taken, wasn't going to hit her brother again. Cam had his arms in front of his face and, somehow, the unexpected nous to lift his foot to Darcy's groin. The dark boy doubled up without warning. Panicking, Fil picked a chair up and was about to deck Cam when Jon burst in the screen door and relieved her of it. He looked around wildly at the wrecked room. So it had happened, and sooner rather than later. There were splatters on the white wall. Cam had a squashed tomato for a face. Darcy was groaning on the floor, the lower half of his face a red mask. Plenty of blood, Jon assessed, but he was breathing and nothing major was damaged, by the look of him. Cam was standing, just, and Fil looked okay. Jesus H. Christ.

'What the FUCK is going on here?' he asked quietly.

Cam shot a fast look at him and took off.

'Fil? What's going on? Cameron, come back here. NOW!' He wasn't so quiet anymore.

'They had a fight,' she said, gulping. It had all taken only a few seconds and her head spun. 'Cam chucked a glass at me, but it hit Darcy—'

'He chucked *what*?!' Jon was halfway down the corridor before Fil answered. He could hear Cam frantically locking himself inside his bedroom.

Jon broke the door down.

For the first time in his life Cam was forced to really confront his father. Two pairs of angry, fearful yellow eyes met. Jon's face was white with rage, and it wasn't the knowledge that Cam would hit back that stopped him lashing out.

'*Get out there*. This better be good, pal.'

Scared shitless, Cam stalked past him to the kitchen. Darcy was sitting propped up against the wall, bleeding like a stuck pig and holding his balls with both hands. Fil stood helplessly with a wet tea towel, ready to bathe his wounds when he was ready. Her legs were shaking. After briefly examining both boys, Jon sat Darcy on one side of him and Cam on the other. He put his bunched brown fists on the table in front of him as a silent warning. 'Now talk,' he ordered.

Cam stared at his reflection in the bathroom mirror. From the forehead up he looked fine. His jaw only *felt* broken, the doctor said, but the blackened, swollen, eyes that came from the punch that broke his nose, well, they'd take five days to settle. His nose looked as though it had decided to go for a little wander off underneath his right eye. Maybe when me eyes are back to normal, Cam thought as he probed his loosened teeth, and me jaw stops hurting the nose will look craggy and Sean Conneryish. Jon had offered his ballpoint pen services again; Cam had declined for fear more pain would shatter his face completely.

Jon had shrugged. 'Your funeral, slugger.' Jon wasn't interested in seeing him for the next few days, he said. Do your work (unpaid for two weeks), he ordered, do your extra work, apologise to Fil for your *stupid* and *juvenile* behaviour, and get outta my sight.

'What about Darcy?'

'I'll worry about Darcy.'

Cam considered himself lucky and did the disappearing act. Work didn't worry him, and now judgment was passed he could endure Jon's disapproval. The real killer was when Lucy phoned. Cam heard the excitement in her voice when she said she was allowed to go out with him; then the flatness when he half-lied, saying his father had grounded him for a week. Well, he couldn't show up looking like this, could he? Lucy rang off casually without making any more plans to meet, which left Cam feeling like killing Jon. Or Darcy. Or himself. Or all three of them.

Miserable, Darcy sat on the step of the caravan. Time to be moving on again, fuck it. He'd have to go and ask Granny Lil if he could camp at her house. A slow rage at his circumstances burned in his chest. *What if Fil hadn't started teasing Cam? What if the glass hadn't slipped? What if he'd thought, instead of snapped? What if Cam had blocked his punches? What if Jon understood better?* Ah, what if, what if, he mocked himself. Jon said it when he arrived: If anyone gets hurt, or anything goes missing – look out. Pretty clear, wasn't it? He picked up his bag and went to get his pay off Jon at the stable, where he was examining Babyface for Queensland Itch.

'I'll be goin' then.' Darcy said in a low voice, shame.

Jon turned around. 'Where?' he said harshly, hiding his disappointment.

Darcy shrugged. Anywhere. He'd fucked up good and proper again. But he shoulda known it wouldn't work, hanging round whites.

'Running away now, are you?' Jon said, 'How many times has this happened before?'

Hey? Darcy took a step backward, still looking uncertainly at Jon.

'How many times have you used fights to give you an

excuse to run away from what's too difficult to solve?'

This was a new one. An assortment of punch-ups and contrived arguments, flashed through Darcy's mind. But Jon was wrong ... people picked on him, that's all. 'It's not ... I just had to.'

Jon looked carefully at Darcy's cut and swollen face. Even if Darcy was very wrong, he wasn't lying. Something big was happening inside the kid. *Sit down*, he gestured at a hay bale, and Darcy sat. Jon chewed a strand of lucerne.

'Darcy,' he said, 'if you want to walk, you're free to go. But I don't know that I want you to. Please tell me why you think you had to break my son's nose.'

'He hit me first. Bust my mouth.' It was obvious, Darcy thought. What's to talk about?

'So? It was an accident.'

'Whaddya mean? He cut me. I get to cut him, that's the Law.'

'Customary Law, you mean? Black Law?'

'Yeah.'

Jon wrinkled his brow. Now what was he getting into? He squatted down on the bricks. 'Go on.'

'It's simple, eh. Payback. He hurt me and if I don't do nothing, that means it's not level. I hadda square it. Thass why I only hittim two times, eh?' Darcy pleaded for recognition that it wasn't a totally random attack.

'Isn't there another way?' Jon asked severely, hoping Darcy wouldn't propose spearing Cam in the leg next time they disagreed. Darcy stayed silent. There were other ways, but he didn't much feel like talking to a whitefella about it. 'What about talk? Compromise?' Jon suggested. 'Compensation, even.'

Darcy shrugged. It wasn't impossible. He struggled to put it into English. 'It's like, it's the blood, eh. That's what's important first up, onetime. Then, after, it's not blood, it's ... like who's right.'

'Like I said, it was an accident. Blame doesn't come into it.'

'Nah,' Darcy replied through his teeth, frustrated at not getting through. 'Not that kinda right. Like who's got the right.'

'The right to pay the damage back?'

'Yeah.'

'So we're back where we started. Violence begets violence?'

'But if he ... it depends. Like if he offered.' Darcy stopped. That wasn't right.

'I'm listening, take your time,' Jon said.

Darcy tried again. 'If he said, okay, you've got the right, I did wrong and you've got the right to spear me or cut me or whatever, then I decide whether to, then it might be okay, eh. But he wouldn't know that. So it's easier just to do it, then it's finish. Like, out home, if there's payback, and it's decided, and you say right, do it now, here I am' – Darcy slapped his front leg as if offering it to imaginary spear – 'maybe they spear im. Maybe just gammon spear him, little bit blood, couple weeks bad. Maybe nothing at all. Whatever.'

Jon's face was blank. Darcy flung his hands around, trying to make him see. 'It's the saying that you're wrong that matters most. Sometimes talk makes it level, sometimes not.' He shrugged. That was the best he could explain. It was about acknowledging what was right and what was wrong – and how could Cam possibly know that? He was just a kid, raised and living in the white world. And living there was like living in a maze with no way out.

'So, it's not so much about punishment, more about recognising your rights in the Law ... and Cam wouldn't know how to start. Well, why didn't you wait and talk when it happened?' Jon asked slowly, beginning to see a chink of light. 'Surely that's Law too?'

'I dunno.' Darcy shrugged. This bit was where it got tricky and he lost the moral high ground. He could hardly say that living in a world where the rules were all wrong for him, hitting people had become his normal response to trouble.

Jon waited. 'I didn't think first, I just did it,' Darcy offered shame-faced. And Cam just a kid and all, and me half a man, he thought.

'Do you feel sorry?'

Darcy considered that one carefully. To his surprise, his answer was honest.

'Kind of, but not that sorry.'

'So you think you did the right thing?' Jon was taken aback.

'I did the right thing for me. Kinda. But the wrong thing for Cam. In my way, I'm right. In his way, I'm wrong. See?'

Jon covered his face with his hands, then drew them down. 'I won't pretend to understand, no. Not really. Not when I warned you about anyone getting hurt.' Then he had a very unwelcome thought. 'Have you had a HIV test lately?'

Darcy shook his head.

'Well, that's priority number one, buddy – that room was swimming in your blood. Get down the medical centre this arv, please.'

'And then?' Darcy was too frightened to ask what was going to happen now. If they pressed charges it'd be grown-up jail this time, no doubt about that with his record. And he'd heard stories about them places, stories that didn't make ya sleep too easy at night if you were a pretty young boy – straight, gay or otherwise. He thought seriously about bolting while he had the chance.

Jon watched Darcy carefully. What's going on in his head? The kid's sweating. 'Shit, Darc, I don't wanta see Cam's face like that! Or yours. I can see you think you did partly right, somewhere. I tell you what ...' Darcy waited for Jon's judgement, heart pounding '... I want two things, no, three things from you. One, I want you to apologise properly to Cam and Fil.'

'Fil?' Relief that he wasn't going to jail again flooded all over Darcy. *Deadly!*

'She saw it happen, didn't she?' said Jon steadily. 'Not pleasant. Second, I want your word that before you get into any more fights on my property, you'll come to me with your problem. And third, you owe me for this. Call it whitefella payback if you want, and don't go doubting that I'll call it in. I'll give you five minutes to think it over. If that sounds unfair – you know where the gate is.'

Jon turned back to the horse while Darcy gave serious consideration to the meaning of *second chance*.

Chapter Eleven

'How many trail riders last Wednesday?' Jon asked Cam from the computer desk. His son looked up, diverted from *Lethal Weapon*, which he was watching with Darcy.

'Um, Governor, Benny ... Donks, Picasso for me, Babyface I think, and I let Samantha Smith take Garbo. Five pays.'

Jon smiled. Samantha was another local female that made Fil despair. 'I bet you did. She's a bit old for you, sonny. Did you put the money in the tin?'

Cam scowled. 'Yeah. Shoulda been one twenty-five.'

Jon went back to his spreadsheet. 'And eight on Saturday?'

'Yeah.' Cam's attention was on the screen.

Jon took out a piece of paper and began adding up the numbers. Trail riders, mostly regulars, who came weekends or Wednesday afternoons, paid twenty-five dollars each for an hour and a half. The riding lessons he gave occasionally paid thirty an hour. Breaking was seventy-five a day, including board. Wednesdays were two hundred clear after petrol, for a long, hard day with a two-hour drive both ways. Sounds quite profitable, he thought, till you take out hay at eight dollars a bale, oats, nuggets, other feed, saddlery that needs fixing, pay for Darcy and Cam, fuel for the vehicles, and worst of all the crippling mortgage payments of close on three hundred a week. When Jon had originally chucked in teaching and done the sums, he'd worked out a compromised dream that he could pay for outright, using his substantial superannuation. They'd been all set to buy ten acres further up the coast, away from Shelley Bay's lucrative tourist market and far more in line with his budget. Then the real estate agent, almost as an afterthought, had mentioned the forty acres nestled in the hills between Federation and the coast.

At two hundred thousand flat, the owners had surprised everyone by capitulating, and Aonbar's Rest was born. Jon and Cam still sometimes recited the saga to each other: the day Jon's boss had asked him not to come to the University in sandals and shorts; Jon's acerbic response, something to the tune that a Mickey Mouse faculty deserved to be staffed by clowns; his drunken decision that night that he'd had enough; Cam's urging that they move to the magical country of Shelley Bay; the way the idea sat snugly in Jon's head like an opal in the dirt, refusing to shift; weekend expeditions to visit Craig that became more frequent and more obviously shopping trips to the real estate windows. The frantic trip, suited and brushed and numbered, to the bank in Brisbane. The purchase. The hunt for suitable horses. Building the stables first, since the horses needed comfort if they were to work. Living in the Thunderbox while they saved enough money to build the house. And the final, triumphant moment at the end of January when they knocked in the last nail of the back veranda, hung the sign on the front gate.

This evening Jon kept adding and subtracting but there was an annoying glitch that wouldn't come out. The tin was short by about thirty dollars. It couldn't be ... could it? When everything was working out so well? His mouth twisted into a grimace. He'd refused to put a lock on the tin when Darcy started working for him, on the principle that if he couldn't trust the boy with money he had no business trusting him with the horses or anything else on the property. If Darcy *had* taken this money, and Jon didn't mention it, there was no harm done other than the kid thinking he got away with it. But on the other hand, if he *hadn't* taken it, and Jon said something to him, well ... Jon looked at the two boys, engrossed in Mel Gibson's exploits. Cam lay flat on his back, looking at the TV between his knees. Darcy was wrapped around a pillow on the lounge. Fil was nowhere in sight.

'Cam,' Jon experimented, 'did you say seven on Saturday?'

Cam's eyes didn't shift. 'Mmm-uh.'

'CAMERON!' Jon bellowed, shocking both boys to attention. 'How many on Saturday?! Seven or eight? Here's me thinking Darcy's flogged half the weekend pays, and you're dreaming away ...'

Darcy paled, turning an odd washed-out grey under his brownness. Cam quickly computed on his hands. 'Seven, it was definitely seven.' His guts were screwed up in a little ball; he hated it when Jon got mad. Cam still hadn't got over the shock of what had happened the other day.

'Seven,' Jon said tightly. 'You're sure of that, now?'

'Yeah. I forgot that Picasso had that sore chest, so it worked out Liz couldn't come.'

'Thank you so much.' Jon was over-polite, turning again to the computer screen. 'Then I guess Darcy can continue in our employ.'

Sometimes it was worse when Jon didn't yell. Generally speaking, Cameron enjoyed having adult responsibilities. Unlike many of the kids his age at school he had his own money, real money, enough to have bought Garbo for eighteen hundred dollars last year. Jon usually treated him more or less as an adult, not telling him where to go or what to do unless it affected his work. The downside was having to cop the same crap as an adult would; Jon didn't make any allowances for him being fourteen. Cam watched another ten minutes of the movie to show he didn't care about Jon's anger and wasn't upset. Then he went to his room to stare at the ceiling for half an hour. What would happen, he wondered, if he said he was leaving home? He honestly had no idea. The fear that Jon would put up no protest stopped him from going downstairs and trying.

Jon glanced over at Darcy. 'On your lonesome, son? Where's Fil?'

Darcy shrugged. She was avoiding him lately. 'Said she had some reading she wanted to do.'

Jon grinned, remembering something, and shuffled in his overflowing drawer. Magazines fell out – *The New Yorker, Punch, Bit and Spur.* 'Do you like reading?' knowing what the answer was going to be.

'Nuh. Boring.'

Jon tossed him a *Campaign* magazine. 'Try that. I doubt you'll find it boring. Even if you do, read it for my sake. All of Federation will know I bought it, and am, therefore, a poofter.' Darcy stared at Jon as the movie credits rolled. The man grinned, white teeth gleaming in a brown face. He brushed the hair off his face. 'Just kidding, son. What I mean is, the tiny minds of Federation will assume that only a queer would take an interest,' Jon closed the spreadsheet and opened another document.

'Oh. Thanks.' Darcy got up. He stopped in the doorway, rubbing his upper arm nervously beneath his T-shirt. He was dying for a smoke, but Jon wouldn't let him smoke in the house, or the stables, so a bloke may's well try and give up, eh. 'Ah … Jon?' Darcy came back into the room again. 'I've gotta go to Lismore on Monday.'

Now Jon stopped typing and eyed him. Was this a ruse to get another day off? But Darcy was a hard worker and seemed to enjoy the horses. Sometimes he hung around the stables after knock-off time, talking to them. Especially Babyface: she and Darcy had developed a bond.

'What for? The glittering lights of the metropolis too much to resist?'

Darcy snorted then looked down at his feet feeling shame. 'See my parole officer.'

Jon was all sympathy, hidden under a flinty face … Ah, the dreaded screws. 'What time?'

'Nine o'clock.'

'Did you tell 'em you're living here?'

'Yeah.'

'Arseholes,' Jon commented. It was typical of screws to give a morning appointment to someone living an hour and a half's drive away. 'What if I give him a ring and make it for later on in the day? And I guess we can probably pick Gunner up Thursday instead of tomorrow.'

'And – could you write me a letter, saying I've got a job?' Darcy asked.

Jon agreed. Then as Darcy made to leave: 'So, Darc, want to tell me what you were locked up for?'

'Stealin' mostly,' Darcy was defiant. 'Bein' black, Granny Lil reckons. Fuckin white kids never get as much time as us mob.'

That figured. Most teenage crime was theft.

Then the boy faltered. 'And ... an assault in Sydney. Put this bloke in hospital. He was okay, but. Just ...'

'Battered.'

Darcy nodded. Bastard had needed it. Calling him a stupid coon.

'Like fighting, don't ya? What did that cost you?'

'Eighteen months all up. I done eleven. Two years parole.'

'Well, okay. I'll do your letter, and ring the bloke.'

'It's a woman.'

Jon wrote down the details. When he was alone in the room, he leant back on the chair and put his feet on the desk. He stared at a calendar which showed the Third World's December in Pakistan, or India or Sri Lanka – he couldn't see, having taken his glasses off. Thievin' ... bein' black ... put this kid in hospital, he was okay but ... six months jail – or what did they call it for kids? Six months in a juvenile detention centre. Sean Lovejoy had gone to hospital too, for three stitches and overnight observation. Thanks to Jon's intervention, Cam would suffer two weeks suspension when school started again. Jon wore a blank expression as he imagined Darcy's future and weighed it in his palm against Cam's. Somewhere there had to be justice, but he was buggered if he knew where to find it.

'Jon.' Cameron peered around the corner into Jon's bedroom, which took up half the eastern side of the house. He was holding a teapot of Earl Grey and toast.

Jon wriggled under his sheet and moaned.

'Jon!' More sharply this time. Christ, it was eight o'clock.

A bleary head poked up. 'What's this?' Jon said in sleepy surprise, 'room service?!'

'Amazingly enough. It's after eight o'clock, you know.'

Jon bounced up to a sitting position, rubbing his leg. 'Crudpuckers! It's that bloody medicine, they're all quacks. Put it down, ta. Did you do stables for me?'

Yes, he had. And Fil and Darcy had volunteered to take the six trail riders out, and Cam had reluctantly agreed. Jon thought about that for a moment and decided it was okay. 'No new ones?'

'Nah, just Sam and John Caldicott and those girls from last week. I came and banged on your door at seven, you know.'

'Didn't hear you.' Jon turned himself out of bed and

yelped as his foot hit the floor. A streak of pain shot into his hip from the wound. He rolled back onto the futon, sweating.

'Dad, you all right? Maybe you shouldn't get up.' Jon gritted his teeth and demanded his walking stick. Cam handed it to him and watched in disapproval as his father struggled to his feet. Stupid bastard. He doesn't care if he croaks but who's going to look after us? Who'd run the school, who'd argue with Dirty Harry? For the first time it occurred to Cam what it must have meant for Darcy having been taken from his parents. He had lots of other relations out west, from what he'd said, but his real mum had died before he could find her. A hole, that's what it'd mean, Cam decided, a big awful parent-shaped hole.

'Can I look in your room, Dad?' the boy asked as Jon was eating his toast in front of Saturday morning *Rage*.

'What for? *Why* do I watch this rubbish?' Jon clicked over to another channel, one showing ads for canal real estate. He developed a pained expression.

'A book.' Cameron didn't feel like explaining about the poem. It was personal. Talking with Darcy about the Aboriginals, that past stuff, he felt … odd. He wanted to keep it to himself.

'Go on.' Those kids are up to something, Jon mused. Ah, well, they'll live. My worry's feeding the buggers for the next four weeks. He sat wondering if he really should sell Picasso to clear the debts once and for all, knowing that it would break his heart to do it. The horse was friend, brother and psychologist rolled into one.

Cameron padded down the polished wood floors to Jon's room and swung the louvred cedar door open. Jon had put hours of work into decorating this place. His bed was a bright blue futon spread across the floor beneath a mozzie net. The end walls were repositories of Jon's books; he'd had to value them once for an insurance claim and that afternoon they'd counted one and a half thousand, without the magazines and newspapers. The back wall, facing the door, was almost book-free, hung with intricate layers of pine shelving holding family photos, Japanese pottery, carvings of South Pacific gods, a New Guinea mask that gave Cam the horrors with its staring cowrie-shell eyes, some small pieces of Aboriginal art and about a million other knick-knacks, all touched with the minor magic of Jon's selecting eye. In the centre of the wall, framed by the other pieces, was a large watercolour of Filomena as a baby, held by her mother. *I had a dream*, Jon had told Cam, *I saw this wall in it, and when I woke up, I wanted it. So I made it instead – my dream wall.* The only other furniture in the room besides the bed and a wardrobe was a large armchair facing the open stained-glass window. Picasso grazed outside.

Now Cam went straight to the poetry shelf. A couple of wrong guesses later, he tentatively plucked Auden from between June Jordan and Paterson. He ran a finger down the index. Here it was. About refugees from the Holocaust:

Saw a poodle in a jacket fastened with a pin,
Saw a door opened and a cat let in:
But they weren't German Jews, my dear, but they weren't
German Jews.

He read the whole of the poem to himself carefully, twice, then replaced the book.

Darcy and Filomena headed and tailed the five riders peacefully clip-clopping around the mountain. A line of sweat flowed relentlessly down the middle of Fil's back; she scratched it with her crop handle, making Governor twitch nervously underneath her.

Blond Sam Caldicott, toes down, elbows out and hauling away at poor old Donk's mouth.

'Look,' Fil said patiently, 'keep your hands down and you'll have more luck.' She rode up beside him and adjusted his hands. Sam, delighted by her touch, resolved to continue riding badly.

'Can we canter now?' asked a fat girl whose name Fil could never remember. She looked up to where Darcy was sitting on bay Babyface. The trail ran fairly straight and smooth for the two kilometres home.

'I suppose so.'

Three of the five went ahead, cantering towards the school. Sam and a small girl of no more than twelve stayed walking with Fil and Darcy. Their horses, heads nodding, threw up fine reddish dust. Darcy was talking to the little girl, Mary, about her ambition to be a jockey. He was telling her it was hard work, lots of broken bones and not much pay. 'But at least you're small,' he added, 'you won't have to starve.' She nodded seriously, hanging on his every word. Fil carried out a reluctant conversation with Sam, bored with his thirteen-year-old acne and infatuated manner. Is that how Darcy feels about me, she suddenly thought in horror. A dumb, boring kid that won't leave him alone? She began to pay more attention to Sam's discussion of some sci-fi show on TV, telling herself never to let him see how much she despised him and – more to the point – his society parents' wealth.

Fifteen minutes later the trail riders were back home. Jon raised one arm to Fil from where he sat on the back veranda. She waved back, wondering why he didn't come down. Skinny Girl unsaddled her horse and stood offering him lucerne scraps from her tiny hand. The others tied their mounts dangerously, reins to the ring timbers, and went to pay Fil in the tackroom. Apologetically, the fat girl produced an assortment of one and two dollar coins, plus a ten dollar note.

'It's all money, love, all good legal tender,' Fil told her cheerily.

The fat girl smiled, and said she'd come again on Wednesday.

When Mr and Mrs Caldicott arrived in their flash car to pick up their sons, Mrs Caldicott raised her eyes at seeing Darcy, and asked where Jon was.

Fil pointed him out on the veranda. 'He was injured breaking in racehorses in Brisbane last week.' She tried to make it sound more impressive.

'Racehorses, really?'

'Yes, for one of the big trainers at Hendra.'

Gemstones flashed as the cheque was written out. 'Thank you, Mrs Caldicott,' Filomena was saying politely when a roar came from the yard.

'Get back and keep your filthy black paws away from my son!'

What was happening? She pushed back her chair and got up. Caldicott, flushed crimson, was standing between Darcy and his eldest son, John. Darcy looked helplessly at Fil.

'What's going on?' Fill asked him.

The man answered, swallowing rage, 'This little prick! Where's your father?'

'On the veranda,' said Fil. But Jon was standing just outside the yard, leaning on his stick.

'Is there a problem?' he asked. His voice suggested there wasn't, or there'd better not be.

'This little queer was trying to feel up my son!' Mr Caldicott looked like he was about to have a seizure. Fil laughed. How ridiculous. Jon regarded the man impassively. Jon was on antibiotics and couldn't drink. His leg hurt. He was lonely. He had debts to worry about. Rich Mr Caldicott was a royal pain in the arse at the best of times. Looking first at handsome Darcy, then at John's plain features, disfigured by acne, Jon felt a surge of recklessness he couldn't resist. Fuck Caldicott and his money.

'Did he enjoy it?' he enquired innocently. 'I can't imagine he's had too many other offers.'

Darcy spluttered. Caldicott turned an unnatural shade of purple and wrenched his son away. His wife and Sam reeled behind them to their expensive car.

Jon shook his head. 'Well? What's going on?' he asked Darcy, who looked sideways at Filomena, then back to Jon.

'*He* grabbed *my* arse. And then the father saw, and he didn't like it, eh?'

Jon nodded. Yeah, that sounded about right. Darcy wasn't stupid enough to harass someone in broad daylight, in public. And John Caldicott had given Jon the eye once or twice, before he'd made it perfectly clear he wasn't interested.

'I thought this was a professional establishment, not a ... bordello for Abo queers!' spat Caldicott from his car window, before bravely speeding around the corner.

Filomena was looking sympathetically at Darcy. Fancy being propositioned by a poof. She giggled. 'He thinks you're gay, when it's his son who's a poof!' She was highly amused. Jon gave her a meaningful look. Darcy, carrying a saddle on each arm to the tackroom, *fuck it, fuck it, fuck it*. Trouble every which way.

Fil didn't get why Jon was glaring at her.

'What's so funny?' he asked seriously.

'Well, it's just ...' Fil was tongue-tied. It seemed to be a permanent condition these days. Finally she snapped in irritation. 'Oh, sorry I'm being politically incorrect, aren't I?'

Jon's face darkened. 'No,' he said in the calm, menacing voice that meant you were sunk. 'No, you're not, actually. "Political incorrectness" is an Americanism that had very little meaning even in the States before it was ignorantly – perhaps maliciously – transferred to Australia. Political incorrectness, so-called, is a mindless label used by the ignorant, the racist and the powerful to silence anyone who questions the status quo. Apart from being intellectually extremely sloppy, it's almost always an attack on free expression. Perhaps you might think about what you're *actually* trying to say instead of picking up cheap second-hand political labels to insult people's intelligence.'

Fil opened her mouth, then shut it again. Jon pointed at the disappearing dust cloud up the drive. 'There's a young boy who can't tell his father the first thing about who he is, or what he wants in life. There's a man so hung up and afraid he'd rather blame anyone else than admit his son might not be what he always imagined. And as for Darcy ...' Jon stopped.

'What about Darcy?' Fil said defensively. Jon lifted one shoulder and bit his tongue – he wouldn't out him. Darcy returned from the tackroom. He'd heard the whole thing, and was sick of the lies. His family knew, the friends he'd had in Sydney, and Jon – why shouldn't Fil?

'I *am* gay, Fil,' he said simply; and threw his empty brown hands wide to the air. 'That's what.'

Fil's face puckered as she understood more and more. She turned, and fled with burning cheeks to the safety of her room.

Ten minutes passed, during which Fil considered the pros and cons of suicide. She wouldn't have to face Darcy. It would end the terrible, shameful knowledge that he would never ever want her. Life sucked anyway, except for holidays and Drago (though he was a mixed blessing, too). Against, were the facts that she would most likely make the State soccer squad if she trained hard enough, that it was a mortal sin, that she had nearly three hundred dollars in her Horse piggy bank, and that Mum, Dad and Cam would be left thinking it was their fault, not hers. She snivelled loudly into her pillow, and didn't hear the knocking on the door until Darcy was halfway in. She flapped her arm at him – Go Away. But she didn't really mean it. Realising this, he sat down against the shut door. 'Fil – it's okay, don't worry. Really; I don't mind. People say stupid stuff all the time, you get used to it.' Kind of, anyway; he thought. Stupidity's different to hatred – this realisation had made his life much easier.

Fil's snuffling subsided. She looked up. Darcy gave her an encouraging smile. She sat up. 'You mean that?' she asked, doubting his generosity.

'S'okay. You couldn't have known.'

That was true, thought Fil. How could I?

'I'm sorry,' she offered. 'I didn't mean ...' Fil felt a bit watery, inside and out. Quavery. She was curious, too, yet terrified to put a foot wrong. 'Um ... why?'

Darcy sighed and clutched his knees. The eternal question. 'Fucked if I know. I was a normal kid, just running around, you know. Then when I turned twelve I thought, well, must be time to get it on with girls, like everyone else. I tried that a few times ... I dunno, it just didn't feel right, sort of. I was confused for a long time, till I met this guy in' – Oops, cats out of the bag all over the place – 'in Sydney,' he went on. 'He was gay, and then I realised I was too. And that's it. End of confusion, happy ever after. More or less.' He shrugged. No big deal. Heaps of blackfellas were gay, 'specially in Sydney. Poofter heaven.

Fil considered this. Certainly Darcy seemed pretty happy, happier a lot more of the time than her or Cam. Though of course they had all the camera shit to worry about, and no idea how to deal with that.

'You must have gay kids at your school?' he asked her. Fil shook her head.

'Oh, well. They'll be there, just in the closet, that's all.'

That made her think. Monica Leitch certainly had short hair, and a hole for a nose-ring they wouldn't let her wear. Dunno about the boys, but.

'Anyway,' Darcy continued, 'don't worry about it. I'm being celibate for a while.'

It's getting worse and worse, Fil thought, a gay celibate – he'll never do it with me, not in a zillion years. She lay back on the bed. 'You haven't got AIDS have you?'

'Nah! Oh, dunno, really, never been tested,' he amended. He still hadn't got down the clinic. 'Anyway, Jon said to ask you, what's for lunch 'cos Cam and him are putting horses away,' he added.

Fil made a mental inventory of the fridge. Low on everything. 'I'll make some sandwiches,' she said, 'but we'd better go shopping this arv.' Suicide could wait, she decided. At least Darcy didn't seem to think she was irrefutably stupid. Incredibly enough.

'I'll give ya a hand,' he offered. Jon had asked him to see she was all right, so that's what he'd do. Swallow his pride and remember what Danny told him: all straights are homophobic, just accept it and you'll be right. Seemed pretty right to him. Ever since he was tiny he'd known to operate on the principle that all whites are racist, whether they knew it or not, so why wouldn't gay stuff be the same? Don't trust 'em, and they can't hurt ya. Only, he was starting to think Jon was different. That was a worry.

CHAPTER TWELVE

Jon stood at the head of the aisle in Woollies. Endless tins of Campbells and Home Brand soup stretched before him on his left; on his right were pasta, beans and rice. Shoppers bearing the irritated look of those seeking to do in ten minutes what will inevitably take an hour surged around him. Teenagers stocked up on improbable amounts of soft drink and junk food. A tired Samoan woman juggled small twins as she shopped, helped by a serious seven year old. Pierced and dreadlocked, a good-looking feral woman glanced mildly at Jon, and then more suspiciously at the straights who were getting their bleached white cancer flour for the week. The feral weighed a packet of dried chickpeas in her hands. Was it worth shoplifting? Jon grinned as she put the peas down, bumped into an old man in bowling shorts and, apologising profusely, pocketed some apricot slices. Better value, she thought happily. Oh, nicely done. Jon gave her an air clap, which she ignored.

Fil and Darcy were peering into the dessert freezers. Darcy was almost drooling. Double-choc ice-cream with pecan flakes. Apricot Pie topped with fresh cream.

Filomena dragged him away. 'Too expensive,' she said. Darcy raised his forearms, whined and gave Jon a puppydog beg. Jon looked at the prices and shook his head. Fil was right.

Fil ticked off items furiously. 'Got everything except the meat. It's cheaper at the butchers and we can get that anytime.' She made a face and poked her tongue out in disgust.

Darcy punched her arm. 'Geez, you fellas, I dunno. Don't yaz *like* meat?' For himself, he liked nothing better than a huge steak, burned to a crisp, with chips, salad and tomato sauce. Mmmm.

'Didn't notice you knocking back my beef casserole the other night,' Jon said to Fil, taking the list. 'What's this? Hundreds and thousands? Icing sugar?'

Fil froze ... I thought I'd make—'

'She's teaching me to cook,' Darcy said quickly to divert attention from Jon's birthday cake ingredients.

They trolleyed their way up to the crowded check-outs, where, apparently from nowhere, Granny Lil appeared.

'Darcy Mango.' She held a string bag in each gnarled hand. Cigarette packets showed through the mesh.

Jon stood respectfully silent, waiting until Darcy introduced him.

'Disfla Jon Menzies, Granny. That one bin lookin' after me for job. And you know Fil, eh?' Granny smiled for Jon and gave Fil the fading tail end of it.

Jon swayed slightly at her tobacco breath. 'Hello, Granny. You might not remember me – I met you during

NAIDOC week at the radio station last year.' He knew better than to shake hands.

'I 'member you, yarraman,' was all Granny said, nodding approval. She spoke to Darcy in a broader accent. 'I bin dreamin' bout you, boy. This business – you know what ya gotta do, don't ya?' She was unsmiling, her voice low but clear. Darcy edged away from her, prompting her to raise a forefinger to him. 'No good runnin' – you know what to do. Funny, though, there's three black boys. I seen three black boys. Dunno how, dunno why, but there's three.' The old woman exploded in a phlegmy cough. She is definitely a witch, Fil decided.

'You okay, Granny?' Jon asked with concern. 'That's a nasty chest.'

'Ah, I'm old, thassall, old. My – (cough) time's gone. You 'member what I – (cough) – said, Darcy, you know what to do. And bring this fella over 'ome, too. I be waitin' – (protracted cough) – there too long.'

And Granny went wheezing on her way. Was it her imagination, or did Darcy look pale underneath his colour, Fil wondered.

'Well!' said Jon. 'Guess I'm under orders then. Where'd you meet her, Fil?'

'Oh, round at the Bridge,' Fil did her best to sound nonchalant.

'What was she talking to you about, Darc? Seemed pretty deep and meaningful,' Jon went on.

Darcy swallowed and looked at Fil. It occurred to the girl that if Granny met Jon at her house and started talking about the camera, Jon would discover everything she and Cam (and Darcy for that matter) had been hiding. What would he say about that? This new worry was absorbing her when Jon suddenly flung himself upon a feral woman with blonde dreads, groping under her orange silk shirt.

'Dad!' Fil couldn't believe her eyes. What was her father doing?

Darcy felt the adrenalin surge through his system. His fists bunched and his pulse raced in his throat. Let anyone pick on his mates and they'd answer to him. He waited before jumping in, though. Specially after the other day; his lip was still swollen. And Jon was big and tough, and this was only – a *girl*?

'Laugh,' Jon said urgently to the feral. She wasn't inclined to humour him. What she was inclined towards was biting the remainder of his left ear off, the half containing his diamond. And then perhaps a little Irish jigging on his face. Luckily for Jon, he was able to overpower her before she could do him much damage.

'Bloody laugh, will you?' he hissed at the woman. 'They've seen you!'

An agonised smile came over her face, mingled with confusion and mistrust. Jon forced some more gaiety into his own face, and held the apricot slices aloft, out of her reach. 'Nyah, nyah, nyah!' He was deliberately loud, as no shoplifter would ever be. The security guard who'd been approaching the woman stopped. She observed Jon's shenanigans sourly, then stalked away.

'Ha! Gottem!' He tossed the packet to Fil, who put them onto the moving belt, still wondering what that was all about.

'Cheeky bastard, aren't you?' said the Feral. Jon

winked and put a quick arm around her. Fil stared. Who was this floozy?

She gave him a smile and dumped the rest of her purchases on top of his. Three onions, rolled oats, a jar of Vegemite, a packet of Tim-Tams …

'What sort of feral eats Tim-Tams?' Jon asked in mock horror.

'The pre-menstrual, don't fuck-with-me sort,' said the woman. 'And that little performance is gonna cost you.'

Jon added up her groceries in his head, then swept off his cap in a low bow. 'Cheap at twice the price, *ma chérie.*'

The woman regarded him, unimpressed. She'd had almost enough of good-looking arseholes, and at thirty-six was thinking of jumping the fence. One more try, though? Just for stupidity's sake?

'*Jon,*' said Filomena in exasperation. 'The *money!*'

The checkout girl was looking at the four of them like they were from Mars.

'Oh, I beg your pardon,' Jon said ironically, 'I didn't realise that you were in such a hurry.' He threw one hundred dollars at her. She threw the change back, and Fil hurried everyone away.

Standing outside on the hot carpark bitumen the feral woman gathered her bits and pieces. 'I suppose I should thank you,' she said less than graciously.

'Think nothing of it.' Jon was airy as he and Darcy packed the stuff into the back of the van. Fil was sulking in the front. 'Can I give you a lift?'

The woman wondered who this guy was. Still, he had two teenagers with him. She'd never heard of a mass murderer who took a black-and-white minstrel show along.

Seeing her hesitate, Jon stuck out his hand. 'Jonathon Menzies' – he stepped away to pat the side of the van, 'Horseman, *bon vivant*, social change agent. This is my daughter Filomena, and my main man, Darcy. At your service.'

The feral finally cracked a smile. 'Social change agent?' She shook hands. 'Ruth Thomas.'

Darcy swung around when he heard her say her last name. *Nuh.*

Ruth read the side of the van. 'Aonbar's Rest. Nice. Oh, well, I suppose you can drop me off at the T-junction.' She dived into the back of the van, flummoxing Jon's plans to talk to her for the next forty years or so.

When they reached the turn-off he pulled over onto the grass and opened the back. 'When can I assault you again?' he asked, eyes twinkling.

Ruth frowned. Men assaulting women wasn't funny. 'What makes you think I'm interested?' she asked, climbing out without ceremony.

'In men?'

'Or in you in particular.' No beating around the bush for Ruth.

'Ah ... never know your luck in the big city,' Jon replied, gazing at the cows.

'You smoke?' she asked him sternly.

'Very little,' he replied.

Ha, she'd heard that before, from men who spent whole weeks staring at walls, zonked out of their brains. Pack of useless mongrels. 'You're a boozehound,' she asserted, hoisting her bag.

'Filomena, do I drink?' Jon shouted.

181

'Like a fish!' came the reply. 'He's never sober. He hits us. Darcy's not black, he's just bruised.' Hey, Fil thought in surprise, I made a racial joke. Darcy smiled at her.

'Teenage conspiracy,' Jon whispered to Ruth. 'I never touch it.'

'*Married*,' she spat over her shoulder. 'Or gay,' she added.

'Single as they come, sweetheart, and my experimenting days are long gone.'

'Don't call me, I'll call you. When I get a phone.'

He shouted as she disappeared: 'Come to lunch next Sunday. Tim-Tams guaranteed.'

She shouted back without turning around. 'If I'm there, I'll marry you!' Not likely. He *was* cute, though. Ah, forget it.

Jon climbed back into the driver's seat. When Fil began interrogating him he turned up *Blood On The Tracks*, and whistled through her questions the whole way home.

While the others shopped, Cam sat on his bed, looking at the photos. Questions rolled around in him like clothes in a washing machine. *Why? How?* For the thousandth time he held the photo up against the light, trying to decide if the stick was a gun, if the man was Hew Costello, if the body *had* to be dead? And, for the thousandth time, the answers were all yes. The eccentric hat-shape on the ground gave away Costello's identity. The stick thickened too much towards one end to be anything other than a rifle, and the body ... he hated to look at it. Face-down, he couldn't see if it was male or female. The thin limbs meant it was probably a child of about twelve, he and Fil had decided. But yeah, it was a dead body all right. Everything added up to murder, no matter how hard he tried to *twist the figures. And one question lay under all the others* – who the bloody hell was the kid?

Exasperated, Cam flung the photo to the floor. Before this crap happened, his biggest problem was working out how to buy a thousand-dollar Nikon camera and travel the country show circuit becoming Australia's premier horse photographer. He had it mapped out: leave school next year, if Jon would agree, by which time he might have saved the dough for his Nikon, then live on the dole until the first cheques started rolling in from the photo assignments. Easy peasy. Cam knew he could pull it off. Hadn't the *Shelley Bay Herald* printed his shots on three different occasions? Then all this camera shit had to descend upon the peace of Aonbar's Rest. If only they could go back and undo the murder ... even go back and take a better photo, so that they knew once and for all what had happened. Fil wouldn't let him tell Jon, in case he made her hand the camera over for free, to the cops or someone. Darcy didn't know what was happening, and had merely said to wait: fat lot of good that'd do. Cam let out a theatrical groan. He imagined Jon's voice: 'Groans aren't going to solve it, son. Action's what's required here, informed action.'

Informed action. What could he do? His gaze wandered to where the camera hung in a Kmart bag on the back of his door. A voice inside him said to take it down. Once he held it, he realised (why hadn't he before? Was the camera's power fuzzing their brains as well?) all he had to do was go to the ruin and take more pictures of the same room. The room – here Cameron felt a cold wind rush past his face – where the killing happened. He looked at the camera. The leather case was only leather. The lens plate was only glass. Somehow, though, something had affected these ordinary materials, this ordinary camera, to make it transform what it saw. *Why? And why us?* Cam had to know. He was frightened by the idea of going to the ruin alone, yet irresistibly drawn to it at the same time. He had an absurd wish to have something new to show Darcy and Fil when they got back. In a dreamlike state, he found his Swiss Army knife, and put its comforting blades in his jeans pocket. Then carrying the camera, he went nervously out to saddle Garbo.

'Hey look, we're missing a horror movie on Channel Three,' Darcy announced that night. '*Mother's Blood.* Cool.'

Screwing his face up, Jon got up to answer the phone. His face broke into a beam when he heard Ruth's voice.

'Not that I'm promising anything, mind you,' she said, 'but there's a party next Saturday night …' He made arrangements to meet her there, heart singing. It had been a long time since he'd felt interested in romance. Splitting up with Michelle had knocked a big piece of his soul, and he often felt Cam's mother Julie had got the rest.

'Who was it?' Cam asked.

'Ruth, that woman from – oh, you weren't there. A woman we met out shopping today.'

Cam raised his eyebrows. A girlfriend for Dad? He didn't know how he felt about that. Most of his friends had stepmothers from hell. Jordan hated his father's girlfriend with a passion. He kept quiet, though, as Jon retreated to his bedroom to work on his journal.

'Oh, come on,' Darcy was pleading.

'Yuk,' said Fil. She hated horror.

'Oh, it looks deadly!' the black boy argued. 'Hey, Cam?'

Cam didn't feel terribly enthusiastic either. Going up to the ruin had given him his quota of fright for the day. Not that he'd been *scared*, exactly, he lied to himself. Like, it wasn't the big deal Fil made it out to be. Okay, maybe he hadn't dawdled, hadn't hung around once he was through the lantana, right in close to the building. That was when that funny feeling came over him ... not fear exactly, but unease. Yeah, unease, that's what he'd felt as he rushed in, snapped blindly with his eyes closed and rushed straight out again. Garbo must have felt uncomfortable too; she'd tossed her head in agitation when he scrambled onto her. She was more than happy to gallop down to the flat ground. Cam shivered at the memory of the cold darkness inside the ruin. Still, it was done now. The photos were developing as Fil and Darcy argued. He'd surprise them in a minute.

'No, I want to watch the basketball,' Fil was saying.

'Arm-wrestle you for it?' Darcy countered.

'No way,' she said, knowing him to be stronger. 'Paper, scissors, rock?' she suggested. When she'd explained the game to him, they both held their right hands behind their back.

'One, two, three,' said Darcy, putting forward paper. Fil looked despondently at the rock of her fist. 'Shit.'

Darcy crowed in triumph, and switched to Channel Three. Low organ chords filled the room, and when he switched off the lights to make it even creepier, Fil was too embarrassed to admit her fears. She'd intended to go to bed and avoid the film; now it was too dark to venture down the shadowy corridor. Stuck, she lay on the lounge facing away from the TV and tried not to listen to the screams and footsteps. She closed her eyes. After a few minutes she managed to fall asleep.

Darcy was enjoying himself. He loved the thrill of fear he got from a good horror show, and this was a beauty. The story was about a woman who went mad after her baby died in childbirth, and then went around murdering other people's kids. Gross. He particularly liked the way she wrote their names in their own blood on the walls of their houses. As the credits played he noticed that Cam had gone off somewhere and Fil was asleep. Then Cam reappeared in the doorway, looking pale as a ghost in the dim light.

'Man, you are *white*,' said Darcy.

'I'm like Billy Connolly, a pale blue person. Got something to show you,' Cam told him. 'Wake Fil up.'

'Fil,' Darcy shook her shoulder. 'Wake up.'

Sleepily, she sat up, complaining. She'd been dreaming about playing in the World Cup with Alan Shearer and Robbie Slater.

'Look!' Cameron said, waving his prints. 'I went back to the ruin today.'

Darcy frowned. 'I thought we weren't gonna do nothing till—'

'But I had this great idea,' Cam interrupted him in excitement. 'To find out who the murdered kid is, we just have to take more photos till we see his – or her, I s'pose – face. Except look – nothing came out.' He showed the other two pictures of grass, trees and a clearing amongst trees in the bush. In the corner of one was something that might have been the angle of a building. Then again, it might not.

'That's strange,' Fil said. 'What's going on now? Darcy – do *you* know?'

Cam waited hopefully, but Darcy shook his head. Anger was rising in him as Cam calmly discussed what he'd done. 'Are they all of the ruin?' he asked.

'Yeah,' Cam said, 'but I took some yesterday here, I haven't checked them yet. Just of the house and that – I wanted to see what it looked like.'

Darcy felt pissed off that Cam had been taking pictures. He'd wanted everything to stop until Granny Lil said otherwise. Well, if these white kids wanted to run around stupid, lettem. Just don't fucken run to me when things go wrong, thassall.

'Get the others, Cam,' Fil urged. 'Let's see what they're like.'

Cam padded off to the darkroom once again. When he returned he looked even more confused. 'Fil ... look. The arcade's gone. I took one of the outside of your room, and it's not there.' He showed her.

Then something clicked and spun in Fil's head. 'When did you take these? Yesterday? And when did we take the first lot? About two weeks ago, hey? You know what's happening?' she demanded, eyes bright.

187

Darcy sat up. 'The ones of my room, before, they'd just finished building the arcade. Remember the date in the photo, and the date on the newspaper in the library?

'Well, the camera's going backwards. As our time shifts forwards, it's going backwards, see? That's why there's only grass and shit in the others – that's what the ruin looked like before it was built, I mean what the land was like.'

Darcy grabbed the photos off Cam and shuffled them till he saw the ones of what should be the ruin. There. A sense of dread came over him as he looked at what he knew was a bora. He dropped the photos to the floor. You fucken idiot, he told himself. Why'd ya do that, you know better. He had a barely controllable urge to check his initiation markings; with a massive effort he sat still, breathing hard.

'So it was just a fluke we took the body picture,' Cam was saying to Fil. 'If we'd been there earlier, or later, we wouldn't have seen anything. I mean, we wouldn't have seen it as it happened.' Fil nodded as Darcy stood up impatiently.

Standing trembling in the middle of the lounge, he blasted the other two. 'Haven't youse learnt *nothing*? None of this is by fluke. None of it's by chance. This is serious. There's reasons for shit like this! That's why I said – wait for Granny Lil to tell us what to do.' He stared with angry contempt at Cameron. This dumb white kid was buggering up what he didn't understand.

Cam's eyes narrowed. He didn't like being spoken to like he was an idiot, and he had half a mind to—

'What isn't by chance?' Jon enquired from the door,

silhouetted against the kitchen light, holding a beer. They stared at him in dismay. Darcy flung a hand away from him in a disgusted gesture: See what you've done now. Cameron swallowed hard.

> *There once were three kids, quite a trio,*
> *Who decided it was time to – flee, oh?*

Nuh.

'What's going on?' Jon repeated, 'You lot have been creeping around on eggshells for days now. I know it's got something to do with that old camera.'

No one spoke for a full minute. Cam finally looked at Fil, who rolled her eyes in a give-up way. 'Go on, tell him,' she said.

'Um ... we found this camera—' Cam began, but Darcy jumped in.

'NO! Let Granny Lil tell him.' At least then it won't be our responsibility, was what he was thinking.

'Granny Lil?' said Jon, puzzled. 'Is she involved?'

'Yeah,' said Darcy in a tired voice. 'She'll tell you.' He refused to say any more than that. Why had *he* got involved? Why had he ever left the bush? That night, he had a nightmare that he was surrounded by Elders and his initiation scars were dripping thick blood onto his toes. He stood in a growing pool of blood, completely alone, as a tall bearded stranger with a long spear took aim at his thighs. The spear was singing through the air, wobbling with speed, when Darcy woke up clutching at himself, screaming.

Chapter Thirteen

Cam sat astride Angel, knees pressed firmly against the tall grips of Darcy's new Syd Hill stock saddle. He rode Garbo in an all-purpose, but the sleek, flat saddleflaps of his own saddle wouldn't help him when Angel decided to cut loose, so he'd borrowed Darcy's pride and joy. He was wedged in tight. If that didn't do it – nothing would.

'Okay,' Darcy said, 'off with ya!'

Cam gathered the reins up and squeezed the chestnut's sides. Angel pranced on the spot.

'Give him a little more rein, Cam,' Jon instructed from the middle of the ring. 'Don't hold him too hard.'

Cameron obeyed his father, and woke up a quarter of an hour later lying on the grass of the Small Paddock. The sun bored into his left eyeball, making him cry out in pain. Why were the trees spinning?

'Cam, Cam!' Jon was saying. Inside the ring, Cam could see Darcy riding the horse mercilessly into the ground. Figure of eights, keyhole turns. Angel was asthmatic with effort, but Darcy drove him on, ignoring his discomfort.

'Fuckin arsehole of an overgrown—' Cam couldn't think of any word bad enough to describe Angel, so he stopped.

Jon looked relieved. 'At least your brain's still functioning. Can you feel your toes?'

Cam nodded. He could feel every part of his body.

'Put him away, Darc,' Jon called, before helping Cam inside. 'Quiet afternoon for you, I think,' he said, settling Cam in front of the TV.

Cam smiled ruefully. 'Just a flesh wound.'

'You can drive, can't you, Darcy?' Jon asked early on Thursday morning as he pulled on his boots.

Darcy nodded. 'Yeah. I'm not s'posed to, but.' Jon smacked his own head. 'Parole, of course.' Like Fil and Cam, Darcy was too young to drive legally. Unlike them, it would blow his parole if he was caught. Jon wondered what to do. Fil had declared at breakfast that she wanted to spend the day taking Governor to Shelley Bay, and having a decent lunch in town that she didn't have to cook herself. Cam had to stay behind to wait for a mare to arrive later that morning, another of Gunner's harem coming over from Bill Barton.

'Ah, well, life is a wheel of pain after all,' Jon muttered to himself. Three hours driving the van wasn't going to leave his leg in good shape. 'See how we go.'

'We got everything?' Darcy checked as they got in the car.

Lead-ropes, blanket, haynet, pellets …

'Yup. Let's go tell some lies,' Jon grinned. Poor bugger,

he thought, having to front the Department.

As they drove up Camelot Street, Darcy began to worry about what the parole people were going to say. Didn't matter what *he* said, they always said the same stuff. Well, he had 'em over a barrel this time, the wankers; he had a job, hadn't got arrested for over six months (and then it was bullshit, ALS eventually made them let him go), *and* he was meeting his parole schedule. Rang them last month when he was supposed to. You're turning into a straight, he told himself in scorn. Ah, fuck it, they'll be sweet. In the back of his mind was the frail shell of an idea that Jon would stick up for him, and – being Jon – his word would prevail. For the first time in his life, Darcy had a white boss looking out for him.

'Nervous?' Jon asked. Darcy looked out the window and saw the St Vinnies shop. He needed some new undies and stuff. Another day … 'Aw.'

'Hey! There's Granny Lil!' Jon said. He waved energetically and tooted the horn before he pulled over. Granny was standing waiting impatiently for St Vinnies to open.

'Granny, how're ya going?' said Darcy unwillingly. Ah, too deadly – *not*. Just who he didn't need to see.

'Real deadly this morning, son.' (Cough, cough). Her creased black face was awash with smiles. 'Course, I'd be better if it was pension day today steada next week. Where you fellas going this early, uh?'

Furtively Jon snuck a five dollar note into Darcy's hand. 'We gotta go Lismore, see that parole fella this arv. You wanta coupla dollars, Granny?' he said, proffering it.

She took it without ceremony. 'Ta, you're (cough) a

good boy. You wanna come stop 'long my house, eh? Come stay with Granny. Teach me some that desert lingo.'

'Oh, they might lock me up, eh?' Darcy said, semi-seriously, avoiding her request. 'That parole mob wanna put me away as it is, specially livin' with blackfellas.'

Granny made a face. 'Oh, tru-u-ue ... well, you gonna come see me soon, eh? That Peter lookin' out for you – now. And we got business to discuss, Darcy Mango. You know what we gotta do.'

Darcy frowned. 'Oh, Granny ...' Couldn't she give him a break?

'Never mind, "Oh Granny". You come see me,' she ordered as the saleswoman swung open the St Vinnies door. Darcy gave a sigh with centuries of foreboding in it. 'Okay.'

Driving away, the boy noticed with some disquiet that Glen Goddard was standing on the footpath outside his shop. He would have observed the whole exchange. Darcy didn't like that fella, not one bit. He was a straight crim, the worst sort.

'It's eight-thirty three here on Bay FM, and a big welcome to all our visitors from all over the world ... not forgetting a big hello to the locals, you good people that make Shelley Bay a very special place to be and live ...' Click. Jon slid a Not Drowning, Waving tape into the deck.

Darcy sat quiet most of the way to Lismore, listening to the drums. He hated anything to do with prison; seeing a parole officer was another reminder that he lived at someone else's say-so. That he wasn't really human, just a black crim. You can't explain that stuff in words, he'd realised, trying to tell Cam one day recently. It was like trying to explain what feeling cold was like. You either knew it, or you didn't. Cam lacked the survival trait of categorical thinking – two legs good, four legs bad. Crim good, screw bad. *Agadja* good, whitefella bad. Suddenly Darcy had the amazing thought that if you were white, and not a crim or a poofter, then you didn't *have* any real enemies. And what the hell would that be like? He found he had no answer.

At five-thirty Darcy bounced up the caravan steps, ripped off his collared shirt and flung himself onto his bunk. He stared up at his pin-up of Keanu. *Yes! Yes!* Another encounter with whitefellas successfully negotiated. The parole woman had liked Jon (everyone did), who'd been cluey enough to take his earrings out and do a heavy straight act for her. Wearing ordinary clothes, with his hair plaited, he'd looked more or less like any regular guy off the street. She'd been suitably impressed with his glowing character references, and so Darcy had attained another month of conditional freedom. Then Jon had reverted to normal, they'd collected Gunner, curtailing his long and enjoyable stay at the Lismore Quarter Moon stud, and brought him back home. Afternoon stables were done; he could relax. Fil said they were having pizza. Life was pretty damn good. Or would have been, he suddenly remembered, if it wasn't for Granny Lil and what she expected of him about this whole camera business. Darcy's exuberance faded as he considered what it would mean to go back again, knowing what he knew now.

Later in the afternoon, as the summer day faded slowly to black, Darcy sat on the caravan step, munching pizza. A fire crackled in front of him, ringed by rocks he'd retrieved from the bush which Jon and Cam had to slash back every couple of weeks to stop it taking over the farm. He watched the orange flames melt and meld together in the dusk, same as at home. Cam and Fil sat watching on milk crates, Cam half in the smoke, Fil, the city-type staying away from the smoke and accordingly swatting mozzies like mad. Darcy grinned. He believed in Aerogard himself.

'How come you'n Dad went so early this morning?' Fil asked, pushing the cardboard pizza box into the fire and sending up a torrent of sparks.

'I hadda see someone in Lismore,' he answered.

'Didn't realise you knew anyone round here. Did Granny Lil say something about your relations one time?'

'Yeah. Aboriginals got relations all over the place, usually.' Darcy explained 'I'm Yanbali, eh.'

'What's that?' Fil asked.

Cam looked askance at his sister, ashamed of her ignorance. 'Don't you know? That's the local tribe!'

'Yeah, well, I'm Yanbali. Kind of. Me mum was Yanbali and when they took me away they did it arse-about. Most people got took from the bush to the city – get 'em away from the blackfellas, see. But me, they took me from the city when me first mum died and gave me to Dad – he's Agadja through his mother. They were giving some of us to black families by then. So I got me dad, and Mum Rita and Mum Gladys, and all the others back home. But my ...' Darcy was going to say 'real' but that wasn't right, was it? '… other family's here somewhere. Up the Tweed, Granny thinks.'

It was one of the longest statements Fil had ever heard Darcy make, and it was blank fact. No emotion intruded, except for a slight amusement about going back-to-front, city to bush.

'You going to try and find them?' Cam asked.

Darcy shrugged. 'Oh, I'll run into 'em, for sure. Won't take long. Not as if I ain't got enough out west, anyway.'

It seemed to Cam a funny way to go about your affairs, having relations you didn't know.

'Speaking of Granny Lil,' he said, 'what're we gonna do now? About the camera and that?' His voice was tentative after Darcy's anger the other night. He stared glumly into the glowing ironbark coals.

'Yeah,' Fil broke in, 'and what did she mean in the supermarket? She kept saying "you know what to do, Darcy, you know what to do" … I mean, do you? If you do and you don't tell us, well, I may as well sell the camera.' She was half-serious.

Darcy made an odd sound, stood up without warning, went inside and slammed the caravan door, making the rickety structure shake. A fruit bat squawked and flew out of a tree.

'Oh, bloody hell!' Fil cried. 'What NOW!' Jesus, he was a temperamental bastard. And it was *her* camera. Why did no one seem to understand that?

Inside the van Darcy sat on the bed, miserable and trapped. If Fil sold the camera, he might as well give it all away. Most likely he was gonna finish up anyway, but while the camera was here he still had some chance of making it through. His head spun with the stress like he was on petrol or pituri. Whitefellas outside, making demands. Granny Lil, making demands. Parole fucken officers making demands. He opened the door again and stood there a dark silhouette. His words didn't make much sense to the others; he was speaking as much to people who weren't there as to them.

'Ya can't make me! Ya can't! I'm not gunna die! I ain't fucken gunna, okay, so ...'

Here Darcy broke into a language that Cam thought was probably Agadja. In the darkness it looked as though Darcy's face was wet. Was he on drugs or something? Cam felt a bit frightened. This was a new Darcy he hadn't seen.

He attempted conciliation, 'Okay, Darc, take it easy, okay, settle down, eh. What's wrong, man?'

Darcy looked straight through him like he couldn't understand English, then leapt down to the fire. He picked up a blazing sapling and thrust it towards Cam's face. Cam carefully stepped backwards, moving slow like Jon said to do whenever someone was hyper. Quick moves and fast talk just made 'em worse, same as horses. Inside, he was packing it.

'Ya dawgs, ya can't make me! Ey? Come and try'n fucken make me, then ...' Darcy gesticulated at the night sky with his flaming stick.

Cam was careful to speak in a low, slow voice. 'We're going back to the house, now, Darcy, okay?' This was all beyond him.

'Sorry,' Fil muttered as they left. But sorry for what exactly, she didn't know. As they left Darcy shouted incoherently: 'I ain't scare … nobody calls me gutless for yufla … I ain't scare!'

It was a bizarre and disquieting display. As they stumbled through the darkness to the house, the only thing Cam and Fil could be fairly certain of was that someone or something had Darcy – if that *was* Darcy – terrified out of his wits. Cam felt a shiver of dread enter his soul, as if Darcy's fear was contagious. He discussed what Darcy had said rationally and calmly with Fil, but that night, for the first time in years, Cam dreamt those old awful dreams; dreams where he stood in a pool of dark-red blood and a man hooded in black aimed a gun at his head. As the man squeezed the trigger and the bullet flew towards him, Cam woke. He lay paralysed with terror for a long, long time.

'… and this's Peter, he's my Robbie's boy.' Granny Lil finished introducing her family to Jon.

Hang on, thought Fil, so he's Aboriginal? But he looks white. This Aboriginal stuff was more complicated than she thought. The more she got into it, the more confusing it became. She'd have to ask Darcy what made you an Aboriginal; it didn't appear to be the colour of your skin or the shape of your nose. Though he'd probably just start raving again. Fil stayed where Granny Lil put her, and kept her mouth shut.

Everyone sat on folding chairs underneath Granny's elevated house. A fan had been set up, using a frayed extension lead, and two camp beds enclosed the lounge area where lunch was to be. Pot plants hung from the beams from which mozzies made their sorties at the visitors' ankles. Fil was fascinated by the way Granny Lil was able to ignore the blood-filled insects dinging to her legs. 'Ah, they won't eat much,' she said, when she noticed Fil watching. Twin cement laundry tubs sat next to a battered fridge, and under it all lay a faded piece of green felt matting. A large TV with wooden legs sat fatly to one side.

Peter smiled a slow, attractive smile from the closest camp bed, a smile meant not for Jon but for Darcy, who looked away. He had bigger problems, and anyway, he had to keep his guard up. Peter's face fell.

'This looks great, Granny. You've been doing too much work for us!' Jon enthused over the assembled salads and barbecue.

Granny laughed, blowing smoke everywhere and making Darcy long frantically for a cigarette. Mozzies whirled up away from the smoke. 'Not me! Veronica done this up on her Weber and brung it over. She be back soon, she gone shop for grog.' Granny's mouth turned down in disapproval. 'Mad for grog, all that lot.'

'Not like you, Granny,' said Peter slyly.

She nodded. 'I never did drink, that's one thing. Smoke, yes. Gamble, oh yes, my word! But I've never bin one for drinkin'. My sister bin killed from drinkin', and since then, nothing.'

''Cept for Christmas,' Peter added helpfully, wriggling his pale limbs on the bed to sit up and get a better view of everyone.

'Oh, well ... yeah, maybe a drink or two at Christmas.' Granny looked like she wanted to change the subject.

'And a sherry on ya birthday, Nan, don't forget that!' Peter piped up again.

Granny grunted and shot him a warning glare. 'Mmm ... Christmas and birthday.'

'And—'

'You shut up, *doolum*-face,' Granny snapped.

Camping-it-up, Peter stuck a bright pink tongue between his lips, raised his eyebrows, and shut up.

They ate extravagantly, cramming down steak and sausages with great puddles of tomato sauce, fresh bread and three different kinds of salads. It was Darcy's idea of food heaven; Fil was surprised to see him picking indifferently at his plate. Jon was telling dirty jokes to Granny's daughter Veronica, who had insisted he share her beers. Cam and Peter were half-listening to Jon, half-watching the NBL.

Fil got up, pretending to refill her plate, and sat down next to Darcy. 'What's up?' she hissed at him.

When he looked up at her, his eyes were haunted. 'I'm gonna die,' he said.

'What!' It was as much as Fil could do to keep her voice down. 'What dya mean?'

Darcy nodded at Granny, who was choking and coughing with laughter at Jon.

'It's why we're here. She's gonna tell Jon what's happened.'

Fil nodded. They knew that, it had been decided the other night that Jon had to know. Or at least that he shouldn't be fobbed off with weak excuses any longer.

'And then ... she'll say, it's payback time. I'm gonna get killed.'

Fil's face wrinkled. 'What do you mean? Don't be stupid. You don't have to *die*.'

'It's the Law,' Darcy said hopelessly. 'Nothing we can do.'

'The law?' Filomena's brain turned straight away to Darcy's recent revelation that he'd spent last year in jail. 'They can't kill you! Not in Australia. You haven't done anything lately, have you?'

Darcy refused to say anymore, getting up to beg a cigarette off Veronica. He then sat staring at the ground, smoking, not joining in any of the conversation. Fil began to wonder if there was something seriously wrong with him. Maybe he was whaddyacallit, paranoid? Although, she reflected, if she tried to tell anyone what had happened to her in the last month, she'd probably be locked up as well.

Granny Lil was sitting quietly sipping beer, listening to Cam talk horses. He was explaining his big ideas on travelling the country as an equine photographer.

'You mean people *pay* you to take photos of their *horses*?' Veronica asked incredulously. 'Ah, well, if they wanta throw their money away, no reason you shouldn't pick it up, eh.'

'It's a nice dream, Cam,' Jon suggested, 'but you can't eat photos.'

Cam rolled his eyes. 'He keeps knockin' it,' he told Granny. 'Tells me to go to Uni instead.'

'I won't stop you,' Jon said. 'I fully expect you to be a brilliant photographer, Cam. And you can take me to dinner at the Shriekerville Hilton on my fiftieth birthday, to prove it. I just think you could go to Art College as well and get qualified.'

'Photos,' said Granny. 'We got photos around 'ere, somewhere. Ron, where those photos? Them one's a yufla?'

Veronica shrugged and ran her fingers sexily through her long hair. She didn't give a shit about photos, not unless this handsome Jon fulla did. Granny gave an exasperated sigh and got to her feet. She drew a photo album out of the old cabinet beside the fridge, scattering the newspapers and car parts that lay on top, and showed Cam the family snaps. He made polite comments, wondering whether he should bother trying to explain to Granny the difference between his Art and these pieces of memorabilia.

Going through the album took half an hour, what with Granny's commentary and reminiscing. By the time they closed it up Fil was beginning to wonder what the afternoon would bring. She looked at her watch. Three o'clock! And they hadn't even started. Darcy was lying silently on the spare bed, asleep or pretending to be. Peter was watching TV with Cam, talking about Jordan and Rodman, and Veronica was making eyes at Jon, who seemed to be rather enjoying her antics.

'Ah ... well,' said Granny finally, after another few minutes of chitchat. 'Time for a cuppa, eh?'

Jon readily agreed and they trooped upstairs. Granny stayed back momentarily, talking to Veronica and Peter in a voice too low to hear. Whatever she said made them leave; Jon saw Peter's Holden backing out the drive a couple of minutes later, Veronica waving and hanging out of the passenger side. *Now*, thought Fil. But *still* Granny didn't speak of the camera or the murder

202

photo. Instead she chatted with Jon about the land rights struggle in the Northern Rivers, and the black families that had harvested the area south of them long before white settlement. Darcy was listening, Fil could tell, and it was interesting enough to hear about the black servants that had worked in every second white home, but it wasn't why they'd come. What could Darcy have possibly meant, he had to die? Filomena felt she'd burst if Granny didn't speak soon.

It was five past four when Jon got slowly to his feet. Cam expected him to say something like: 'Well, Granny, thanks very much for the lunch, hey? We hafta run I'm afraid, the horses have to be fed and looked after.' Cam could picture Picasso, the equine alarm clock, drumming on the loosebox door for his dinner. But Jon was just going for a piss. When he got back he sank again into the lounge as if he had all the time in the world. Cam groaned inside and Granny must have sensed his impatience, for she leaned back in her chair. Suddenly her eyes lost their cheery hospitality. Seriousness descended on the room as though a switch had been flicked.

'Okay. It's time for talking. You lissen, Yarraman. This girl' – here Granny swung around to point at Fil – 'this girl, she your daughter, eh?'

Jon agreed that yes, Fil was his daughter. He hoped so, anyway. Granny ignored this quip. 'Well, she's got aholda something don't properly belong to her, something old. I dunno how. Says she found it up in the hills. Well ...' here Granny paused and looked at Jon, reluctant to let the knowledge go. It had to be done though. And if it had to be a migloo, this one was better than some. 'There's sites up there, sites no one knows about. Sacred places. She's talked about an old house – well, there was trouble with a bora and a house up there before, too. Old Mr Costello.'

Jon suddenly found he couldn't breathe.

'He was a friend to blackfellas when we lived down 'ere. 'E was a good man, but hignorant, they say, like all migloos are hignorant. He lived with a black woman, I believe, not from 'ere, from somewhere else, but my Grandad's people, they let 'im alone, let him be. Then when was time to move on, he went too. It was all okay, till he found gold in the creek. Sent him *womba*, it did, and he ...'.

Fil shot an urgent inquiring look at Darcy, who twirled his index finger beside his head. Crazy. *Womba* meant crazy. Crazy for money. Granny must mean.

'... and he built his house up on the high ground, eh. Built it on a bora, see. Well ...' Granny's sour expression held all the disapproval of the tribe distilled over centuries. Jon leaned forward, both hands on his temples. Ashamed and fascinated at the same time, he didn't know what to say.

Granny dragged on her smoke and went on. 'Then there was trouble, some sort of trouble. Maybe they speared 'im. Maybe them old ones was lookin' for 'im, after that. I dunno, somethin'. Then he went away, and they never heard of 'im again. Just disappeared. No one'd go near the house. Murri too scare, see? Oh, we know it's there, we know where it is. But it's no good for us now. So, I reckon this girl, she's gone in and taken this old camera 'way. S'not her fault, zackly. She didn't know ...' Granny scratched her white hair to demonstrate the point. 'But there's trouble mixed up with it. It's *Business*, you know? She's just a kid, I dunno why it come to her.'

Jon nodded, silent and a little afraid for Fil. Fil sat petrified on her kitchen chair. Granny's voice was like a menacing song, a song of doom and dread and loss. Why had she ever taken Angel that morning? Why couldn't she do what she was told? And (with an unreasonable, irrelevant anger) why did bloody Hew Costello have to go and do the wrong thing? She and Cam looked at each other, knowing full well what had mysteriously gone wrong on the mountain. Murder, that's what. But who was murdered? And why? And what did it all mean, a hundred years later?

'... and ever since then, they, these three, they bin seeing things they shouldn't. 'Specially Darcy. I can't tell you everything.' Granny checked with Jon to see if he minded that. He didn't – not yet. She went on in a puzzled, uncertain voice. 'But Darcy, he's gotta go back again, find out what's wrong. I keep seeing three black boys, three. Could be ... dangerous. I need to see you 'bout that. He your boy?' Granny asked.

That stopped Jon in his tracks. He lifted his head. She must have known Darcy wasn't his biological son, so she was asking him to take responsibility for Darcy, to be his adoptive father more or less. Jon had no idea what kind of danger Granny Lil was referring to. Go back? To the ruin, the bora? It didn't sound so dangerous to him, and if he *had* to, he had to. His was only a support role at best, Jon realised.

'Ye-eah. If that's all right with him, it's all right with me,' he said, looking Darcy squarely in the face.

Darcy's eyes darkened as the man spoke. He was so very frightened of whoever the other two black boys might be, but having Jon be his boss, lookin' out for him, was more than okay.

'Well then,' said Granny, 'that's all I need to know from you.'

Bursting with unanswered questions, Jon and Cam stood up, and Granny ushered the Menzies downstairs. Darcy stood at the top of the steps, feeling flushed with relief, when an iron hand clutched his upper arm.

'Not you, Darcy,' Granny said. 'We gotta talk.' His heart was in his mouth as he waved the others goodbye.

Three black boys.

Swallowing hard, he wondered if he'd ever see the Menzies again. Grim-faced, Granny Lil took him inside, sat him down, and started talking.

In the van, the only sound was the wipers sloshing left and right. It was ten minutes before Jon said: 'I'm not going to grill you. This is more Granny Lil's business than mine. She called me in – as a courtesy. But it's that old camera, isn't it?'

'Yep,' Fil said.

'It's not stolen?'

'No. Taken, but not stolen. I mean, no one owns it,' said Fil miserably, wondering what was happening to Darcy. He wouldn't *really* die? Would he? No, it was ridiculous to think so. 'We haven't done anything wrong.'

'Something's up, though, or Granny wouldn't have a bee in her bonnet about it,' said Jon thoughtfully. 'I don't know if I should ask you to tell me anymore or not. What do you think?'

'Oh, she and Darcy both keep going on about payback and ... oh, I dunno, stuff I don't understand,' interrupted Cameron, wiping condensation from the inside of the windscreen. He was on the verge of telling Jon about the body in the photo, but before he could, Jon nodded.

'Yeah ... well, if you need me, you can yell, you know?'

'Yeah. Thanks,' Fil said, comforted even though she knew this was out of Jon's field.

Cam shut up as the right moment passed to mention the murder. He sat tightly on the back seat, frightened for Darcy, for Fil and for himself. Nothing had improved since Jon came back from hospital. He thought it had, then it all spiralled back to him again, worse than before. Now Jon was saying leave it to Granny, and Darcy was stuck with her, that creepy old woman, doing God knows what. And would any of it answer the question – *who* was the murdered kid? Cam stared at the rain, silver streaks against a dark grey sky. For the first time in ages, he felt totally powerless.

Chapter Fourteen

When they got home Jon ran in his workboots through the heavy rain to the front door, unlocking it. He waved the others inside and they dashed through the downpour. When they were safely indoors Jon shook his hair, throwing silver raindrops all over the kitchen tiles. Fil put the kettle on. As it hissed softly below the drumming of the storm, Jon reached for the phone and dialled Angel's owner.

'Hello, Kate, Jon Menzies here.'

The woman spoke briefly for a minute and Fil fussed with biscuits and milk.

'Yeah, actually that's why I was ringing. Mmm, how does two hundred sound? I'm sorry I can't offer you more, I know you paid an arm and a leg … Well, if you're sure. Okay, see you then.' Jon put the phone down. He turned to Fil and grabbed her in a great bearhug. 'Congratulations are in order, my dear.'

Fil shrieked as Jon spun her round and round. 'Why?' she asked breathlessly when he put her down.

'I've just bought Angel. For two hundred bucks.'

Jon stood, tall, handsome, wetly shining in front of her, expecting her to be happy and excited. Like hell.

'Oh … congratulations,' Fil said. 'If you think they're merited.'

'He'll be another Picasso by the time I'm finished with him,' Jon boasted.

Oh yeah, thought Fil, pull the other one. That horse is gonna kill someone, the way he's going. But she didn't say it. 'Cam, tea's ready!' she yelled.

Jon stood in the kitchen wearing his black jeans and a bright shirt.

'You lot gonna be all right tonight?' Jon asked absently.

'Of course!' Cam snorted derisively. 'Are you?'

Jon grinned with huge anticipation and patted his own bum with two hands. 'You betcha, boyo. Romance is in the air.'

'We need milk,' Cam said smoothly. 'If you're coming back early tomorrow.' He broke into a grin as Jon pretended to cuff his head.

'None of your cheek. There's the number of the party if there's any trouble. *Ciao.*'

The van revved in the yard, and he was gone.

'What'd you think of this woman?' Cam asked Fil and Darcy. 'Was she nice?'

Fil thought for a moment, then slowly replied: 'Ye-eah, she was okay. I think. Feral, but. But she was okay, hey, Darc?'

Darcy nodded. Jealous though he was of the woman, he had gotten a nice vibe off her. She was okay. 'Yeah, she's nice, Fil. Pretty, too,' he added for Cam's benefit.

Fil sighed. Yeah, that'd be right, another Elle McPherson. Federation was full of them.

When he walked into his bedroom after Jon left, Cam looked up from habit at a framed black-and-white portrait of Garbo. He'd constructed the shot with her fine-boned head high in the dark stormy air, ears pricked. A zig-zag of lightning crackled behind her, illuminating her blanket of spots. It was his best picture ever, printed by Australia's leading horse magazine in their annual issue. They didn't pay him anything, of course, but his work had been seen by thousands, maybe tens of thousands of people. Cam glowed every time he remembered it, even tonight with so much else to worry about. His room was full of photos, pinned to the walls, stacked on his table. As books were to Jon, so photos were to Cam. They dominated the room – you didn't notice anything else once you were inside. Even Cam's images of Charles Barkley and Michael Jordan were arthouse shots.

Carrying after-dinner cups of coffee, Darcy and Fil came into the room. At least, thought Cam, Darcy's okay. That funny stuff Fil mentioned about him saying he had to *die* must have been crap.

Darcy stared around at the photos. Each one – the horses, the people, the landscapes – reminded him he was about to break every Law he'd ever been taught. He sipped his drink, wishing cameras had never been invented.

Fil joked heavily to start their discussion of serious matters. 'So, you're still with us, Darc.'

Darcy started, then realised she was joking. 'Yeah. So far.' He was glum.

Cam rifled through loose prints on his desktop. 'Here's the ones from the other day – see, Fil, the arcade's gone.'

Gingerly, his sister picked up the photo. As Darcy looked over her shoulder, his rough stubble grazed her cheek, and Fil felt like pheromones were radiating off her. 'How come,' Darcy asked, 'it showed an arcade? This must've been all bush out here.' Filomena explained that the house was built from the materials of the old arcade building, they thought that was why the camera was showing them the arcade rather than the site of Aonbar's Rest.

'Here's the others, the earlier ones.' Cam said, pushing towards them another bundle. Darcy took them, one by one, as Fil sifted through them slowly. The mystery horse/pony/cow. Hew Costello in the arcade. The body.

'That's the dead body there,' Fil said casually.

Darcy's eyes widened. 'That one?'

'Mmm. Oh!' Realisation dawned. 'Didn't we ever show it to you before?'

Darcy shook his head. As far as he was concerned, he didn't want to know about anything with dead bodies in it. Cam and Fil had forgotten that when the first shots had been developed, Darcy wasn't involved. They'd never directly asked him if he wanted to see the photo of the body. Which suited him just fine. Now, however, it was staring him in the face. He regarded the photo uneasily, grunting when Cam showed him what they thought was the gun, the man's hat fallen off (probably in a fight, Cam suggested), the unnatural posture of the victim.

Darcy held the photo a little distance away and squinted. Momentarily overcome with pure interest, he forgot to be afraid. 'He's *black*,' he said.

'Who's black?' said Fil.

'This kid – look.' Darcy's long thin index finger was resting on the body's legs. 'See how skinny that leg is, and how long it is from foot to knee? See his ankle bone sticking out, and the tendon? That's a blackfella's leg. And look at the colour.' The photo was black-and-white, which really meant, of course, that it was a blurry range of blacks, whites and greys. The profile of Hew Costello showed up a light grey, verging on white. The hat was a dark grey, the gun black. And the body, which Cam and Fil had never thought of in terms of colour, was a darker grey than Costello by three or four shades.

'Isn't that just the light in the picture?' Fil asked Cam.

He made a fish-mouth. 'Hard to say, could be, could not.'

'I'm tellin' ya, that's a blackfella,' Darcy insisted.

'How can you tell just from his legs though?' asked Cam sceptically.

Darcy waved his hands and shook his head at this opposition. 'I dunno, you just can. You see enough blackfellas, you can tell, eh? Which means,' he added thoughtfully, 'this is the second black boy. Granny Lil said she saw three. I'm one and this is another.' This revelation eased Darcy's fear slightly. It showed Granny Lil was on track, at any rate. They weren't flying one hundred per cent blind. Now he just had to worry about spear-wielding Elders and bleeding to death. Great.

'Listen, what's this Fil said about you *dying*?' Cam

asked bluntly, as though he'd read Darcy's mind. 'You're not gonna die!'

Darcy sighed, looking at the floor. How could he make Cam understand? Knowing it to be impossible, he spoke anyway. 'Look, Aboriginal Law says do this, or else. Don't do that, or else. Granny says someone's got to go back and find out why the camera's doing this shit. She's tried to go back herself – that's why we had to wait.' Here Darcy glared at Cam. 'It didn't work. She couldn't get back, so either something got in the way, like you fucking around at the house, or it's not meant for her, it's meant for us. She doesn't know. So, because I'm the only one that can go back, it's up to me. Only ...'

'What?' demanded Fil through a mouthful of coffee.

'... to find out who got murdered, and who did it and why, and how we're involved in it. I've got to go to the house, eh? And the house is on a bora, like she said today.'

'But you're Aboriginal,' said Cam. 'It's not like with Hew Costello, he was white.'

'Don't matter,' said Darcy. 'S'not my Country, not properly, and I'm not broken in for this Country. Only know a few words of Yanbali. And both my parents had white blood, see. I'm more'n half-white. Some of 'em call us yellafellas. They'll probably kill me if they catch me.'

'Who?' Cam and Fil asked together, confused.

Darcy looked at them with scorn. Fear was making him irritable, and in the back of his head was the idea that if Cam hadn't gone to the house, taking photos when he shouldn't have, Granny might have gone back instead of him, proper way. 'The Old People! Didn't you listen to what Fil said? The camera's going *backwards*! If we wait much longer I'm not gunna be going back to a nice little town with shops and goldmines and that shit! It's tribal times! Killing times. Blackfella's Law.'

Darcy stopped talking, his eyes bright with fear. Cam and Fil stared at him. They hadn't properly thought out yet what it meant, the camera going back in time as they went forward.

'Christ Almighty!' Cam eventually managed to say. 'I'm sorry, Darc, I didn't even think ...'

'Mmm, well, bit late to think now,' the Aboriginal boy snapped. 'Damage done now.'

'Are you gonna do it?' Fil asked, finding it hard to believe he would go back when he was so obviously terrified.

Darcy ran his fingers through his curls. They didn't understand that he had no choice. 'Haveta. Granny says I haveta. The camera wouldn't have turned up unless someone's supposed to do something. Youse can't. I ain't got no choice, see. If I run, it'll catch me. Same as you can't sell it – it's come to ya.'

'What've I done?' Fil murmured to herself. 'I should have stayed home. It's me, isn't it?' she asked Darcy. 'It's my fault, for going onto the bora?'

Darcy shrugged. 'Well ... you shouldna. But ya didn't know. It's no one's fault, exactly, 'cept maybe Hew Costello's, 'cos they told 'im not to build his house there. But see, maybe there's a reason you was let in? Something we don't know about.'

Fil thought back to the first day when she'd stolen Angel and ridden off. After she fled from the creepiness of the house and was standing outside ready to go, it was true – there had been something pulling her back inside. She hadn't wanted to go, not really, she'd been drawn there almost against her own will. It made her feel shivery, remembering.

'So …' said Darcy, extremely reluctant, 'if I'm gunna hafta go back, the sooner the better. Tonight. If I can be quick and get back during whitefella times, it's better, eh. The Law's not as strong when there's whites around, and there'll be more places to hide, that sorta thing, more people around the area and that. Granny's coming here dreckly, so she'll be with me when I try. You got the camera, haven't you, Cam?' It was a formality, the question that sealed his fate.

'Yeah,' Cam answered, looking up briefly to the back of his door where he'd hung it for safe-keeping.

But the camera bag was gone.

Darcy followed his gaze. The shock on Cam's face told him all he needed to know. 'You've sold it!' Darcy shouted at Fil, 'I told you not to! You've sold it!'

Fil cowered against the wall, horrified. 'I haven't! I didn't – don't be stupid, I wouldn't sell it, not after – I *didn't*!' She was pale and sweating, waiting for him to believe her. Darcy continued to rant. As if it wasn't bad enough having to go back and face the spirits of the fucken dead, without having his plans interfered with now, at the last minute. Yet, he realised, after a minute, standing there shell-shocked and craven, Fil looked as surprised as Cam.

Darcy stopped shouting and stood facing the other two. His heart was hammering. 'Well, where the fuck is it then?' he demanded of them both. 'Vanished into thin fucken air? What've ya done with it?'

Cam looked at him dumbly. 'It was here on Wednesday,' he said pathetically. 'I went to the ruin on Wednesday.'

'Wednesday,' Darcy echoed. 'A fat lot of good *Wednesday's* gonna do us on Friday night, eh?' He couldn't believe the camera was gone and kept looking at the door, hoping it would materialise. This was far worse even than having to go back and face the ancestors. How, for instance, was he going to tell Granny that her only hope of recovering some ancient lingo and lost songs had disappeared off a mig teenager's bedroom door?

'So where is it?' Fil thought aloud in a quavery voice. 'Would Jon have taken it?'

Cam shook his head. 'Don't ya remember him telling Granny he'd only ever seen it that time when Goddard …' He stopped; his mouth hung open on the word. And Darcy suddenly remembered the look on Goddard's face when he held the camera that day. He'd seen that look on the Johns that handled him. All-encompassing desire.

'That sleaze, he's wanted it ever since he knew about it,' Fil said softly. 'And now he's got it.'

'You reckon?' Darcy asked. 'When could he have got it, but?'

They went through the hours since Cam had brought the camera back from the ruin.

'We went shopping,' said Fil, 'and then after that we were all home that afternoon. Wednesday night we

216

watched that crappy horror movie. Thursday I went riding and you went to Lismore, but Cam was here the whole time.'

'Ah ...' said Cam uncomfortably. 'Actually. I, um, when Mark dropped that horse round, I put him away and fed him and then I took Garbo over to Craig's to get some mull. I was gone about an hour and a half.' He felt terrible. First he buggered up Granny's efforts by doing what Darcy told him he shouldn't, then he took off from Aonbar's Rest and allowed the camera to be stolen while he was buying choof.

'And Thursday morning me'n Jon drove through Federation and Goddard saw us going,' said Darcy slowly. 'And he heard us telling Granny – she was standing outside St Vinnies – we were going to Lismore.'

'That's it, then,' said Fil, 'Why d'ya go out, Cam? Dad would kill you if he knew you left the place when you were supposed to be looking after it. Jesus, you can go to Craig's any time.'

'Well, why'd you steal Angel that day?' Cam countered as guilt rose in his breast. 'If ya hadn't ...'

'But I wasn't in charge of the place,' she argued hotly.

'Oh, cut it out, youse two!' Darcy said. 'Where's the bloody camera, that's the main thing? We need to get it back. And quick, too.'

'It'll be in the camera shop, I suppose,' Cam said. 'That's where Goddard keeps his collection, out the back. And since we can't prove it's ours, there's no reason he shouldn't put it there. Camera collectors are all crazy anyway – he'd put it there probably even if it had Fil's initials on it.'

Darcy snorted. 'Let's get cracking.'

'Where to?' Fil asked.

'The shop, of course. I told ya, we need to get it back, asap.' Darcy stood waiting impatiently, until it dawned on him that these kids had never done a b & e. 'Ah, root my boot,' he said heavily. He'd have to spell it out in one-syllable words. 'Goddard's got the camera, right? It's Friday night, yeah? All the coppers in town are gonna be waiting for the drunks at the pubs and nightclubs – they're not gonna expect a break-in at the camera shop until the early hours of this morning. Now's the perfect time to hit it and get the camera back. Are youse comin', or do I have to do everybloody thing meself?'

Cam swung unhesitatingly to his feet. He had to redeem himself. Fil sat on the bed wondering what to do.

'Fil?' he said.

She sighed. This holiday wasn't what she expected *at all*. 'Coming.'

Darcy rang Granny Lil, then they headed to the highway.

Chapter Fifteen

'Where was Jon's party?' Fil asked Cam when they'd hitched to the outskirts of Federation, 'It wasn't in town, was it? I don't want to run into him.'

Cam shook his head. 'Nah, it'd be out in the bush.'

'Full moon.' Darcy commented, drawing to a halt beside the War Memorial. 'That's good. Good in Murri way, anyway. Not so good if the cops are after us. Now lissen up, you two. Cam, give us your watch.' Darcy strapped the Seiko to his wrist where it flopped loosely. 'Okay, emergencies. If the cops get me, ring Granny Lil. She'll ring Legal Aid for bail. If they get youse, give ya name and address, then ask 'em if you're free to go. They've gotta say yes, else they've gotta arrest ya. If they're chasing any of us, head for the back of the battery warehouse, okay? The scrub's real thick there, but it's close enough to here so they won't think we'd go there. We can sneak down the beach to the Bridge from there. Meet us there after.'

Fil looked at Cam, impressed. Darcy really sounded like he knew what he was doing. Maybe they could pull this mad scheme off after all.

'Right, Cam it's five past ten. At quarter past, I want you to go make some trouble over there, on that side of the square, okay, near the pub. Pick a fight or something.'

Oh, yeah, great, Cam thought, just perfect.

'Fil, you come with me and just sit outside St Vinnies. If the alarm goes off, you stand around like you're having a good dorrie ...'

'A what?'

'A dorrie ... ah, a sticky beak. And don't run off whatever ya do. The coppers turn up, try an get in their way. Pretend you're charged up, make a real bloody nuisance of yourself, okay? Give me a bitta extra time.'

Fil and Cam agreed on their roles, and said a tense goodbye to Darcy. Dressed in black jeans and a faded navy-blue T-shirt, he quickly disappeared over a high wire fence behind the row of shops. Pick a fight, thought Cam. Jesus, I can't do that. He decided instead to start flinging the rubbish bins around, making a spectacle of himself. They'd all think he was drunk or tripping. Fil took up her position on the pavement, people-watching. There was a steady stream of partygoers and nightclubbers on Camelot Street, some young kids, an older crowd. She didn't see how Darcy could hope to break into a burglar-alarmed camera shop, but he'd sounded confident. After all, he was the criminal, not her. She sat and watched the dock of the War Memorial as it ticked to eight, then ten, then fifteen minutes past ten.

Suddenly, on the other side of the square, she could see Cam behaving like a crazy. He was doing a brilliant job – everyone around was fascinated by his antics, including the bouncers at the Federation Arms pub. They stood, arms crossed, watching for now but ready to pounce if he ventured too close to their territory. A garbage bin crashed to the ground in front of the Fair Dinkum Bargains store, spilling papers and drink cans all over the footpath. Cam adroitly weaved away from an irate passer-by and stood yelling abuse at a parked car. People were giggling and pointing. Cam threw a short but convincing fit on the grass of the square, then picked himself up and started walking on his hands in circles. It was twenty-five past ten before Fil even remembered what Darcy was doing. Finally, Cam drunkenly staggered past her with a big wink. Fil got up after he passed and made her way to the battery factory. When they reached the scrub she found Darcy sitting cross-legged, smoking, the camera bag strapped to his back.

'Piecea piss,' he said casually. 'But I couldn't get that Minolta, Cam. Sorry, they're chained on.' Darcy sounded sincere in his apology, as if he really had intended swiping an expensive Japanese camera for his mate while he was at it. In contrast to the black youth's studied nonchalance, Cam's chest heaved for breath and he sounded like he was about to have an asthma attack. He collapsed in a heap beside Darcy.

'Speak for yerself,' he muttered, 'I'm dying. And (gasp) don't worry, it's a Nikon I want, anyway.'

Darcy laughed softly. 'How 'bout you, Fil? You okay?'

'Yeah,' she answered. 'Howd'ya do it? So quick? What about the alarms?'

'Ah, trade secrets,' Darcy said, 'and a cunning way with this.' He held Cam's Swiss Army knife high before tossing it back to its bemused owner. 'Might be a bit blunt now.'

'I had that in my pocket this arv ...' Cam said, astonished.

'Me too,' said Darcy. 'Lucky I'm an honest thief, eh? Come on, let's get to the Bridge. Best if we get up the ruin before this moon goes.'

'Is Granny coming with us?' asked Fil. 'She's a bit old to go crawling around the bush at night, isn't she?'

Darcy shrugged, pretending not to care one way or the other. 'Yeah, but she wants to see what happens. If anything ... goes wrong, maybe she can help.' His words reminded Fil that they weren't just having an exciting Friday night jaunt in town, but were to engage in serious Business. Dangerous Business, for Darcy. 'And,' he added practically, 'she's gotta car. It's a bloody long walk up there.' He hauled Cam to his feet, and they set off towards Knockrow Street.

Granny wheezed beside Fil in the front of Peter's mangled Holden as it made its way noisily up to Mill Road. The girl shifted uneasily on the cracked vinyl of the seat. The bottom of her legs were sticking to it – why was she sweaty now, at night? The car rocked gently from side to side, the suspension shot to the shithouse.

'Just up there I think, next to that little track,' she said suddenly.

Darcy braked and the car lurched to a one-sided halt. 'Wanna get them drums fixed, eh, Granny,' he said, lighting a smoke.

He, Fil, Cam and Granny all piled out onto the grass, and after the tricky business of getting Granny through the barbed wire fence, set off up the slope towards the ruin. It was only a ten-minute walk from the road, but with Granny coughing and staggering along beside them, it was closer to half an hour before they reached the bottom of the cliff. Granny peered into the lantana bushes. Her eyesight wasn't good even in daylight, and though the moon was a bright white disc hanging low above them she couldn't see many details. Darcy shifted his weight from foot to foot as he chain-smoked, rubbing his upper arm with his free hand. Fil and Cam stood back a little, waiting to see what Granny would do.

'Yep, this is it all right,' she muttered after a minute's straining to see. 'See the dish?'

Fil looked around in vain for grubby porcelain remnants. More alert, Cam followed the track of Granny's pointing forefinger and noticed for the first time in the moonlight that Costello's house sat squarely in the middle of a large shallow depression. All around the house (assuming it ran round the back where the bush was overgrown and they couldn't see) lay a slight rise in the ground. It created a shadow-circle within which lay the house. 'What is it?' he asked, feeling ignorant but needing to know.

'Dance ground,' Darcy said unexpectedly, throwing his cigarette butt well away from the area. 'That's good, means it ain't an initiation circle. Blackfellas been stomping here for years and years and years, till the ground's worn down flat with dancing. The circle there, that's for watching – it marks the edge of the bora.'

Then *that's* why, thought Fil, excited, that's why once I got outside the lantana, it's not as creepy, why I felt better when I ran out the first time … that's why it didn't feel scary to Cam till he went inside. Seeing the physical evidence of the bora gave her a sudden tingling shock. It's *real*, she realised in a rush, this black magic weirdo stuff, it's all real. Till then Fil had been able to keep a small part of her normal, sceptical self apart from what was happening to her, able to believe that somehow a rational explanation for the photos would appear. Standing in front of the sacred circle under the full moon, that part of her melted away; a strange new respect entered in its place. Puzzled, she followed the others as they crept through the overgrown bushes to face the house.

'Darcy.' Granny said simply.

Darcy stepped up to her, eyes shut, chin thrust forward. The movement looked, thought Cam, like a man stepping forwards for the hangman's noose. Granny lifted off the boy's Nirvana T-shirt to reveal a chest deeply marked with cross-scarring. Fil and Cam both stared. Cam sucked air through his teeth and winced – how the hell did those thick lines of scar tissue happen? What sort of dreadful accident had Darcy experienced? It looked like he'd ridden into a barbed-wire fence, yet the lines were neat and straight. Fil had read in one of Jon's books about the practice of scarification, and seen a photo of an old bearded man bearing the marks of initiation, but it had seemed a million miles – or years – away from here and now. She had no idea that under his ever-present shirt Darcy bore the same legacy.

Granny reached into her pocket and pulled out a white tube. She daubed Darcy's face: two horizontal stripes on each cheek and a vertical one from forehead to chin. She silently waved Fil and Cam away, and they stepped back. Fil looked at Darcy with wonder. The black youth they knew had disappeared. An awesome, timeless man stood there in his place, a man she didn't know. The pupils of Darcy's eyes seemed suddenly to swallow the whites, making his gaze entirely black. Fil looked away, frightened. Granny got her and Cam to sit cross-legged alongside her, a little way from the house, backs to the bushes, then she pulled a pair of clapsticks out of her black vinyl handbag and rested them in her lap. Goosebumps ran riot on both the Menzies' necks when she took a breath and began to wail. Cam shivered, but his yellow eyes gleamed with expectation.

As they faced the ruin, they could only see the outline of Darcy's back under the glistening moon. For a full two minutes he was stockstill while the wailing went on and on. Then slowly, very slowly, he raised his arms to the side. He began to tremble, starting with the fingers, movement creeping up his arms until his whole body shook. Still wailing, Granny brought the sticks together with a *boom!* that made Cam jump where he sat. His feet itched to get up and dance – ridiculously, since he knew nothing of dancing.

Clap. Clap. Clap. Clap. The sticks echoed and rang in the narrow space between the watchers and the cliff-face. A long, thin high-pitched singing broke from Granny's mouth, wordless, meaningless but full of sorrow. Darcy stomped one thin leg on the damp ground, then the other, bowing his head, arms still a-flutter. Granny's song was a taut rope pinning him to the solid earth.

'He's a bird,' Fil whispered to Cam, who nodded. He

could see it too. A brolga. The bird walked, feathery and tentative, around the whole of the clear space in front of the house. It shook its sinewy head at the house, asking with its beak: Is it safe? It jumped away in fluttery flight when it feared danger, then pranced forward again to ask and ask, and all the time it danced Granny wailed in that reedy voice of nothingness. As Fil watched, she began to feel as if she was falling back, falling away from the world into the blackness of space. Everything was dark; she could no longer see Cam or Granny. Who was that over there, dancing? She couldn't tell. A great pain was tearing through her chest. Fil lost consciousness. Just before she did it seemed to her confused mind that she too had joined the dancer.

She floated above the others. The pain had gone. There was Granny, singing and clapping, with Cam sitting on the grass beside her. Neither had apparently noticed that she was flying as high as the gums. Darcy/the strange man/the brolga was walking into the ruin holding the camera. There's danger there, Fil thought with an odd calmness and clarity. Danger for whom? Don't know. For some reason she could see through the walls. Darcy was raising the camera in front of his face, now he was clicking the button. He fell to the ground inside, jerking and shuddering. Then he lay still. *He's dead*, thought Fil. But before she could think any further, the ground began to rush upwards to meet her.

Why's someone sticking needles in my neck? Fil wondered angrily. Why isn't Mum telling them to stop?

Or Cam? Stop it! She opened her eyes to discover she was lying on the back seat of the Holden on top of a scratchy gum branch.

'What's happening?' she asked.

Darcy looked over at her from the front seat, his normal, unpainted brown face a study in relief. 'Hey, she's awake!' he told the other two.

The car slowed as Cam stopped speeding to hospital. 'What's this bloody branch ...' Fil started to say, before realising that she was gripping it for dear life in her left hand. She shook her head. 'Okay, tell me, Darcy – what's going on?'

Darcy grinned. Not dying had improved his Friday night no end. And now he was safe from 'em, forever and ever. 'I'm not sure where you ended up,' he mused, 'or where the branch came from. But I went back and seen Costello and the boy, before he died. And an Elder, too. Boy, have I got a surprise for *you* – tell 'er Cam.'

'Darcy reckons the boy is, I mean was, Costello's son,' Cam said tightly from the front seat.

Fil frowned. '*What?*' This was too much. 'How do you know?'

Cam pointed at his own dingo eyes. 'Yella terra. He's got yellow eyes, like me, and Dad, and Grandma, and Hew Costello, Darcy saw him in the house. Hew Costello was telling him a bedtime story, cosy as anything. And he called him "son".'

Fil gaped at Cam. This didn't make any sense. 'So he's not black after all?' she asked Darcy.

'Yeah! Well, brown that is. Like me,' he retorted. 'A yellafella. A black yellafella.'

Chocolate-dark Granny burst out with laughter. Darcy scowled. Being mixed-race was a hassle.

'But that's even worse!' Fil cried out in disgust. 'That means he killed his own son.'

Darcy shook his head, forehead creased into a dark frown. 'I dunno, Fil. When I first seen that photo, I thought, yeah, this migloo killed a black boy, but I dunno. I just can't believe that no more, not after seein' 'em together, you know. He loves – I mean loved – that boy. I can't work it out.'

'Then what ... so who's the third black boy?' Fil was bewildered. Why did Hew Costello have a black son? And then kill him?

Darcy shrugged. He felt released from caring much, now he'd been told to keep out of it by the Old Man.

'Maybe it was an accident.' Cam broke in excitedly over the top of Darcy.

'Yeah, it had to be an accident! What do you think, Granny?' Fil asked. Granny sat stiffly in the front between the boys. She grunted noncomittally.

'She wild 'cos she couldn't go back,' Darcy told Fil. 'She wants to take the camera and go back and get her own sing, own dance. She cranky now 'cos it's finished.'

'What's fin—' Fil began, but was interrupted.

'I don't see no accident,' Granny told Cam in a very clear, definite voice which said – you, I don't *mind* you, but don't go forgetting your great-great-grandfather murdered blacks. He looked at her uncomfortably. They all fell silent.

★

Granny and Darcy dropped Fil and Cam at the moon-silvered gate of Aonbar's Rest before heading to Knockrow Street. Crunching up the gravel drive to the house and stables at half-past midnight, Fil felt weak and tired.

'Cam, I'm buggered,' she said, stopping. Her brother looked down at her. She was pale and looked as though she hadn't slept for days. She didn't look sick, just bone-tired.

Fil shook her head and slumped to the ground. Cam, seeing her exhaustion for what it was, picked her up and put her to bed. He only wished he could sleep that soundly, without bloody footprints and murderous gunslingers dogging his nights.

'A death,' Granny said bluntly to Darcy over his morning coffee, 'needs a death. You know that, boy. Same's the Bible, eh? Eye f'r an eye, tooth f'r a tooth.'

Darcy shook his head weakly. 'But Granny, it feels wrong. Like maybe he didn't kill him, even. It don't feel right.'

Granny snorted sceptically. 'You bin hangin' around them whitefellas too long, startin' to believe they all angels, that's your problem.'

Darcy said nothing. Was she right? Was he starting to lose his culture, turn into a black-hating black, a coconut?

'Darcy, use ya head. There's a black boy dead and a migloo holding a gun. Oh, I know' – her tone softened – 'I know ya don't wanta think ya friends are descended from a murderer. But think about it, boy. They all got blood on their hands somewheres, somehows.'

'I bin having nightmares,' Darcy confessed. 'I seen this Old Man, he wants ta spear me. And last night I dreamed I seen blood everywhere, pools of blood, even after I went back.'

Granny nodded. 'Mmm. Well. There's trouble somewhere, eh?'

Miserable, Darcy had to agree.

'If the dead boy's his son,' Fil said to Cam, leaning over the stable door as he groomed Babyface's shining flanks, 'then ... he's our great-grandfather ... and the boy would have been Dad's Mum's half-brother, wouldn't he? Isn't that our cousin? Or great-great-uncle or something?' She tried to draw the family map on the stable wall with her finger, but failed.

'Mmm, I think so,' said Cam uncertainly. 'So we had a black relation once. Is that why Costello disappeared out of the family history? They didn't want to talk about it? And why all this has happened to us?'

'Must be,' said Fil. She could think of no other reason why they would have been picked by ... whatever picked *them* to find the camera.

'Wonder what he was like?' Cam asked with a small smile. 'Darcy said the boy looked about twelve in the house. He said the house looked a bit different to what it does now, too. The wall of the bedroom's in a different place, and it goes out onto a kind of paddock where the lantana is. He said he saw the pony, that grey one in the photo. Outside in the little paddock.'

'How long was I out for?' Fil asked, aware that Darcy

had been able to pass a lot of information on to Cam while she was unconscious.

Cam paused with the grooming and thought. He rubbed his forehead. Losing sleep to nightmares was catching up with him.

'Oh ... ten minutes. Maybe a quarter of an hour. We carried you to the car downhill, and then we'd gone about a kilometre or two ... not that long. How are ya, anyway?'

Fil nodded. She felt okay this morning. She didn't mention what she'd experienced when she fainted. She didn't know how to begin describing that to Cam. Maybe Darcy would understand; for now though, she'd hold it close inside.

Chapter Sixteen

Darcy looked over his shoulder. Fil was washing up at the sink, Cam drying. Jon in front of the TV. No one took notice anymore when he went to the fridge, they were used to his massive appetite. His body was making up for years of living on damper and cool drink. Surreptiously he sneaked a large piece of Jon's birthday cake into his left palm, taking an extra dollop of icing with his right index finger. Yummo – Black Forest gateau with whipped coffee cream icing and roasted almond flakes. *Excellent.* Him and Fil made a deadly pair in the kitchen.

He sat down in the lounge and didn't meet Jon's eye. The two of them watched the rest of the midday ABC news in silence, Darcy saying nothing because the political intrigues were boring to him, Jon sulking because he had been stood up by Ruth on his birthday yesterday. He had been all abuzz that morning, Darcy remembered, dressing carefully, shaving on a Sunday, hastening back with the trailriders instead of letting them linger over their last few minutes of horsy heaven. Then there had been an embarrassing half-hour of waiting for her to show at lunchtime, until Jon pushed his chair out and threw his hands to heaven, crying melodramatically. 'Oh, my Ruth, why hast thou forsaken Fil's chocolate gateau? Well, two, four, six, eight ...' and they'd all plunged into the roast chook and then the cake. The food was enough to make the kids forget Jon's disappointment but Darcy had noticed he was quiet all afternoon and less flamboyant than usual over dinner. Poor bugger, he thought, it's awful when ya want someone and they don't want you back. That *sucks*.

Fil lay on the lounge reading a women's magazine as she drank her post-lunch cup of tea. 'Eeyugh,' she said in distaste. 'Listen to this, Dad, yuk! The Voodoo clans of Haiti believe that blood is intrinsically magical, having properties of prophecy and contamination ...' She went on to describe several gory uses of chicken's blood for magical spells.

Jon shrugged his shoulders, unmoved. 'So tell me it's any worse than bullfighting in Spain, or breeding battery hens without legs in the US. But no, they're black, and African by descent, so what *they* do is voodoo – spooky.' Jon made scary hands and ghost noises.

'But blood! That's revolting,' Fil said with a screwed-up face.

'Blood is a universally emotive substance, whether it's used for positive or negative effect. Every theology has its blood, or blood substitute,' Jon said.

Darcy frowned. What did that mean? Jon was cool, but couldn't he stop talking like a bloody dictionary? Cam merely nodded; he'd obviously got whatever the hell Jon had said. Darcy felt shame not to know what the big words were.

'I have nightmares sometimes with blood in them,' he said, trying to make it sound as if he knew what they were talking about. 'Scary ones.'

Cam sat up quickly. 'Me too! They're friggin' horrible, eh. The last one, I was standing in this blood, splashing around in it, and this guy wearing a hood had a gun pointed at me. He was just pulling the trigger, and I could see the bullet coming for me here –' Cam pointed at his forehead – 'and then I woke up. It was so scary, I was shittin'.'

'Guilty conscience,' said Jon, grabbing Cam suddenly and punching him semi-softly in the stomach. 'Comes from not doing what you're told, Sunshine. Banquo's ghost. When shall we three meet aga-a-ain, in thunder, lightning or in rain?' he cackled, rubbing his hands at his son.

'When the hurly-burly's done,' Fil crooned quickly, stooped over witchlike with a forefinger raised wisely. 'When the battle's lost and won.' She'd done *Macbeth* in Grade Ten. Darcy scratched his head at this. Migloos were all mad.

'Mine sounds like yours,' Darcy told Cam. 'I'm standing in blood too, it's dripping out of me. But it's not a gun, it's this Elder with a beard, trying to spear me. And the spear's flying towards me in slow motion, and I wake up just before it hits me ...'

Cam looked at Darcy as his voice fell away. 'What did yours look like?' Darcy asked in an unsteady voice.

Cam shook his head. 'Couldn't see. He had this hood on. But the bullet – I can see it spinning through the air.'

'The spear wobbles in the air,' said Darcy, sweating. 'Oh, shit. It's happening again.'

'Hey?' asked Jon, 'what's happening? Oh.' He stopped, seeing their faces. 'Don't tell me. I haveta ask Granny, right?'

Cam nodded, whitefaced. Darcy sat down and buried his head in his hands. Jon chose to ignore him. The school would go to rack and ruin if he let every little hiccup stop the work. He was behind the maintenance schedule as it was. 'You lot gonna help me with Angel this arv?' he said.

'Yo,' said Darcy, looking up. Maybe a bit of hard work would take his mind where he wanted it to be: in the real world.

Cam got to his feet. 'S'pose so. But I ain't riding the maniac, not after last time. Now he *needs* a bullet, the prick.' Tough talk to hide his fear.

'Don't worry, I'll be doing the riding,' said Jon, whose leg was now completely healed, showing only a bright pink scar over his ankle. 'But I'd better have some stretcher bearers around, I reckon. I might have met my Waterloo here. Two hundred bucks of useless, oversexed beauty ...'

'Garn!' said Darcy in mock disbelief, prancing on his toes. 'Who offered you two hundred bucks lately?' He dashed from the room, hotly pursued by Jon threatening to bash him for his insolence. Darcy slowed down when he got outside, choked by laughter.

What? thought Cam as he went to saddle Angel. He hoped that Dad wouldn't let Angel go to the rodeo circuit. The horse was too fine-bred for that kind of treatment, even if he was an evil-minded bastard.

An hour later they were back inside. Jon winced as Fil

probed his shoulder with a sterilised needle. Two semi-circles of tooth marks were raised red on his brown skin. Tomorrow they'd be purple, the day after, black. And where the skin had been broken by Angel's savage yellow teeth, the sawdust of the breaking yard had worked its way underneath, rubbing agonisingly against raw flesh. Jon gritted his teeth as Fil tried to extract the major bits of sharp curly wood.

'Lift your arm for me,' she ordered.

Jon tried. 'I can't,' he said. Fil took his left elbow and gently felt the movement of the shoulder joint.

'*Aaow*!' Jon cried out, snatching his arm back off her. He felt the damage with his other hand, reaching awkwardly over his left shoulder. 'Bloody hell,' he said as his fingers came back with red smeared on them.

Cam looked steadily at him from across the room. 'That horse is dangerous,' he said plainly. 'He's thrown you, Darcy, me and Fil. He's busted two girths, kicked me, and now he's biting. And if me'n Darcy hadn't been there ...'

Every other time Cam had raised this topic before Jon had leapt to Angel's defence, but this time he said nothing. It was true. Darcy had leapt off the fence and played rodeo clown while Cam helped drag Jon, in semi-shock from the fall and the pain, clear of Angel's hooves and teeth, grinding sawdust into his wounds in the process.

Jon set his mouth in a straight line. 'I know, Cam, I know. Just give me a while to get used to the idea there's a horse I can't ride. That'll do, Fil, the rest can work their way out. You boys do the afternoon exercising and feeds for me, please. I'm gonna have a lie-down.'

Darcy and Cam decided they may as well start the afternoon strapping early. Fil accompanied them. She felt as though she'd hardly ridden at all these holidays, after dreaming all year in Melbourne about spending the summer on horseback. Her time was slipping away. Less than a month till she had to go back south to the cold. She begged Cam for an eensy-weensy ride on Garbo and he surprised her by agreeing. The three teenagers rode for the rest of the afternoon along the lower banks of Desperation Creek, Darcy leading Gunner beside Governor, Cam on Babyface leading Picasso, and Fil blissfully enjoying herself on Cam's bouncy little appy mare.

Darcy rode into the stableyard to see Jon sitting in the tackroom, staring at the wall. 'Ey, Boss!' he said, dismounting and putting Governor in his box. The big grey tossed his head and shuffled his hooves, playing around with Darcy, who growled affectionately at him then took saddle and bridle and put them away on the racks, wondering what Jon was doing sitting still. Normally he was a hive of energy in the stables, doing three things at once. Now he just sat, still and silent.

'You okay?' Darcy asked in an offhand voice.

Jon brushed his long hair back and looked up at the boy. Darcy stood tall and young and strong in the doorway, a picture of health. The only thing that marred his appearance was a trace of white sunblock in the creases between nose and cheek. In contrast, Jon felt old. Old and hurt. Depressed, even.

'Yeah. It's Angel ... he's too good to let the rodeo stick him in a paddock and rot. And I hate to think of bloody Pekinese chowing on him.'

'Mmm. It's a bugger,' Darcy said. Horse that looked like that, but was totally useless. Out west they'd just turn him loose, let 'im go feral, but that wasn't practical here.

Fil and Cam rode into the yard, Jon stood up. 'Ah, well, I'll think of something. Let's feed these nags.'

Jon remained quiet as the four of them mucked out and groomed and fed the horses. When the last loosebox was filled with dean yellow straw and two rows of heads were deep in the feedboxes, Jon spoke to Cam. 'Can you fix yourselves up for dinner, Cam? I've got something to do in town. It'll take a half-hour or so.' His voice sounded oddly strained.

Cam was taken aback – going to town at this hour? 'Yeah, sure. Want someone to drive ya?'

'No, it's okay.' For some reason Jon wouldn't look him in the eye. Cam watched his father put the van into gear with his right arm and drive slowly out to Mill Road.

When Cam put the dish full of stir-fry in the middle of the kitchen table Fil sniffed it dubiously.

Darcy eyed the gooey mass of rice, overcooked vegetables and semi-raw meat. He took a small portion onto his plate and chewed hard. Involuntarily he made a sour face.

'Well, youse know what you can do, don't you!' said Cameron, growing heated. 'It took me half an hour to chop all those veges and youse reckon you aren't hungry.'

Fil grinned. She knew that feeling, all too well. 'Settle down, we'll eat it,' she said, forking the bits of meat out of the serving dish and getting up to cook it more thoroughly. 'Just fry the meat first, next time, not last.'

Cam flapped a dismissive hand at her. Bugger 'em, he thought, he was an artist not a kitchenhand. 'Darcy, want a beer?' he asked. Darcy nodded.

'Getting into my Heineken again?' Jon accused from the door. 'At least leave me a couple this time.'

'Where'd you go? I suppose the doctor's would be too much to hope for?' Fil asked him as she threw him a green can. He caught it neatly in his right hand.

'To see my not-so-illustrious acquaintances at the Ulan's clubhouse,' Jon replied. 'A charmless bunch, but useful in some circumstances.' From behind his back he drew a .22 rifle, aiming it carefully at the ceiling. 'I'm sorry Darcy. We're gonna have to terminate your employ.'

Darcy drew his chair back in a panic and bolted to the bathroom where he slammed the door shut. He locked it, then flattened himself against the wall of the shower cubicle.

'Hey! Darcy, it's a *joke*!' Jon called after him, lowering the gun. Poor kid. You stupid bastard, he chastised himself, not to think that Darcy had seen real shootings and carryings-on. He went and persuaded Darcy to come back and sit down.

'What's it for?' Fil asked, half-seduced by the power of the rifle. Cam sat down and began to eat stir-fry as though there was no tomorrow. He knew what it was for ... *Angel.* If he ate quickly enough, maybe these sudden hot tears wouldn't spill. I'm nearly fifteen, he thought, I can't cry. I won't cry.

That night the family sprawled in the lounge, half-watching *The X-Files.* Jon snorted and hissed at the thinness of the plot, irritating Fil, who was a devotee. Cam sat nursing his indigestion.

'Da-a-a-ad! I'll bloody murder you. Shut up!' Fil yelled. Jon was obligingly quiet until the show ended, then: 'Criminal drivel,' he said. 'What have I spawned? I knew I should never get TV out here.

Cam faked a heart attack. 'No TV! *Aaaagh.*'

Darcy grinned at Cam's acting, then, noticing the affectionate looks passing between the two yellow-eyed males, thought of the Costellos. Curious, he asked: 'Hey, Jon. What would it take for you to murder Cam?'

Jon frowned. 'What sort of question's that? You still thinking about that rifle? Nothing ever could. Why? Thinking of knocking him off and blaming me, are you? Got bad news for you, son – you're not in the will.'

'Just wondered.'

Jon peered at him over his glasses that he wore for the computer and which he sometimes used at night when his eyes were tired. That was his uniform – jeans, his blue peaked sailor cap outside, glasses when he was at the computer, shirt off to cook. It never varied. 'Murder's a funny thing to "just wonder" about, Darc.'

Darcy looked away, catching Cam's eye as he did so. He wasn't about to say any more but simply sighed as he saw what was going to happen. Maybe he'd even wanted it.

A torrent of words broke Cam's month-long dam. 'Yeah, it's this business with Granny Lil, Dad. Someone's been murdered!'

Jon leaned forward immediately, staring at his son. His hands gripped the sides of the lounge chair. '*What!* Who? Where ... and why the fucking hell didn't you tell me earlier?'

'It's okay,' Cam said rapidly. 'Not *now*, I mean this kid, he got killed a hundred years ago.'

'Oh,' said Jon, leaning back in relief. 'Christ, I thought you meant Darcy'd murdered someone.'

Darcy stood up to leave, not angry but apprehensive. He looked straight at Cam – strange for Darcy, who in the traditional Aboriginal way often avoided people's direct gaze. 'Cam – I know things're different now, but if you're gonna tell him, you be the one to tell Granny Lil, okay? It's not my responsibility.'

'Yeah, I know,' Cam acknowledged Darcy's warning. But it'd be okay – Cam had a strong gut feeling that Jon should know as much as they did. 'We don't really know *who* he was exactly,' Cam began telling Jon, and as the night shadows lengthened outside on the veranda, his father learned more and more – about the ruin, the camera, the photo of the body and Darcy's quaint little knack of popping back to the nineteenth century now and then. When Cam finally drew to a close, it was late.

Jon flopped back in his chair, the tension of listening for nearly two hours on top of his shoulder injury making him giddy with tiredness. His head spun. He didn't know what to say. 'That's some story, Cam. I believe you, but I can't think really straight at the moment. The first thing

I'm asking is, how do you know Costello killed him? What happened to the burden of proof? I mean, you don't even know the kid's name, let alone the details.'

'Well,' Cam argued, 'it was just before the turn of the century, the frontier was right here in Federation, and the photo shows a black kid dead and Hew Costello with a gun. Black murders were a dime a dozen back then. What're we supposed to think?'

Jon nodded, unhappily acknowledging his logic. 'Yeah ... it makes perfect sense – except that the boy's his son. Not that murdering your offspring's impossible, of course. And it would certainly explain,' he said in distaste, 'why Costello drops out of the family tree so suddenly.'

'But we don't really know,' Cam answered Jon's earlier question slowly. 'It's just that ... well, the photo ... it just looked that way to us.'

Fil and Cameron both turned towards each other in wonder. For ages now they'd assumed that Costello was the one who'd killed the boy. Other explanations immediately began to fight for air below their doubts.

'A bushranger could have come to the hut to steal his gold, and shot the boy; and Costello got out his gun to drive him away,' Cam suggested.

Fil pursed her lips at him. 'Or the boy had the gun for some reason,' she said, 'and Costello snatched it off him ...'

Jon rose wearily to his feet. 'I need to sleep on this. If it's too much for Granny Lil, it's definitely too much for me. Let's talk about it tomorrow morning.' He staggered off to bed, leaving Fil and Cam discussing their great–great-grandfather's possible innocence versus his probable guilt.

'Why don't we ask Darcy to go back again?' suggested Fil doubtfully.

Cam shook his head decisively. 'Nuh. When you blacked out, Darcy was saying he ... saw something. An Aboriginal Elder. I didn't really get what he meant, but Granny did. This person said Darcy didn't belong there, and he wasn't to come back. Oh, he was so happy; hey? Haven't you noticed how happy he's been since Friday night?'

'I suppose ... but why?' asked Fil. "Cos he saw the guy? I thought he'd be shittin' himself.' Darcy had been pale and sweating as he smoked in front of the ruin, thinking he was about to die. Why would he be happy to see spirits?

'He was,' Cam said. 'But he was told not to go back, see? Now Granny can't make him. No one can. So, he doesn't have to do it anymore. And they didn't kill him like he thought they would.'

Fil fell silent. If Darcy wouldn't go back, and the camera couldn't return to the time of the murder, they were stuck. They'd have to figure the mystery out themselves.

'Hatches, matches and despatches,' said Ann briskly next morning, sweeping an arm across a wide stack of roughly indexed boxes. 'Go for your life.'

Cameron cast a despairing glance at Jon and sighed at the thousands of unsorted small white cards that lay in front of them. Fil raised her eyebrows. It'd take *forever*. And it was a nice sunny day, too, perfect for the beach. Or riding.

'Aren't they supposed to be computerised these days?' Cam moaned.

'Sorry,' said Ann. 'We put them into the boxes when we thought we were getting the money, but the council hasn't managed to deliver yet. Too busy building themselves Taj Mahals and subsidising mangrove developments.' There was a bitter tang to her words.

Cameron couldn't help watching her perfect brown legs. He sighed and they all turned to the equally hopeless work of the cards.

But by a massive lucky fluke, the second box Fil sorted through contained Hew Costello's records. She drew out the age-yellowed card. 'This is him! Hew James Costello, born 1863, Moreton Bay, Queensland. But there's nothing about any marriage here.' That figured. Blacks weren't legally able to marry whites until much later on, she'd discovered in her reading, and if Darcy and Granny Lil were right, the boy's mother was Aboriginal. 'But listen to this: issue living or dead. Edward Hew Costello, born 1887, Federation, New South Wales. Death by Misadventure, died 1900, Federation, New South Wales. That's him! Edward. He was' – she counted on her fingers – 'thirteen.' Under 'mother' was a blank space.

'Death by Misadventure,' echoed Cameron. 'Could mean anything.' They looked at each other in deep dissatisfaction.

'Is that all there is?' asked Jon. 'No death certificate or anything?'

'Nup.' The card Fil held was their only link to Edward Hew Costello, whose bones presumably lay somewhere in Federation Shire.

'At least it doesn't say *murder*,' Cam said hopefully to Darcy, who was hanging back, letting the others sort through the cards. Writing and reading weren't his strong suit, despite the nuns' efforts back home.

'Yeah, but how many whitefellas ever got tried for murdering blacks?' argued Darcy. 'Death by Misadventure – that could just be a nice easy way of covering it up, eh?' He was irritated beyond measure by that little white piece of paper Fil held. Typical white way, eh? Write something down about something important, but make sure no blackfellas can understand it, and it doesn't tell ya what ya really need to know. He stalked to the window. Goddard's Photographic was down the street. At least we got that right, thought the black boy. did something proper way onetime.

They trooped back to the van and Fil drove them back to the money-makers, the horses. Jon decided the stables needed scrubbing out. All day long, while Fil rode Gunner to the beach then lay around the house reading, Darcy, Cam and Jon shifted straw, moved horses to the paddocks, scrubbed down walls and bricked floors, then returned the occupants to their luxury accommodation. It was late afternoon before they staggered inside to Fil's cheesey brown-topped lasagne and salad. Jon's left arm hung uselessly by his side. Angel's was the only box they had left alone. 'Leave it,' Jon had said, 'it doesn't need doing.'

Cam was afraid to ask why, and Darcy was too tired to care.

★

Next morning Cam tossed in bed, wishing Jon had strangled Maxwell like he'd promised to a million times. The mutt regularly got into the chook run, making a hell of a racket chasing them and putting them off the lay for a week. And it was always at the crack of dawn.

'Will you BLOODY Shut-UP!' Cam yelled out of his window, ready to haul a heavy black Doc Marten. Maxwell ran under the van, canny enough not to be a visible target; a month ago Jon had got him flush in the ribs with a tin of baked beans. Then Filomena banged angrily on Cam's wall for him to shut up.

'Four-forty-five, you PRICK!' Cam, who'd caught sight of the alarm clock, yelled at the dog for good measure. It was just daylight, that beautiful dear cool light that you get in the sub-tropics before the day's heat arrives like a blast furnace. Cam lay undecided and irritated for a minute, then got up. Riding at dawn was a joy few people experienced, Jon had said when they moved to Federation, so make the most of it while you can. Cam pulled on his clothes and went out to get Garbo. A bit of a gallop down the beach south of Shelley Head would be perfect to get rid of this adrenalin rush. With the saltwater spraying under your horse's hooves and the smell of the sea in your nostrils, you could pretend you were immortal.

Out in the caravan Darcy jerked into wakefulness. Where was he? Which screw was yelling? He forced himself awake enough to remember he wasn't locked up anymore. What the bloody hell was all that noise? He pulled the orange nylon curtain aside to see. To complicate things further, he spied Jon walking out of the stables leading Angel in an old rope halter. *Hey?* Darcy rubbed his eyes and looked out towards the Small Paddock. Jon tied the horse to a young tree.

Cam reached in to unbolt Garbo's loose box, bridling the mare quickly as she nickered good morning to him. He didn't bother with a saddle; they'd swim in the dawn coolness of Shelley Bay. He led her clip-clopping gently out through the brick courtyard, noticing with curiosity and disquiet that Angel wasn't in his box. Turning the corner, he suddenly saw Jon about thirty metres away. He was moving to stand directly in front of Angel, who was tied to a sapling in the Small Paddock, his front fetlocks hobbled. The horrible cross-mark of death was chalked in white on his chestnut forehead.

A dark green trail showed where the man and the animal had brushed dew off the grass as they walked into the middle of the paddock. The next few seconds seemed oddly familiar to both boys watching from their different vantage points. They also seemed to take a long time. Cam forgot that Garbo was next to him, her leather reins fast in his right hand. It seemed nonsensical, somehow, to turn an ordinary corner on an ordinary day and see something being shot to death as the sun came up. To Darcy, viewing the scene in silence through the glass of the caravan window, it had the atmosphere of television. Cam, there in close-up, wanted to scream out 'No' but found his voice wouldn't work. He could only stand stupidly watching as Jon did the rational thing with a useless and dangerous horse.

Apparently, Jon had finished saying his goodbyes to Angel; now he prepared to destroy the handsome animal without pause. He tossed his blue cap aside and drew the .22 to his right shoulder, squinting, sniffing some moisture out of his sinuses, not quite tears. Angel tried to toss his head and snort, but his lead-rope was tied too short. As the horse flicked his ears forward and was unmoving for a short moment Jon's rifle cracked. The chalk cross exploded. What had been Angel sank to the ground, legs kicking out convulsively. The sapling he was tied to bent in a semicircle: Jon lowered the rifle and wiped his wet face; the gun barrel was now pointed innocently towards the ground, damage done.

At that exact moment Cam realised with an eerie prickling sensation why he had a feeling of *deja vu*. The sun behind the man's figure. The rifle, held by the butt in Jon's right hand. The hat lying on the ground like a rock. And all of it blurred, almost obscured, by the tears he himself was blinking back. Silhouetted by the rising disc of the sun, it could have been Hew Costello standing there. *The pony*, he thought in a single second of wild revelation. Costello's shooting the pony. Wasn't the dead boy wearing spurs? Wasn't he crumpled as though he'd fallen? Costello wasn't shooting the boy. He'd tossed his hat aside to see properly as he shot the pony after the animal had thrown and killed his son. Cam couldn't breathe, he was so certain. And that's why Darcy had to go back – to see that Costello was Edward's father, and that he couldn't have murdered the son he loved. Cam's heart thudded madly behind his ribs.

'It's the photo,' Fil said from behind him in a small voice.

Cam swung around. 'I know!' he replied joyously. 'I know! He isn't, wasn't, a murderer!' he replied.

'What are you kids doing up at this hour?' Jon asked, walking towards them with the bloodied halter in his hand, 'I didn't want you to see, Cam. I didn't want anyone else's life on my hands. I had to do it,' Jon showed Cam his open, pleading palms.

'It's okay,' said Cam, smiling strangely even as he started to sob for Angel – beautiful, savage, useless, unrideable Angel. 'It's okay, Dad. It's solved everything.'

Jon didn't quite understand what Cam meant, but ushered his kid inside anyway, away from the mould of the horse's dead body. Silver streams splashed shamelessly down his face as he walked across the grass, rifle and halter in his right arm, his left around Cam's broad young shoulders.

CHAPTER SEVENTEEN

It was five o'clock the following Tuesday. 'Phone. Jon!' Darcy yelled to where his boss stood undressing in the laundry. 'STD!'

Jon had stripped off his muddy work jeans and was standing in his undies, talking. Fil's heart sank. It would be Michelle for sure, saying what flight she was arriving on, and when Fil should be sent back home on the East Coast train. School started again in two weeks. Yuk.

'No! Really? That's fantastic. Congratulations,' Jon was saying. 'What's his name again? Yeah, we can organise that – three hundred fifty each? Pure-bred mares, of course.' He talked for a little longer, then hung up and ran and jumped for the ceiling, whooping. 'You helliferocious little beast! Cam! Cam!' Where *was* the boy?

'Who was it?' asked Darcy through a peanut paste and honey sandwich.

'Joe Mentink. A guy that used to have a couple of quarter-horse mares at Bill Barton's last year. One of Gunner's yearling's has won Best of Show in Sydney.'

Jon's face split open in a huge grin. 'He's sending three more mares up this week to be serviced. We're gonna be rich, kiddo! That horse is going to be real busy.'

Cam appeared in the hall, towelling his hair.

'Remember that black mare that came from Bill's last year for servicing?' Jon asked him. 'The really nice tall one?'

'Yeah. What was her name? Ebony.'

'Well, her foal just won Yearling Best of Show in Sydney on Sunday.'

Cam laughed. No way! But Jon was serious. Their little orphan Annie, Gunner the wonder-horse, rescued from a grotty paddock at *his*, Cam's insistence, was going to be famous. Unreal.

'His fees just went up to three-fifty for new mares,' Jon declared. 'We'll be knocking them back with a bloody stick once the news gets out.'

Fil held up two green apples from the fridge, and everyone trooped out to the stable to admire Gunner, stroke his bay coat, and feed him slices of apple.

'That's enough,' said Jon, 'can't give him colic, he's got a lot of work to do in the next few months, paying off the farm.' He gave the bay a last unbelieving pat. Hard to accept that you could translate horse's semen into solid earth and buildings, but it was amazingly, miraculously true. The offspring of Gunner and Ebony was going to make a new beginning for them all. He had accepted a verbal contract for a thousand and fifty dollars over the phone – and that was just the beginning.

'Can we buy some Sara Lee now?' Darcy asked hopefully, stomach rumbling.

'Sunshine' – Jon clapped him on the back, making him stumble forward – 'we're going to have Sara Lee coming out our ears. It'll be the land of milk and honey around here from now on.'

Darcy threw his head back and yelped at the sky. 'Yeee-ha! There is a God!'

'And she's looking out for us,' said Fil, who had started reading *The Female Eunuch*.

'This is it,' Jon said with fake nonchalance, showing a piece of paper to Granny Lil and the kids. Granny peered closer. Bill of Mortgage regarding the property adjacent ... blah blah blah. And across it in big red letters: CANCELLED. Jon turned to the bonfire Cam and Darcy had built from the Thunderbox, and waved the paper at it. His reflection danced blurrily on the side of the new aluminium van that was now Darcy's home. They'd had to pay the guy in Lismore extra at five-thirty that afternoon to open up and sell it to them on a Saturday. Jon had insisted that it be in place for the barbecue.

'Dad! Don't!' cried Fil. Surely you were supposed to hang onto things like that?'

Jon grinned at her. 'Ah ... will he or won't he? Will he or won't he?' He dropped his hand, however, and shoved the paper carelessly into his jeans pocket. Ruth dug it out again and folded it neatly before putting it back. If she was going to have a landed-gentry boyfriend, better be certain about it. Poverty held no attractions for her after three muddy years in a yurt.

'Lord and Master of all I survey. One day, kids, all this' – his hand described an arc – 'will be yours …

'One day it was all ours,' said Granny haughtily from where she sat on a milk crate, 'and maybe it will be again.'

'You're right, Granny,' Jon said instantly, with dignity. 'We should change the name, eh? To a Yanbali one?' No one could spell Aonbar's Rest anyway – he kept getting oddly addressed mail for Antlers Nest and the like. The price of whimsy.

'Oh, that's all right,' Granny waved his idea away. 'Just make sure the door's always open for blackfellas, eh.' She sipped carefully at her can of Bundy and Cola.

'Granny,' said Darcy, sitting next to her, nursing a beer. 'You know before the other night, and before we knew about the pony and that—'

'Mmm.' Granny didn't like being reminded she had been wrong about Costello.

'Well, Cam and me had these nightmares, bad dreams about getting killed and that. Why dya reckon that was? They were almost the same …'

'Bad dreams,' she murmured darkly into her drink. 'Bad dreamin'.' Then she looked up slyly at Darcy. 'You a good boy, eh, Darcy?'

He nodded uncertainly. Yeah, well, most of the time. Depending on what you meant by good, of course. He'd never murdered anyone, raped anyone, really bad stuff like that.

'You got good eyes, Darcy, nothing bad hiding there. But everyone's got something to hide, something to make 'em worry. Everyone's got sompin' on they conscience. "Judge not lest ye be judged" … cos we all guilty, somewhere. Like the migloos, they all livin' on our land. And blackfellas too ... so to me, sounds like you need to work out what you done wrong, and put it right, eh?'

'That's what Jon said!' Darcy answered back in displeased surprise, remembering when the Menzies had done that crazy witch-muttering in the lounge. 'Said it was Cam's guilty conscience.' He got up and took that idea to the other side of the bonfire to mull over for a while.

'I bin go funeral today!' Granny announced loudly a few minutes later, cigarette smoke hovering around her like a mist.

'Oo finish up?' Darcy called over the flames.

'That old one, up ...' Granny gestured with her chin to the north. 'Ve-ery old lady. eh? She be ninety years old last Christmas. Count her age by Christmases, she did. Anyway (cough) I bin go talk her daughter at funeral and yufla know what she told me?'

Everyone shook their heads, intrigued.

'Her aunty, the dead (cough) one's aunty. She useta live in the bush with a migloo man, long time ago.' Ah, Granny thought in satisfaction, *that* got their attention. 'She bin have twin boys, little arf-caste boys with yella eyes ...'

When will they stop talkin' like that! Darcy thought angrily, but kept listening.

'But when they (cough) grow up, 'bout this size' – Granny pointed at Cam – 'one boy die inna accident, kill by yarraman, and the mother (hacking cough), she too sad for her country, eh? She take her other jahjam and go home to her people up there, past the river. That boy's name ...' – here she paused with a fine sense of drama – 'his name Darcy. Darcy Hardacre.' She cackled at Darcy who was standing rigid beside the fire. His mother's maiden name had been Hardacre. 'That boy your great-great-uncle, Darcy. And *'is* father – Ew Costello! This mob your family. You Hirish, boy!' Granny bent over in a fit of furious laughter that turned to coughing.

Darcy sat down on a stump, feeling weak as he looked from Jon to Fil to Cam. They weren't *closely* related, but still ... his white relations? Jesus. He'd never even thought of lookin' for that mob.

Fil stood up and walked towards the house, followed by Cam. They appeared to be arguing.

'Ah, let them go,' said Jon, frying steaks on the hotplate. 'They can sort it out themselves.' He gave the meat another poke, then went and sat beside Darcy and started talking family trees. Ruth took over the barbie and chatted to Craig. Being stoned, he was easy to talk to if you didn't mind long silences. Granny mused into her fresh drink, crooning an Elvis song to herself.

Then the Menzies kids reappeared. Fil held the camera bag and stood facing Granny. 'Granny? I want to give this back.'

The old woman raised her eyebrows and took the bag, weighing it as if it contained oranges. 'So ... you finally worked it out, uh?'

Fil nodded, ashamed it had taken her so long to realise the camera didn't really belong to her at all. Cam watched, amazed and a bit sad to see it go. After all that time clinging to the camera. Fil was voluntarily handing it over. Well, good for her, he supposed. It wasn't healthy to want something that bad. Not an inanimate object, anyway. Horses were different, as he'd told Lucy on the phone yesterday, they got into your system.

'Darcy said you wanted to use it, to get some old songs or something?'

Granny laughed. 'Too late for that, now. D'is just a camera now, luvvie.'

Fil shook her head. 'But ...'

'You'll understand one day.' Granny put the camera down unceremoniously beside her stash of UDLs and the subject was dosed.

Cam went over to Darcy and Jon, who were discussing the function of the conscience. Darcy wasn't terribly surprised to find Jon agreeing with Granny's assessment of his nightmares. He stared at the ground where the browned-off grass of summer was rubbing away under their feet, revealing fine grainy sand mixed with the volcanic earth. The firelight shone on small grains of rutile in the sand. Darcy mentally threw his hands in the air. Was it the wine cask they'd passed around, or was he back to the same place he'd been at Mrs Long's, somehow? Doing stuff he didn't understand in a world that made minimal sense. He looked pleadingly towards Jon, who gave him a rueful shrug. Jon knew of poetry that almost explained it to his own satisfaction but he didn't think Darcy would get it, not that way.

The rest of the night was devoted to eating, drinking, boasting, storytelling. Ruth dragged out Jon's old guitar and sang 'American Pie' and some Sinéad O'Connor songs. Predictably enough, by one o'clock, Cam was vomiting his beer into the bushes. Soon after that they all dispersed to bed. Craig crashed in the lounge and Ruth drove Granny home, promising to be back for their dawn ride on Monday morning.

'But you asked Ruth!' Cam protested hotly on Sunday night to Jon, whose face was creased with the tension of another tiny battle. 'Why's it one rule for you and another for me?' He couldn't believe Jon didn't want Lucy to come on their ride. It was all right for his bit of feral fluff to tag along, but when he, Cam, wanted to invite someone ...

Jon sipped at his coffee, thinking furiously. *A Human Pattern* abandoned in front of him. He'd wanted the dawn ride to be a special occasion, a celebration of finally owning Aonbar's Rest, a confirmation of the family before Fil had to go away again and the coming year was swallowed by school and work. Darcy was coming, obviously; he was now family by history and blood as well as his new life at the riding school. But Lucy? A girl he'd never met and barely spoken to? Jon checked his own behaviour. Maybe he just didn't want Cam to grow up and be a man? Afraid to see his little – well, young – boy changing? No, he decided, it felt wrong to have strangers come, that was it.

'Yep. You're dead right, Cam. It'd be hypocritical.'

Cam waited to hear the old lecture from his childhood: But I'm the boss around here. When you have your own place you can—

'So I'll ring Ruth and ask her not to come.'

Cam did a double take. He hadn't wanted *that* – he liked Ruth, he had reluctantly discovered. But he liked Lucy, too, and it was the perfect excuse to impress her with his riding, his wit and his reasonably cool family. 'Ruth'll get the shits!' he said, wondering if Jon would actually do it.

Jon smiled. 'I can explain it – there'll be plenty more rides with Ruth for me, I think. Not many more with my kids, though. You lot'll be too big to hang around your old man in a year or two. And anyone who can't forgive a simple error of judgment – well, it ain't me you're lookin' for, babe …' He went to make the call to Ruth's neighbour, then calmly sat down again with his coffee and poetry. People worried about such little things. Didn't they know life was short?

In the greyish blackness just before Monday's dawn, Jon, Fil, Cam and Darcy rode silently over the ridges separating Shelley Bay from the sleeping outskirts of Federation. In front Picasso, just a shadowy outline to the others, arched his long bay neck under Jon's reins. He yawed at the bit, pretending he would like nothing better than to rear up and unseat his rider.

'You fool,' Jon told him gently, drawing to halt on top of the last ridge. The beach below was completely deserted, all the early-morning joggers staying farther up towards town on the other side of the massive headland that towered above them. The surf boomed below onto the hard flat beach; white wave-caps showed up brightly as the light changed minute by minute from night into dawn. Beside Jon, Fil sat lightly on Gunner (the wonder-horse), her mount chunky with stallion's muscle, his broad blaze standing out starkly from his dark head. Darcy and Cam rode up and the four horses stood in a row, nearly touching, their riders shielding their eyes when the sun began to break the horizon's dark edge with its long reaching fingers.

Jon drew his breath in sharply. 'Well, my dear ones, welcome to The End of the World,' he said, drawing a silver flask out of his saddlebag. 'And now for the Cup of Truth.' He passed the wine around. Cam and Fil were long used to his rhetoric; since they were tiny they had never found his ritual naming of objects and events strange. It's odder, really, thought Fil, to leave things un-named ... to go wandering through life without autographed guideposts. Like blind people, having to let others see the world for you.

'The Four Horsemen of the Apocalypse,' said Cam, swallowing a mouthful of wine and feeling it going acrid into his empty stomach. He wanted to gallop.

'Youse always say stuff like that,' complained Darcy, made brave by being included on the ride. 'Why can't ya talk like normal people?'

'Cos we aren't normal,' Fil said, feeling it to be true. 'We're different. Normal people are being woken up by their rattly alarm clocks to get in their pollution-machines and drive to their boring little grey lives. And we're here.' She pointed at the slap and suck of the blue sea. 'Who'd be anywhere else? We're the chosen people and it's our Golden Country!' She tried out Jon's style and bravado.

'I'll drink to that,' Darcy said as she handed him the flask. 'More like my country but, cuz.'

'Ha!' Jon said to Fil as Picasso became restless, shifting underneath him and wanting to run; his yellow eyes held an evil gleam. 'Hubris ... the Menzies' disease. Special, eh? Chosen people, eh? That's a big claim, Bella. You want to take yourself out of the madding crowd, show me ... show me something I can remember.' He taunted her with silence, waiting for her to renege on her claim. Please don't, he begged inside himself, please don't give in. Don't let me bully you ... I know it's there.

Watching his sister squirm under Jon's merciless interrogation, Cam searched his brain for some lines of Will Ogilvy, one of the bush ballads he used to recite as a kid. He stood in his stirrups and in a gesture that felt somehow right he held the flask to the rising sun:

We are heathens who worship an idol
We keep for our pleasure and pride
We are slaves to the saddle and bridle
Yet kings of the earth when we ride ...

'Fair.' Jon inclined his head in salute. 'Middling fair. Fil?'

Shakespeare, she thought, racking her poor brain, you did *Macbeth* only last year ... She shook her head. All she could think of was 'great Thane of Fife'. Jon was right. She wasn't special at all. She was just a bloody pretentious kid.

'Darcy?' Jon accused.

'Yo?'

'Perform, Son. Show the rising God what spirit you're made of.' Jon pointed at the dawn.

Darcy shook his head violently. Fuck that.

'Ah, but I insist,' said Jon, smiling strangely. Darcy shook his head again. No way.

'Have you forgotten that you sold your soul to me, son? It's payback time,' Jon said plainly.

Darcy's heart sank. He looked into Jon's eyes that were hard and yet soft at the same time, and could see there was no way out. *Okay. Fine.* He'd been put on worse spots than this, by men wielding knives, men wrapped in red ochre. He let Babyface's reins go slack and jumped to the ground. Fil watched his thin brown legs stalk to the edge of the cliff. Framed by the blue ocean, he stared into space for a moment, thinking. Then he turned and stepped onto a granite ledge a little above the others, where he clapped slowly, standing fully erect with the sun rising behind him. As he sang his eyes bored down blackly into Jon's. The slow rhythm of his hands and the rich anger of his voice contained a restrained violence he'd never before shown the Menzies.

Terra Nullius, Terra Nullius,
Terra Nullius is dead and gone!
We were right, we were here,
You were wrong and we were here.

Jon smiled at finding himself bested. He nodded approval and turned back to his daughter. 'Well, Fil?' Found anything more remarkable about yourself than the ability to get on a horse and ride to a beach? No?'

She flushed a deep red and found her anger. 'What about you? You're the one who encouraged us to think

261

we're special. You're the one that'd never let me watch cartoons in the holidays, or listen to music without analysing the lyrics, or ... anything normal, practically! You're the one who told me about Ghandi, and Mandela and ...' She stopped; a bitter note was creeping into her voice as she felt belittled by Jon's demands for instant greatness. Just add a sunrise.

'Quite so, and all in vain, it seems,' he mocked.

Fil was close to tears. Why was Dad doing this to her, today of all days?

'Just you, then. Send the others away,' Jon told her.

Fil made an upturned mouth. What was he going to do? When she asked them, Cam and Darcy rode down to the sand and cantered off to swim at the inlet. Waiting till they were several hundred yards away, Jon began; he didn't take his eyes off Fil from the beginning to the end.

'You were happy when your mother said you could come and stay with your devil-father this year, weren't you, Fil? And I was happy, too. I could begin to know you as an adult, not as the child you were when Michelle left. But when you arrived, I was ... I didn't know what to think. You weren't what I expected, and I had to sit down and work out what that meant for me. Your life has been shaped by your mother – that's as much my decision as hers. I could have moved to Melbourne, insisted on seeing you other than the odd holidays, but I didn't, and when I made that decision I had to give some of my dreams and illusions away. Then you came here for the full summer holidays, the grown you, and I saw it as a chance for both of us.'

Fil looked up at her father, her eyes full of tears.

He went on stonily. 'I gave Darcy a job with us, mostly because he needed one, but also because I could see him as a ... conduit. You needed shaking up, Cam too, but less so – he's less insular than you by nature. And a parent can only do so much shaking up before his kid begins to hate him. Fil, sweetheart, part of life can be mucking around in classrooms or sitting in trendy cafes talking about the faults of the world, but not all of it. Life, in my opinion, is about constantly running into brick walls, and falling over and getting up again, about making hard decisions and dealing imperfectly with difficult situations. When Darcy showed up something told me he'd take you there, to where it's all a bit more real. I wanted you to step outside yourself while you were here, to do the first and hardest part of becoming an adult, put yourself in someone else's shoes and figure out why they're the way they are. So when Darcy arrived I thought, well, here was someone who'd known another life to yours, someone who'd lived in busted houses with busted people, with violence, someone who thought fancy food was a luxury, not a necessity. Someone who knew something about jail, and a bit more again about being frightened. And yet had stayed human through it all.'

Jon turned from Fil and spoke as if to the sea. His jaw twitched and his voice dropped. 'I hoped knowing Darcy might humble you, that it might temper your pride, valuable as that is, with the spice of shame and the knowledge that we're all terribly flawed – you, me, everyone. But it hasn't worked the way I hoped. The failure is mine as much as yours.' He gestured towards the overhanging headland. 'Did you know that they chased people like Darcy over cliffs just like this one, all up and down this coast, all over Australia? People like us killed them, massacred them. Some of the Darcies chose to jump rather than stay and be raped or killed or enslaved as we decided fit. Some of us protested it; many more of us turned away and saw nothing, remembered nothing. A rare few, a *special* few, wrote it down, or didn't stop talking about it. They bore witness. Here, I brought this to show Darcy,' Jon put his hand into his saddlebag and brought out a book. 'If you can at least grasp this, but don't tell me how special you are, not in front of Darcy, not without something to back it up next time. And maybe you might have a think about why those people who *aren't* so special never got a chance to be.' He thrust the book at Fil, then rode roughly down the bank to where Darcy and Cam were.

Fil, trembling close to shock, looked dully at the book of poetry Jon'd been reading lately. He'd handed it to her open at a poem called *Nigger's Leap, New England*. She read it three times, the first two struggling with the meter, the third grasping more of the sense. Then she looked up to see the others as distant dark figures down on the beach. Jon sat on Picasso, looking calmly up towards her. Fil turned away from him and tears spilled down her cheeks as she cried for herself, for never knowing her father or her brother properly, for never knowing the people in the poem. She rode down to the waiting sands and handed him the book back, sniffling.

Jon took it, his manner serious but kind. He reached over and put a hand on her back. 'It's okay, Bella, it'll be okay. I was like you once, thought I was the renaissance and the people's revolution rolled into one … it's the hardest thing in the world to learn, how ordinary we all are. But you need to know it before you can try to overcome it. Yeah?'

His daughter nodded, only slightly, but it was there. A truce. Pax Menzies.

Fil felt a bit better, realising that harsh though his judgments were, Jon didn't despise her after all.

'Good. Come on, I'll race you to the inlet,' he challenged her.

Fil instantly swung Gunner around and drew her reins up close to his nuggety head, ready for revenge. Gunner pranced on the spot, eager to be off. Jon did the same on Picasso. Their horses were evenly matched, Picasso bigger and taller but carrying a heavier load. The horses spurted away towards the water where Darcy and Cam were swimming. As they galloped, Picasso gradually drew ahead and Jon gave him a loose rein. Darcy and Cam looked on, spellbound, as the leggy bay animal pounded through the shallows towards them in the grey dawn.

'He looks like he's flying, man, like a fucken superhero or sumpin. Like he's flying over the water,' Darcy said. They both marvelled at the beauty and power of the horse thundering towards them, silhouetted by the sunrise, spray shooting up from every hoofbeat. Jon was crouched low over his neck, barely visible.

'That's who Aonbar was, you know,' Cam said, rubbing Garbo's neck. Her fine ears flickered at his touch. 'Aonbar was a magic horse that could gallop over land or sea.'

'Yeah?' Darcy was intrigued, imagining a horse racing over the waves.

'It's an Irish myth.' Irish, thought Darcy, some of me's Irish. Some of me's in this whitefella here, and his Dad, and his sister. How can that be? He gave Cam a word in return.

'Yarraman's the word for horse round here ... but there never was horses till the whites came.'

Yarraman, Cam was thinking as his father reached them, rolling the word around in his mouth. *Yarraman's Rest.*

Fil came up behind. 'Second,' she panted.

'You okay?' Cam asked her gently. seeing her reddened eyes. Jon could be pretty merciless sometimes. He'd spoken in an aside but her answer was deliberately clear, loud enough for Jon and Darcy to hear. 'Yeah. As okay as a bloody migloo ring-in'll ever be,' she said, looking straight at Darcy.

The black boy laughed. That's the way. She'd got it right now, not shame 'bout being white, but honest about it. And about whose place it still was, till they all sorted something out. 'Ah, yer right cuz.' He smiled a wide Aboriginal smile for her, splashing water at her with a dark hand. Drops of the Pacific slid down the girl's face, salting her eyes, her mouth. The ocean mingled with the water of her tears. The sun was up properly now, and Jon turned Picasso around. Time they all went home and started another day.

Glossary

Terms offensive to Aboriginal people:

Abo   slang term for Aboriginal person, offensive

arf-caste   half-caste

full blood   Aboriginal person with no non-Aboriginal descent, often regarded as offensive

yellafella   mixed-race Aboriginal person. Term used by traditional Aboriginals and often regarded as offensive by others

Other terms:

Aboriginal   a person of any degree of Aboriginal descent who identifies as Aboriginal and has the support of an Aboriginal community

ALS   Aboriginal Legal Service

b & e   break and enter (in order to steal)

book-up   a form of bush credit, often exploitative

bora   a sacred Aboriginal meeting place where Business is conducted

broken-in   initiated in Aboriginal Law

bud   brother or friend

charged up   drunk

child person who has not been initiated in ('been through') the Law

clapsticks musical instrument used by women

cool drink soft drink, eg Coke

Country land of traditional significance to an Aboriginal person; usually of great emotional and psychological significance

crook sick

cuz cousin or by extension, friend

damper bush bread

deadly good, highly prized

disfla this person here

donger type of cheap accommodation

doolum louse (Bundjalung and related languages)

dreckly immediately

finish up to die

gammon (1) not serious, joking (2) not authentic, no good

grog alcohol

jahjam baby or child (Bundajalung language)

Kriol A form of non-traditional Aboriginal language

Language Aboriginal language, as opposed to English or Kriol

onetime used for emphasis

Out West the remote Australian bush, 'outback'

payback retaliation for injury or offence

pituri Aboriginal intoxicating plant

quack medical doctor, qualified or otherwise

ring-in substitute or fake

saltwater mob Aboriginal people of coastal Australia

shame ashamed, remorseful, embarrassed

skin   a form of traditional Aboriginal social classification

susu   milk or breast

swag   portable mattress for camping

the Law   traditional customary practices, incorporating both religion and punishment, but much more complex than either

time   time spent in prison

toyota   vehicle of any make

whitefella   non-Aboriginal *or* (occasionally) not of the Aboriginal group in question

womba   crazy

yandy   marijuana

yufla   the people being spoken to